PURPLE JESUS

PURPLE
JESUS

a novel
———

RON COOPER

bancroft
press

ISBN 978-1-890862-70-1 $21.95 (cloth)
ISBN 978-1-61088-004-6 $14.99 (paper)

Published by Bancroft Press ("Books that enlighten")
P.O. Box 65360, Baltimore, MD 21209
800-637-7377
410-764-1967 (fax)
www.bancroftpress.com

Book and cover design: Tracy Copes
Author photo: Sandy Scott

Printed in the United States of America

For Sandra
as always

PART I

"One cannot step twice into the same river."
—Heraclitus

ONE

Purvis shoved an empty condensed milk can across the dinette table toward boney, bluish Armey Wright. "You got more room in here than I thought, old man," Purvis said. "I guess some things are bigger on the inside than they look from the outside. That's more work for me."

Purvis slid another condensed milk can across the gray mica tabletop. It stopped on the edge, hovering over Armey's lap. "Touchdown!" Purvis said. "Now you supposed to make a goalpost with your fingers for me to kick the extra point, but we can skip that part."

Armey's head was tilted toward his left shoulder as if he were coursing a distant sound. His glasses, with the one blackened lens, had slipped to the end of his nose, exposing one eye squinting, the other completely white with just an outline of iris. One shiny hand clutched the front of his green coveralls as if trying to unsnap them.

Purvis stood and picked up the crowbar off the top of the stove. "I'm going to try that room with all them books in it," he said. "They got a liberry in town, you know. I might have to come back tomorrow if I can't find it there." He kicked aside empty condensed milk cans and stepped over the pots (a two-quart and a stew size), a skillet, three coffee cans (one filled with spoons, one with finishing nails and wood screws, and one with empty aspirin bottles), and two blue willow plates (now broken) he had dumped from the screened pie safe.

PURPLE JESUS

If only the storied million dollars had been in one of those coffee cans, where normal people keep their rainy-day money, Purvis wouldn't have to tear down half the house. This was all Armey's fault, Purvis thought. The old man knew this day was coming, what with everybody knowing he was rich and all, so why'd he have to make it so hard? Nobody likes to ruin a house like this, but by God, Purvis was not the one who hid it.

Wallpaper peeled; boards fell. What kind of fool stuffs a fortune in the walls? Not Purvis. With that money, he could buy some Easter presents sure enough. He could get his father that airboat. His mother could have a dryer so she wouldn't have to hang his drawers out on the line anymore. His brother DeWayne could quit work at the hash plant, and they both could sit around drinking Michelob and not turning a lick for a year or two.

The rest of those Wrights were no better than Armey. When they finally came to check on him and found him dead, they'd probably be too stupid to even know how to look for the money, much less where to find it. And if they found it, they'd blow it on more of those sooners. Running around the country dogfighting—how much sorriness can one family hold?

The floors sloped as if the house had been built on a bevel. Purvis's ankles ached from leaning. He plopped down on a pile of books and wondered how it stayed stacked. And the dirt—maybe Armey thought dirt would just roll out the door, and he would not have to sweep. Purvis opened another can of hot Pabst. "You could've at least had a Frigidaire that worked!" Purvis yelled. "But I reckon you didn't need one, living off all that canned cream."

He looked at the books at his feet. *A Treasury of Humorous Verse. The Mysterious World Under the Sea. Religious Symbols of the Orient. Aristotle for Everyone.* His cousin, who'd gone off to college, once told Purvis about Aristotle. He was some son of a bitch who lived thousands of years ago and was supposed to know everything. Purvis's cousin said he wrote about how the soul is all the body can do. That didn't help out Armey very much right now—his body was doing a pile of nothing.

Purvis returned to the kitchen. "I got about all I can stand of this today, old man. Gonna be too dark to see before long anyway." He slid another empty milk can across the table, which knocked the one still teetering into Armey's lap. "I should've come out here a week ago and used this wrecking bar on you. That'd been better for you, quicker at least, than poisoning. Look." He held a can in front of Armey's eye. "See that little plug in the middle of the bottom? That's lead they stop it up with when they vacuum-fill the can, you dead-ass. What kind of groceries is that, anyhow? If the lead hadn't got you, you would've give up the ghost from misnutrition, you scrawny dead-ass."

Armey couldn't be more than a day or two dead, Purvis figured, since he didn't stink and no flies were crawling on him. His old watch was still running, the kind with the stem you have to wind every two or three days. That watch made good on its lifetime guarantee, and he wore it with the face on the inside of his wrist, just like Purvis's tenth-grade art teacher, from New York or somewhere like that. Unnatural was what it was, bending your hand back like a woman to tell the time.

"I'm gone now. Anything you need, besides somebody to stick your dead ass in the ground?" Purvis moved around the table and adjusted Armey's glasses to sit straight on his nose and not make the old man look so pitiful. He nudged the head upright, but it fell forward, as if Armey were reading the label on the can in his lap. In the back of his coveralls, two inches below the collar, was a small hole.

Purvis stuck the tip of his latex-covered pinky into the hole and felt it enter into Armey's back, stopping on something solid.

"You double-dead bastard! Why'n't you show me your new—what's it called?—orifist before I worked my day-late self ragged looking for what money someone done already stole? Goddamn *Aristotle*!"

The back porch was a clutter of rust and decay: a twenty-horsepower Johnson outboard motor with no top, a sling blade, a shovel, a grubbing hoe, a bush axe, two foot tubs, cane poles, more empty milk cans, a partial roll of chicken wire, radios, a typewriter, a rocking chair missing an arm, rat traps, a Phillips 66 sign, an unvarnished shotgun stock, and a foot locker with screwdrivers, drill bits, saws, hammers, and wrenches. A stack of cinder blocks led to the yard. The forty yards from the house to Wadboo Branch had grown up so bad with palmettos and elderberry that the creek could not be seen. The train trestle was just a dark line running behind the cypresses. The walk of boards, which would probably crumble like dry-rotted sponges beneath your feet, had surely borne no walkers in years.

What a sorry way to be, Purvis thought. You got to have something in life— a hobby like fishing, or a woman to fuss at you. Why not go ahead and slit your throat instead of just sitting at a little table nursing cans of cream, nobody even missing you until maybe they notice you don't show up at the store for your pack of Red Man this week? Whoever put that bullet in Armey's back did not know what a friend he was to the old man. Not long ago either—he wasn't stiff yet, and some dogfighting Wright was already running around throwing away Armey's money.

Purvis checked to make sure he had left nothing. He'd returned the *GQ* magazine inside to exactly where it had been. The crowbar was in his right hand, and his left held the plastic sack with his beer cans, three pairs of latex gloves, cigarette butts, and a tiny roach from the joint he smoked while crapping in the bushes. The FBI can analyze shit, he'd been told, so he was careful to go outside where it would not be found. Cigarette ashes were safe, though. Not even the FBI can trace those, although they can analyze your spit on a butt. They put it under a high-powered microscope and find a pattern. Then they use a computer to match it up to all their files, one for everybody in the world, and a little card prints out: Purvis Driggers. Cordesville, South Carolina. Twenty-four years old. Unemployed. They *would* say that, because the government thinks working a bunch of jobs here and there does not count as employment. The good thing is that unemployed means no taxes. You don't pay taxes on stolen money, neither, especially a dead man's stolen money.

Purvis walked toward the creek. After a good night's sleep, he'd think more clearly and come up with another plan. For now, he just knew something had to give.

TWO

The old Cadillac Fleetwood made clicking noises each time Reverend Pyron turned or accelerated. Martha thought the car smelled like a wet dog.

"You best take this thing by J. C.'s and have one of them boys look it," Mrs. Pyron said. "It's not supposed to crack like that. You going to strand us out somewheres in the woods and we'll have to walk the roads like trash."

Reverend Pyron popped the cigarette lighter from its hole by the ashtray, pulled it up to his Winston, and took a long drag. "That's just a rod. They do that."

"What's a rod? They not supposed to be quiet?"

He pushed the button to let his window down an inch. "You don't mind if I smoke, do you, Martha?"

Martha turned the page of the *Celebrity Life* tabloid she had picked up from the stack on the backseat, which also included copies of *Star Inquirer*, *Real Life News*, and *National Reporter*. "Not if you got another one."

"Now you know better than that, honey," Mrs. Pyron said. She shifted her eyes in the sun visor vanity mirror to see Martha. "The Reverend has been wrestling with that demon for years. The Lord's helped him get down to two packs."

"The Lord helped your daddy grow tobacco," Martha said. "I believe he did pretty good."

Mrs. Pyron clamped down her tweezers and yanked a hair from her eyebrow. "Everybody's got to live, honey. The Lord understands that, and my papa never missed a tithe in his life, even in the hard times when we lived off cornbread and milk. And *he* didn't smoke."

The Cadillac *tick ticked* as Reverend Pyron turned onto Wadboo Road. He slowed and looked into the rear-view mirror. "Why's Bone staying so far back?" the reverend said. "He don't know where we going and liable to miss the turn."

"That cracking's getting louder," Mrs. Pyron said. "Didn't it sound louder to you, Martha? Now roll that window up, Necessary. You blowing Martha's pretty hair."

"I don't care if it gets messed up," Martha said.

"That's what I say about mine. Ha!" Reverend Pyron ran his hand over his shiny scalp and looked into the mirror again. "There's Bone with the rest of them idiots all spaced out like they trying to get left." He pressed the gas, and the car sped up, *tank tank tank*.

Mrs. Pyron put her tweezers into her purse. "They all know where we going. Maybe one of them'll carry us back home when the motor falls out of this thing." She turned to look into the backseat. "Where's the camera at, Necessary? I told you not to forget it."

"It don't matter, Polly. Their memories of this day in the spirit won't fade."

"But Martha's gonna be so pretty in that white gown. I just wish her daddy could've been here. How long since Gamewell passed, honey?"

"Three years," Martha said without looking up. "Not long enough. He wouldn't've come out here no way."

"Honey, don't talk ugly. And what about your husband? Didn't you tell him?"

Martha closed the magazine. "We divorced, and he's the last person I'd want to see."

"You don't mean that, honey. The Lord will forgive you for that divorce and everything else today. Then you and, what was his name?"

"Young."

"You and Young can get married in our church, a real marriage in the eyes of the Lord this time." Mrs. Pyron licked her forefingers and smoothed out her eyebrows. "Now don't keep them under too long like you did that Metts boy last time, Necessary. Him coughing and crying and his daddy diving into the water and breaking his arm."

"You got to wet them real good," the preacher said. "Else it won't take."

Martha made a popping sound with her lips and turned to see the line of cars trailing behind. Suckers, she thought. All of them thinking a dip in a muddy creek will solve their problems. It might, if they stayed under and drowned.

As the others emptied from the seven vehicles parked on the road shoulder, Martha watched Reverend Pyron stand on the railroad track and look toward the trestle. He was a short man of small frame, but with a big gut and no neck, who could not button the collar of even his double extra-large shirt, which clumped under his arms. The folds of extra material pinched around his waistband, and the cuffs were rolled up three or four times. Martha imagined him walking that track with a strangling tie and a binding shirt until he fainted from heat exhaustion and fell on his face, breaking his front teeth on a railroad spike. In real life, he thumped a cigarette butt toward the ditch and returned to his car, where Mrs. Pyron handed out white polyester-cotton gowns to all the others.

"Y'all that's getting baptized, just slip these on and then reach under and pull off your other clothes," Mrs. Pyron said.

"Do I leave my drawers on?" Kaylene Bunch asked.

"We all know you don't," Johnson Rondeau said.

"You behave, Johnson," Mrs. Pyron said. "Everybody leave on your underclothes, just put the rest here in my trunk. Won't nobody mess with them. Y'all that's already been baptized can leave your regular clothes on underneath."

"Where's my flip-flops?" Jodie Craven asked. "I can't walk no railroad track barefooted, and I ain't getting my pumps messed up."

Martha stood in front of the Fleetwood, away from the rest.

"You doing okay, sweetheart?" Reverend Pyron asked. "Need me to hold your clothes for you?"

Through the sleeve of Martha's gown wriggled a hand, dangling a bra. "Here."

"Don't play with me, child."

"I'm nobody's child."

A scream came from near the Cadillac. "Merciful God! Something burnt my foot!" Jodie Craven hopped on one leg. The adults ran to her.

"A cigarette butt," Mrs. Pyron said. "Necessary, is that yours? It's a Winston."

"Nuh uh, I throwed mine way out yonder."

"Nobody else is smoking here."

"It's already blistering up," Jodie said. "Somebody's got to tote me."

"It's all right, baby," Reverend Pyron said. "Sister Honey Jo's gonna talk the fire out of it. Don't be scared."

A woman in her sixties, with gun-barrel hair and a port wine birthmark on the left side of her neck, sat on the ground and took the girl's foot into her hand. She mumbled, passed her other hand over the foot, and blew on it. As the others surrounded her and the girl, and prayed aloud, she twice repeated the fire exorcism. The prayers all stopped as if on cue, and Harlan Lisenbee picked up the girl and helped her toward the tracks.

"It's still burning," Jodie said. "And look at it, crusting up like a meat skin."

"Sister Honey Jo's got a gift of the Spirit, baby," Reverend Pyron said. "You got to let it work."

"Been better if she got some dadgum salve," Jodie said.

The group, in twos and threes, walked past Martha to the tracks. Some of the boys balanced on the rails, while most adjusted their strides to stretch from tie to tie. Martha followed, stopping to place onto the rail a Bicentennial quarter her father had given her when she was a child. She wondered why she had kept it this long. One of the women began to sing, and the others joined in.

On Jordan's stormy banks I stand . . .

Martha reached into the front of her gown and pulled out a thin necklace. She twisted the little metal ring to remove the silver cross, laid it beside the quarter, and pressed both with her thumbs as if setting jewels into a mosaic. She stood, placed her feet onto the rail, steadied herself with outstretched arms, and stepped foot before foot, as if measuring the track, toward the singers.

I am bound for the promised land . . .

THREE

A moan skimmed along the water from downstream near the trestle. In the fading light, Purvis was too busy pushing limbs and vines out of the way with the crowbar and watching for cottonmouths—they bite just for meanness—to hem up the sound in his head and name it.

Several yards from the creek bank, with the woods for cover, he worked through sassafras saplings, over tupelo roots, and away from Armey's house as quickly as he could. When he stopped to pull a thorn from his neck, he noticed the sound growing louder. Purvis squatted to listen: voices, maybe singing. He crept to the edge of the woods and could see people, twenty-five or thirty of them, dressed in white and gathered on the other side of Wadboo under the trestle. A few were in the water, and the rest stood on the gravel embankment. They sang, and Purvis could hear "Jesus calling" but not much more.

Reëntering the woods now, he tried to move faster but quieter. He made it to his side of the trestle and came back out to the edge. They still sang the same song, and this time he could hear it clearly: *Softly and tenderly Jesus is calling, calling for you and for me.*

It's the Holiness, Purvis realized, out for a baptism like they always do around Easter. They did them three or four times, and usually during the week because of everybody's work schedules. That might be Aunt Raylene's bunch, but you wouldn't find her out by Wadboo, scared as she'd been since she'd seen that big gar sideswipe the boat. Last year, she tried to get the church to raise money to buy a big above-ground swimming pool to put behind the fellowship hall. She'd seen a TV program about ancient Christians and how they baptized indoors—Jesus might have done the same thing for all we know, she said. She just couldn't see risking slipping into Wadboo to get fished out down in the rice fields, if a gar didn't get her first, when water is water anyway, but she was outvoted.

The man doing the dunking, who had to be the preacher, had his back to Purvis, but he did not look like Aunt Raylene's End Times Holiness Church preacher. This guy looked bald, and the water was up to his chest. The End Times preacher waded out only to his waist, better to protect his swooping, shellacked hair.

Calling, oh sinner, come home.

The song was pretty. Purvis was glad they sang the same verse and chorus over and over—he nearly had it memorized. One part had him stumped, something like "See all the mortals she's waiting and watching," but that made no sense. Then again, none of it made sense, with Jesus thousands of years dead as dirt.

As the preacher started dunking people, Purvis sat down in the mud, feeling calm, and a little bad about Armey, who probably never came down to the water at all, much less to listen to some good singing. He wondered what the monks at Cainhoy thought about these Holinesses, a kind of Christian different than monks, dunking and singing at the foot of the abbey. He wondered what the monks would think of a guy ripping boards off a dead man's walls to try to find a million dollars. He knew what the church people would think, but he also knew some of them would grab a crowbar in a second and yank a plank or two for an offering that kind of sweet.

Purvis had not eaten since some Frosted Flakes that morning, but these other things kept his mind off his stomach. A joint would be really nice about now, if he knew nobody would see the burning tip.

Another sound pierced through the song—the train. It could be fun when that trestle started rumbling and shaking the hell out of those baptizers. Gravel would fall down onto them, and doves and bats would fly out from under the support beams, the *whop whop* of their wings amplifying off the embankment to make them sound like buzzards.

With the sun dipping below the top of the trees, the failing light turned on the mercury vapor lamps on either side of the trestle. The glow fell onto the group and all over the next wader in line. She was about Purvis's age and slim, but her arms looked strong, and her hair beamed purplish-black. Her white gown had been splashed, and it clung to her chest. If he had binoculars, Purvis was sure he could see nipples.

Something was different about her. Wasn't just being more beautiful than the regular Holiness heifers, either—it was something in her face.

The train whistle blew again. One of the women said, "Oh, Lordy!"

"Come on in, Martha," the preacher said. "The church and the Good Lord welcome you home."

Earnestly, tenderly . . .

The preacher drew her to him and said something Purvis couldn't make out. Martha covered her nose and mouth with her hands. The nearing train's wheels scraped against the rails.

You who are weary come home . . .

"I baptize you, Martha—"

WoooOOT! The whistle blew. The train clanked over the trestle. Beams groaned. Birds scattered. Baptizers ducked. The rumbling and creaking and coughing of the train filled the whole swamp.

What last name had the preacher said?

Martha rose from the branch, spreading her arms out like those snake-neck diving birds, when they perch on a limb after chasing fish. She turned—quick but not jerky, like two invisible people held her arms and lifted and spun her—to watch the boxcars cross the trestle. The gown clung to the slope of her hips. When she lowered her arms, which seemed to fold like the blades of a feeler gauge, the top of the gown slipped down over a shoulder. Purvis wondered if the hollow of her neck would feel cool to his cheek, if her skin would smell like a mix of the muddy creek and her purple-black hair, if a bead of creek water that slid to his lips down from her ear would taste as sweet as condensed milk.

Had he seen her face before, a face that shifted like the elusive colors on a fish scale? Was that a scar at the corner of her mouth? She wore the same expression as when she went into the water. She had not cried like the pre-dipped, nor was she smiling like the post-dunked. She smirked. That was it—one side of her mouth curled up into a wild look. Couldn't the preacher tell she was smarting off with her face? Could anyone look at that face and not fall in love with it, the face of Martha Something?

The bushes rustled at the border of Purvis's vision. He looked across the water to a point about twenty yards from the baptizers. A brown outline of a face nested in the myrtle bushes. Purvis glanced downstream, but Martha was gone, hidden among the other white gowns.

So he looked again at the brown face. It moved and gave him a better look— hairy and stretched, huge eyes, and a crown that seemed to come to a point.

The Hairy Man! The stories were true!

The ape-man supposed to haunt this swamp was no ignorant peckerwood's myth. This was no lie brewed up to keep vandal boys or young lovers from wandering too deeply into the wild, to get lost or pregnant. This was the real thing, watching the dippers, his monstrous thoughts heaving in his pointy skull.

What could Purvis do? If he yelled for the church people to run, he'd risk giving himself away. Or, the Hairy Man might vanish back into his stomping grounds, unseen by the others, and Purvis would look like a fool. Maybe he could throw a rock at the beast to scare him away, but that might anger the ugly thing, and he might attack the church people. Even the Hairy Man could recognize beauty, and he would jump with his gorilla legs over those plain holy-roller girls to get to Purvis's love and drag her away to a hellish den.

Something rolled in the water, something brown and fat, not three feet from Purvis.

"Godamighty!" he cried. He could not help it. A day spent working beside a dead man, finding his true love, and seeing the Hairy Man all merged into a burst of nerves. He jumped, fell over a cypress knee, and banged his shoulder on a tree trunk. "Fish-eating Jesus! River-bastard dog! Church up my *ass*!" He ground his teeth and clutched his shoulder. Purvis thought all the otters, those shad-and-shit-eaters, had been killed from Wadboo the year before. Or maybe it was that humongous catfish that ate Jervey Villeponteaux's bluetick.

Stretching his head up through the bushes, he saw the Holiness bunch looking in his direction. They were motionless, as if posing for a picture, not stretching their necks or straining forward to see the source of the cursing, but simply awaiting its end. He looked upstream—no sign of the Hairy Man. The Holiness people lost interest and sloped up the embankment. With the long gowns hiding the working of their legs, they seemed to glide like boats. What a peculiar sight they would make, floating down the track a half mile out to the road. A voice began to sing, and the rest joined in by the second bar.

Have you been to Jesus for his cleansing power?

Wet Martha stopped and turned to the water as the others continued their ascent. She seemed to glow brighter now in the aura of the mercury vapor. She must have been looking for Purvis. He was tempted to jump into Wadboo and swim to her. He would tell her that no one was so beautiful, that those Holinesses were not good enough for her, that he had saved her from an ogre.

Are you fully trusting in his grace this hour?

She would throw her arms around him, cradle his scraped shoulder, and tell him she would always make him happy.

Are you washed in the blood of the lamb?

Purvis watched Martha walk up the embankment and out of sight.

From the trestle, the rails looked like a pair of wires stretching away and up toward the full moon, which made the evening seem lighter than it had been an hour earlier. The church people were long gone now, and probably the Hairy Man, too. Purvis should have already started his three-mile walk home to eat, he hoped, some leftover supper. He had come home late too many times recently, and his mother warned him she was tired of saving him a plate that he didn't touch. He could sure use it tonight.

If he cocked his head the right way, one of the rails would glow like a flashlight—that's all the Cordesville Light was. The story of the ghost woman looking for her dead train engineer husband was sure enough horseshit. The moon on the tracks is what it was. His cousin said it was swamp gas, maybe phosphorous, like the sailors in the olden days called Saint Elmo's Fire. That was horseshit, too. What the hell *is* a saint, anyhow? His other cousin, the one who had gone to college, said it was the power of suggestion—people seeing what they wanted to. If you go there thinking you'll see a ghost light, then sure as bulls' nuts knock, you will. What Purvis knew was when he looked in the moon's direction, he saw a reflection on a rail. When he looked down the rails away from the moon, he did not see it.

He stepped to the edge of the trestle and dropped his bag of trash into the water. As it spun on the surface, he thumped a cigarette butt at it but missed. The bag slowly gave in to the current and eased downstream. It looked white on the dark water, like Martha's baptismal gown—Martha, floating like a boat. Not a Jon boat with a little Johnson outboard on it or one of those big ski boats with a tall Evinrude shooting up a rooster tail, but a sailboat, like the one that sometimes skims around in the cove of Lake Moultrie on holidays. Martha, a sleek sailboat that never sinks, changing her course at will by zig-zagging with and against the wind, mistress of water and air. Purvis would never have to worry about drowning with the Martha boat coming to his rescue.

He knew she was not really a boat. He remembered the word for this sort of thing—*metaphor*. Sometimes people do not understand that a metaphor, like a story (a parable, like they said at Sunday School when he used to go), is not real, but just a way to talk about what *is* real, a way to understand things better. Those ignorant Holinesses do not understand this. They probably thought Wadboo was a purple stream of lamb's blood, like that could really wash you clean. A boat seemed like a good metaphor for Martha. That was what Purvis needed, a good metaphor.

He walked to the home side of the trestle. Somewhere out there, the Hairy Man squatted on matted haunches, the evening's images rolling around in his horrible skull. What kind of sense did those white-clad figures, moaning at the water, make to that fearsome thing? Or maybe he'd been watching Purvis—picked up *his* scent and flanked *him* along the branch, thinking Purvis, and not the baptizers, a threat to the dank slough he considered home. Maybe he would follow Purvis a while until a nerve tightened and he sprang. Did the train actually scare the man-ape, so he wouldn't wander up to the track, and so Purvis would be safe between the rails? Or had the beast grown used to the thunderous machine, like a yard dog loses its fear of a lawnmower?

"I know you out there, you hairy freak monster bastard," Purvis said. "Now I'm coming through. You just stay out yonder, unless you want a crowbar laid to your shaped-up head."

Purvis walked into the night, sometimes striding on the ties, sometimes balancing on the rails, as wild forms paced about his head like beasts in a dark pen.

FOUR

"The Hairy Woodpecker is a humble bird, retiring, preferring solitude, unlike some of his cousins, who are louder both in color and habit. He is of medium size, about nine adult inches in length. His distinctive feature is the white band down his back. He also has a sizeable beak in proportion to his body, distinguishing him from the Downy. Along the side of his face run two white stripes that, in some examples, meet at a red patch behind the head. These I take to be the males, for in the kingdom of birds the males are highly adorned while the females are unremarkable. He has rows of spots on his wings as do similar species.

"My soul leaped as I spied one at dusk today near the river, the first of these elusive creatures I have seen in years. He scrambled along the underside of an oak limb. His chatter offered wise counsel, echoing Our Savior's word to those who would seek to inherit the Earth: meek, meek."

—Fra. Phillip.

April 17, in the Year of Our Lord 1938.

The azaleas were the wonder of the abbey's gardens this month. They were well placed by the wildflower quarter, which was Abbot Christopher's favorite. "Our Savior was a carpenter, but I wager he fashioned many a hearty hoe," the abbot liked to say.

Most of the fourteen monks at Cainhoy Abbey were pleased with their newfound emphasis on gardening since the abbot's arrival a year earlier, but

Brother Andrew did not share this fondness for soil and seed. He did, though, enjoy walking through the gardens as much as anyone did, particularly on his way into the woods and down to the water, like today. With each step, his binoculars, which were his one special indulgence, bounced against the journal under his cloak.

"Skipping supper again, Andrew?" Brother Bernard said, squatting by the lilies. "I hear it's succotash and brown rice. What's the etymology of that, *succotash*? Do you know?"

Andrew stopped and smiled. Even with his back turned, Bernard had easily guessed the footsteps he heard were Andrew's. Who else would walk through the far end of the garden, away from the buildings and toward the woods, this late in the day?

"Arabic?" Bernard said. "Perhaps French, via Algeria." He stood and tapped his garden trowel against the palm of his thick hand. "I have to look that up, or it'll plague me through the night." He wiped his brow on the gaping sleeve of the hooded shirt that hung low over his jeans. "I had an interesting discussion yesterday with a couple of the old-timers—Brother Garrison, Brother Albert. It was about the extent to which we take liberties with the Rule. I wish you'd been there, Andrew, but I think you were on one of your wanderings. "

Andrew had heard this before. It wasn't just the old-timers—Bernard, too, thought that Abbot Christopher let the brothers follow "their innovative forms," as Abbot Christopher put it, to the point where their common routines and services, the time-honored and once-central features that bound them together in the Spirit, had become marginalized.

Bernard placed the trowel into a canvas bag. "Brother Albert pointed out that work and prayer is the Cistercian way. He called Abbot Christopher a Christianized Gandhi with his 'We must follow our own paths' and his tolerance for your missing compline and vespers a few times. But even the good abbot remembers that we are cenobites, and I am sure he wishes you to at least take all your meals with the brothers." He removed a plastic water bottle from the bag and drank a squirt. "What are you looking for out there in the swamp, anyway, with all those wild things?"

Andrew's smile was barely noticeable behind his long beard. He gave a quick wave, his index, middle finger, and thumb forming an L, and stepped toward the woods.

"Bless you, Brother Andrew. I'll sneak a bowl of succotash out for you."

Cainhoy Abbey's three thousand acres served as sanctuary not just for a few humans but also for an abundance of wildlife. Deer were thick in the sloughs by the water. They were plentiful on the other side of Wadboo Road, too. On Saturdays in the fall, the hunting club across the road raised excitement or irritation from the brothers, as deer often escaped the hunters' guns and dogs by crossing the road into the abbey, and the dogs would follow. Most of the brothers found these noisy intruders foul disturbances of their contemplative work.

But Brother Andrew loved the hunting dogs. When they would spill into the abbey behind a deer, he would whistle for them, a high-pitched melismatic cascade of notes—a talent he'd developed since deciding to extend his vow of silence indefinitely. The dogs came to him every time, and he would loop his belt rope through their collars and tie the dogs near the welcome sign. He would sit with them, whistling a low monotone to soothe them.

Occasionally, he glimpsed a fleeing deer bounding over shrubs, the white tail high like a banner. Once, just after he took up archery, he was practicing alone in the woods when a huge buck hopped by not ten yards from him. The buck had such a lead on the dogs that it slowed its pace, knowing it would soon swim the branch to safety. The deer's neck lay against its chest in a wad of muscle. Atop its great head rode a knotted cage of white antlers that extended as far as a man's outstretched arms. Brother Andrew raised the bow and drew back the string until the notched end of the arrow touched the right corner of his mouth. A wild hunger coursed through him, uncovering primitive and feral urges he had long forgotten, creating fear and trembling that Andrew had only read about from the mystics of the past.

Andrew dropped the bow, caught the dogs, and spent the rest of the day drunk on the thoughts whirling through his head. Is mine a contradictory life, imbedded in forest yet alienated from nature? he thought. Have I abstracted myself, stepped back as a spectator, forever cut off from a world that I can neither possess nor renounce?

The woods along Wadboo Branch were quiet that afternoon. A red-winged blackbird displayed his crimson epaulets on a live oak, perhaps the very one in which Brother Phillip spied his hairy woodpecker over half a century ago. Andrew had not hiked out here for a week, and he expected more activity. Dusk is prime time for birding. Jays squawk and harass other birds. Cardinals *chip chip* in the ferns. The small ones—vireos, warblers, and sparrows—seem brighter in the twilight, more easily discernable.

Most glorious of all are the woodpeckers. Their incessant dedication to work, their singular resolve at detaching a scale of bark or boring into a dying trunk, the smaller ones' taps whirring too rapidly to count and the larger pounding like axes, echoing off the hardwoods—all their beautiful habits seemed special messages to those who truly saw and listened.

How fortunate Andrew was to happen across the journal of a previous brother who heeded those lessons. This cracked leather volume of yellowed, unlined paper that had sat hidden and untouched in the abbey's library for decades provided Brother Andrew an unspeakable joy. It contained no prayers, no theological treatises—at least none outright—only short, random entries recording Brother Phillip's hikes, one or two a week over a decade.

The writing bespoke a kindred spirit, one who also leaned toward a pantheism that the church considers anathema. Walking to and fro and working in the abbey with the journal discreetly tucked under his cloak and against his heart gave Brother Andrew the peace that accompanies having one's unorthodox views legitimized by another. Could a year of Brother Bernard's watering and weeding, of Abbot Christopher's sitting on a bench before cornflowers, phlox, daisies, clovers, and forget-me-nots, compare to just one paragraph of Brother Phillip's journal?

Andrew arrived at the edge of Wadboo Branch, sat near the bank, and opened the journal.

"The sun's slow ascent was unbefitting for this morn on the cusp of Spring. The woods were dark and silent as truth, as if the Earth had grown tired of effort, until a cloud shifted and a single shaft of light peeled back the pewter layers of fog to reveal red, black, white, the proud banner of the red-headed woodpecker. He labored intently not five paces in front of me—"

An odd sound seeped through the thick slough downstream, drawing Andrew's attention from the journal. It was not a boat, nor the howl of some dog still lost from the hunt days, and it certainly was not a bird. It was—singing. Andrew could not make out the words or even the language, but he could tell a number of voices were involved. He cupped his hands over his ears and held his breath. It came from his side of the creek, somewhat farther inland, moving toward the water.

. . . and go with me . . . Promised Land . . .

He moved closer to the trestle to hear better. The harmony was rough and probably more instinctive than practiced. He heard an odd intonation in an upper register, like a man singing falsetto or counter-tenor.

On Jordan's stormy banks, I stand and cast a wishful eye . . .

About thirty men, women, and children, all dressed in white gowns, inched down the gravel embankment from the tracks to the water's edge. This was a baptism, the sort common among the rural congregations where Andrew—he was "Tom" then—grew up in Florida. The sun was setting, and he was well-protected by myrtle and elderberry, but just to be safe, Andrew pulled his brown hood up over his head for extra camouflage and placed the binoculars to his eyes.

A bald man entered the water up to his chest. He murmured to the group and occasionally burst out with "Blessed Jesus!" or "Blood of Christ!" He said an elongated "Amen" and the others stopped singing. Andrew could hear most of what the man, who had to be the minister, said.

"Who will be the first . . . Brother . . . how about you?"

A young man of about twenty, weeping maybe, stepped into the water.

"Brother Hayman," maybe, "because you have . . . Satan and have accepted Christ Jesus as your Lord and Savior, and because . . . Holiness Church by your own . . . I baptize . . . name of Almighty God in the manner that . . ."

The minister bent the young man backwards until he was submerged, and with a brief struggle, brought the boy back to his feet. The others began another song.

Softly and tenderly, Jesus is calling . . .

Andrew had heard that these immersions still took place in the Low Country swamps of South Carolina. These people could very well be Pentecostals.

As a child, Andrew was taught to be wary of them. "They say they're holy," his mother said, "but they're mean. They carry knives." These worshipers follow their own path, but where does it lead? Did immersion in a pewter-colored branch put them directly in touch with one rough edge of providence?

As lights switched on around the trestle, as the sun set, and as Andrew heard the moan of an approaching train, a young woman took her turn at immersion. She stood out from the others, not just because of her blue-black hair and beauty that even a brother could not ignore, but also because of something in her countenance, something captivating but elusive.

The minister called her to him. "Martha . . ." A blast from the train muffled the young woman's last name. It sounded like *omelet*. Once the minister submerged and raised her, she carried herself from the water with the same poise. That was it, *poise*. Glowing in the artificial light, she stepped up to the water's edge with the elegance of a heron and turned to watch the train cross the trestle, as if bidding goodbye to her original sin.

"God almighty!" someone yelled from the other side of Wadboo Branch. The voice continued with "Jesus! Fish!" and perhaps an oath. Andrew turned his binoculars toward the sound and saw the bushes rustle, but could not see the shouter.

So, other spectators were in attendance as well. This pleased Andrew, but he still felt self-conscious. How would this look—a monk out spying—even to another spy? He moved a few feet back into the brush as the small congregation filed up to the tracks, stepping on the wet hems of their clinging gowns. A voice started a new song, and the rest soon joined.

Have you been to Jesus for His cleansing power?

Andrew sat on the ground for a long time. The soft glow of a full moon replaced the ashy streaks of twilight. The abbey's official hours called for rising at 3 a.m. Andrew was a fit man, but he had missed the 8 p.m. retirement too often lately and was feeling tired.

But rather than turn back, he walked to the water, hoping the trestle lamps would allow him to catch sight of a heron spearing a frog. As he reached the muddy edge, he heard a splash downstream. Something rested on the surface of the water under the trestle, but the lamps and the moon did not provide enough light. Then, movement above—a man, talking to himself, walked on the trestle toward Andrew's side of the branch.

The man was soon out of sight, leaving Andrew a moment of solitude to muse on the events of the evening.

From the bushes stepped a snowy egret, cautiously placing its golden feet into the water. It stood in the glow by the trestle, pure white, motionless, poised. Just as suddenly, the bird unfolded its wings and flew under the trestle toward the wide ocean.

As he made his way through the woods to the dormitory, Andrew whistled a low hymn as a prayer for the baptized, benighted souls he had seen earlier. He thought of the poised young woman with blue-black hair and wondered who had gotten more from the water that night.

FIVE

The train roared overhead and blew its whistle just as Reverend Pyron was saying, "I baptize you, Martha Umphlett . . ." She had waited to go last, half-hoping she might be overlooked. Maybe no one would notice she was dry. Maybe the preacher would tire out and save her for another day. Her mother would never know the difference.

She was underwater for what seemed a long time. Above her hummed the dampened voice of Reverend Pyron, around her pulsed the tremors from the creaking trestle, and on her breast lay the preacher's cupped hand. It squeezed, then flattened, the palm running around the nipple. Daughter-fucker, Martha thought. A man's a man, a tittie's a tittie.

Reverend Pyron pulled Martha up from the water. Over his shoulder, she saw something roll in the water a few yards behind him. Maybe it was an alligator that would clamp onto the preacher's white, hairless leg and drag him under, no time to yell, just submerge as if swallowed by the water itself. Weeks later, somebody catfishing off the bank would feel the hook snag on something, raise the cane pole, remove a belt buckle from an alligator turd, cuss because it had pulled the chicken liver off the hook, and chunk the Bible-shaped hunk of brass back into the water. She spat into Pyron's face as she turned to walk to the bank.

She stopped at the edge and looked back at the train disappearing into the trees. Can you actually jump a train like they say in those old songs? That would be one way to leave this shit-hole and a four hundred-pound crying mother. With her luck, she would probably pick a train that ended its run somewhere like

Galivants Ferry, and what good would that do?

"Godamighty!" and some slurred cussing came from across the branch. Probably one of her teenage cousins, Martha thought. Two or three of them had spied on her since she returned home two weeks ago. She saw them peeping from behind the pump house a week before. One darted between the Piggly Wiggly aisles, trying to discover what a bad woman like her ate.

The bunch moved up the embankment as Violet Hood started singing.

Have you been to Jesus for his cleansing power?

Martha walked ten yards behind the pack. This far back in the failing light, no one could see her nipples through the wet gown—besides, now, she wouldn't have to fake the song. When they got back to the road, Martha searched the granite rocks by the rail.

"Harlan," Martha called. "Give me your lighter a minute."

"It's in the car with my clothes," Harlan said. "Let me run get it."

"I got one," said Mitch Bodiford, who had been baptized two years before. "Look, it's got a mermaid on it with a pistol in one hand and—"

"Just give it here." Martha snatched the lighter from him and kicked the rocks around her feet. "Make yourself useful and help me look."

"What we looking for?" Harlan asked.

"A flat quarter and something else I put on the track," she said.

"What something else?"

"Just whatever you see that's flat."

Mitch pulled off his white gown. "I see something that sure ain't flat."

"Here's the quarter," Harlan said. "It's mashed good. Hey, y'all see that otter?"

Mitch spat onto the rail and spread the little puddle with his shoe. "Couldn't been no otter. They shot them all last year. One's tacked to a plank at Flippo's."

"Y'all come on and get dressed now," Mrs. Pyron called. "We got to get back to the church."

George Washington's distorted face was smeared across the silver oval that had been a quarter. Martha turned it over in her hand several times, then flung it into the woods. She kicked around in the rocks once more. Lost in the dark like about everything else, she thought.

✳

Some women stood shoulder to shoulder, forming a partition for the baptized women and girls to change into dry clothes. The men and boys took turns dressing in the L formed by the Fleetwood's open door and front fender. The wet gowns were placed in a tub in the back of Tunk DuPree's pickup where all the children had clumped for the ride back.

"Now everybody go straight to the church," Mrs. Pyron said. "I know y'all are hungry, and we'll get you your certificates, too."

The Craven girl sat with her foot sticking off the side of the truck. "Can we stop at the dadgum Handy Mart for some ice for my foot? God in the sky, I believe the burn is spreading."

The Cadillac *tock tocked* as Reverend Pyron U-turned.

"Take this blessed thing to J.C.'s tomorrow," Mrs. Pyron said, "or you *will* have to pedal me around town on that tricycle." She turned to Martha. "How you feeling now, darling? Just think, Sunday morning you can take communion and join the church."

"Drop me off at the house," Martha said.

"But, sugar, we got chicken purlieu and—"

"Drop me off!"

"All right, then," Reverend Pyron said. "But remember, the Lord's got a plan for you."

Martha lay her head against the car window and peered out at a moon, distorted by the glass to look like a flattened coin, its silvery glow finding her wherever she went.

SIX

Even the towels stuffed around Purvis's bedroom window couldn't keep out the sound of Spessard piddling about the shed at 6 a.m., same as every morning since retiring the year before. Rubbing his temples, Purvis groped along the top of the dresser, hoping to find a pack of cigarettes. He felt the ashtray, and some larger object beside it. He raised up onto his elbow and saw a trophy sporting a miniature running man. Most of the gold paint had flaked off, and the left leg of the track star was missing. Purvis had run second leg on the 4 x 440 relay team for First Baptist when he was fourteen. The team took first place in the Santee Regional Association tournament that year. Why would Purvis's mother have kept the grotesque little figure for ten years, and why would she prop it up at his bedside?

The bedroom door cracked open. "Shug, you up?" asked Arlene, Purvis's mother.

"What do you think, what with Spessard banging every piece of metal he can find out there?" said Purvis. "How he can make such a fuss just carving them ugly stump monsters is what I don't know."

"Lots of people think they's pretty," said his mother. "And you need to get up anyway. Beasley called. Lum Hereford done quit again, and Beasley needs you to drive until Lum comes back. And you ought not to call your daddy by his name."

"I hate that propane. That smell hangs on my clothes and headaches me."

Arlene took a step into the room. "But you know how to do the hook-ups and all and people needs their gas to cook. It won't hurt you to work. What time did you get in?"

Purvis lit a cigarette. "Early. I sat out in the shed thinking."

"Well, get dressed. DeWayne's coming to take you in."

"You put that trophy on my chest o'drawers?"

"Your daddy found it out in the shed," said Arlene. "I thought it might look sweet sitting up there. You need something in here. He couldn't find that other one."

"What other one?"

"That other foot-race trophy, third place."

"Second," Purvis said.

"That's right. That Tillman boy got first, didn't he?" The front door creaked open and closed. "There's DeWayne now."

The familiar *tot tot* of mallet to chisel came through the window. As a boy, Purvis had spent many Saturdays and Sundays lurking about the shed as his daddy reattached an electric cord to a toaster, refinished a mahogany chifforobe, or repaired a chainsaw engine. Spessard had the boy recite the names of tools: rafter square, ball pean, nail set, wrecking bar, jack plane, bastard file, channel locks, coping saw, miter box, vise grips, Phillips-head, flat-head, stud finder. Purvis liked the sounds of the names, especially when his father pronounced them in his heavy country voice. "You got a basic two kinds," Spessard said, "sharp and blunt, but that don't mean each fellow ain't got his ownliest thing he's supposed to do."

As he lay in the dark, the family sleeping, the night birds croaking, creatures emerging from the woods and pacing the yard outside his bedroom, Purvis would assign personalities to the tools, make up stories about them, let their sharp and blunt names roll across his tongue, and sink into the secret and safe world of brave Ball Pean and swift Jack Plane, heroes nobody ever messed with.

Purvis sipped coffee in DeWayne's Isuzu Pup. "I hate this saccharine shit," he said. "Since Spessard stopped drinking tea, Mama don't buy sugar anymore.

Just picks up a handful of those little packets from the free coffee table at the grocery store."

"Then buy some damn sugar," DeWayne said.

"Shut up." Purvis looked through the cassettes in the shoebox, wedged between the gearshift and the seat. "Since when are you listening to all this country shit? Alan Jackson. George Strait. I got to get you some Judas Priest. I hate that propane."

"They're not my cassettes."

"That truck's hot and loud as preachers in hell. Hooking up to tanks on those trailer tongues, where some sooner's liable to come chasing out after you. And stink? I don't see how those other boys can stand it. Something about that gas gives me the headache, like a damn woodpecker's trying . . . what do you call them big pointy-headed woodpeckers, them real big ones?"

"Godamighties."

"Like a godamighty trying to bore a hole out my temple. Maybe if I wore one of those masks like when I was laying insulation for Cribb it might help."

"I tell you what would help. You getting something permanent so you can get the holy hell out from under Mama and Daddy. And don't tell me about stink."

"It ain't the stink. It's the chemical-reaction headache. The rendering plant don't work on you like that gas gets me." Purvis sipped his coffee. A few drops spilled onto the seat.

"Wipe that up!" DeWayne said. "I just had this thing detailed."

"You can throw away as many forty dollars as you want for J. C.'s to detail this thing, but you never going to get the smell of that ground-up dog and horse out of it. I can't believe Sylvie gets in here."

"It don't bother her. She don't hardly got any sense nerves left from all them treatments."

Purvis lit a cigarette and pretended to have a problem rolling down the window. He shouldn't have mentioned DeWayne's wife. The doctors pumped her full of medicine even though they said there was no hope. The rendering facility, which ground, cooked, reduced, and packed twenty-four hours a day, provided DeWayne a flexible schedule, so he could drive Sylvie to her treatments twice a week and stay home with her on her worse days. Purvis did not want to hear about it again.

"You know a girl named Martha?" Purvis asked.

"Martha what takes your ticket at the speedway?"

"No, this one's got all her hair. And long, purpleish-black."

"The onliest other Martha I know is Umphlett. She was in school with me, but I think she got married and moved off. Her daddy was Gamewell the sheriff, and I believe her mama was a Wright."

"You mean a Wright like Armey Wright?" asked Purvis.

"Yeah. Why?"

Purvis told DeWayne about Armey—breaking in, tearing up the walls, finding he was already dead.

"Had to been killed by one of them same Wrights," said Purvis. "Always shooting one another. Remember Browning? Used to be the fishing guide. Shot his brother's elbow out, left his arm flopping. And that girl that shot her mama in the foot, something about her mama called the baby by the wrong name? I need to figure out which one got in there before me."

"Jesus' striped ass!" DeWayne said. "You need me to pop you upside the head, messing around with them Wrights and you don't even know it was one of them. Keep away from that whole bunch. And just because he wasn't stiff don't mean it just happened. Rigor mortis—that's what it's called—don't always set in right away. Might take a day or two, and when it does, it don't always last. People bring in horses and cows and things to the hash plant that were dead for a couple of days and sometimes it's wore off."

"But he didn't stink yet. And the real funny thing was, when I stuck my finger in the hole—"

"Finger in the hole? Goddogit! I *got* to pop you one now."

"My pinky barely fit," said Purvis, "so it must've been a small caliber like a .32. And there weren't no blood around it. Maybe all that cream in the can he was drinking dried him out. But that ain't all." Purvis held the coffee cup out the window and shook out the last few drops. "This shit ain't worth drinking.

Listen—I saw the Hairy Man last night."

"Dog-dammit God! That too? This is why you stuck up Mama and Daddy's ass all day, you no-working bastard. Who the hell wants to hire you and have to hear that kind of crazy talk? Crazy. Even old Beasley can't work you no more than a week at a time, and you out in the truck."

"Remember that book from the library about the Abominal—ain't that how you say it?—Snowman in China or wherever it is he stays?"

"That kids' book?"

"It was all they had. But if he'd been brown instead of white, he'd be what I saw. I'm going out there to check if them monks is due for propane, and I'll find out if they ever see that monkey fucker scooting around there. I'm not scared to talk to them, you know. You missed the road."

When DeWayne pulled onto a dirt road and put the truck into reverse, it bucked and cut off.

"Ow! Me with a busted up shoulder from yesterday and got to ride in this Japanese jumping bean," Purvis said. "When you going to fix this rice burner or junk it?"

"God up a dog's ass of a flooding—" The truck backfired, whisked a nimbus of pale blue smoke from the hood, and cranked. DeWayne backed the truck out of the dirt road and back onto the paved road.

"It's like this," said Purvis. "Where there's a Hairy Man, there's got to be Hairy Women. There's got to be Hairy People families. Hell, it's got to be a whole Hairy People town up in there, and that means the monks would have to be seeing them."

"If they did," DeWayne said, "and I'm saying *if*, they won't tell you. They don't want crazy peckerheads running all around there trying to shoot one."

"*Somebody's* got to shoot one."

"Nobody's going to, because they don't exist."

"It's the onliest thing that makes sense. Ockham the Razor."

"Do what?"

"That's one of a whole lot of things you don't know." Purvis picked out a cassette. "One tape that's worth a shit in here. Why don't you get a CD player?

Ockham the Razor was a philosopher who lived thousands of years ago and he said cut out the extra stuff, because the simplest answer is the best one."

"You learned this before or after you flunked out of tech?" DeWayne looked out ahead. "You need to go in the front at Beasley's or back around to the yard?"

"I better go in the front and see Beasley first. Turn at Goodyear. No, this is something Greazy told me about."

"Here we go. Listening to Mr. College Boy again."

"He's a damn professor," said Purvis. "Anyway, which one is simplest, that bunches of people, including me, keep hallucinating, or we all seeing something real?" Purvis pushed the cassette into the tape player.

"What's simple is you and the other idiots," said DeWayne. The tape player started. "Dwight Yoakam? You rag on all the other singers, then you play Dwight Yoakam?"

Purvis held up the cassette case. "I like his name. A man could go places with a name like that. Yoakam. Yoakam the Razor."

Lum had filled the truck tank with propane before he decided to quit. That was at least one hook-up Purvis didn't have to do, but the list Beasley gave him was long. By noon, his head would be pounding, and no way he could wait until quitting time to roll a doobie. Swinging by Markham's Mobile Home Village and Resort first made the best sense; otherwise he'd have to backtrack. Plus, saving the monastery until later would give him that whole stretch of road to smoke his joint.

But some things just can't wait. Not with the Hairy Man out there.

The oak canopy shading the long driveway to the abbey's few buildings was the only vestige of the plantation that two centuries earlier belonged to "President" Henry Laurens. As Purvis remembered from the mandatory South Carolina history unit in high school, Henry Laurens was president of the Continent of Congress, or something like that, and many in the state felt he deserved the title Father of His Country. Now, he lay buried near a clutch of alien flowers, tended by alien Catholics, whom Huguenot Laurens may have filled with mini-balls as happily as he would have Cornwallis.

Downshifting under the mossy oaks, Purvis thought about how this place, where he used to sneak in and shoot squirrels, was wasted on a pack of nutless monks and ten thousand chickens. You could make some good money off all that timber. You could rent out the land to the hunting club during deer season. Wadboo could use a good boat landing on this side, too. Throw up a few picnic tables and a crapper, and the same people who pay to see those rusty plows and muskets and cracked maps that pass for a museum in town would hand out five bucks a carload to drive through the tree tunnel and sit by the water or stick up a badminton net. Call it "Laurens Park" and you'd get rich.

Purvis drove past the gift shop, chapel, dormitory, and library to the chicken houses. He saw two monks in the garden, and one more, who stopped and nodded, walking by the dirt road. The propane tank was between the chicken houses and the open shed, where the compost piles were kept. Purvis would have to swing wide to the edge of the woods and back in, maybe pull out and re-aim, to maneuver through a slim gap between the buildings. Whichever monk set this up, Purvis thought, did not figure on having to fill the tank. As he pulled off the dirt road and a few yards into the trees, he saw a tall monk standing in the woods, motionless, holding what looked like a fishing pole.

Purvis backed the truck through the gap. The cab was between the buildings, and he could open his door only a few inches to squeeze out. How did Lum manage to flatten his two-hundred-and-seventy, maybe -eighty, -pound mass through this hole? Maybe he'd taught one of the geldings here how to hook up, or offered him a smoke he could smuggle off around the compost shed. Catholics smoked, Purvis's mother had told him, and do not even think it a sin.

Purvis could smell the compost as he loosened the hose from the back of the truck. The smell was a welcome mask for the propane fumes. The chicken noises—not cackles, more like purrs—were broken by a quiet "Good morning." Purvis spun around to see a man behind him holding a pitchfork.

"Hey," Purvis said.

"We weren't expecting you so soon. The regular driver was just here."

Purvis looked the man over: thick glasses, jeans, denim work shirt, shit-covered boots. He must have been under the shed, turning the compost and mixing in wood shavings.

"Lum quit, at least this week," Purvis said. "The schedule might be off for a while, so I figured I ought to come top you off. Run out of heat and them chickens quit laying, don't they?"

"That's true. I'm Brother Michael, or just Michael. Appears that you know your way around, but please say if I can be of service." He turned toward the shed.

Purvis pulled the hose to the tank. "Thank you. Hey, listen, can I ask you something? Let me just get this going." Purvis attached the hose coupling to the tank, walked to the truck, and turned on the valve. "Okay. Listen. You know anything about the Hairy Man?"

"Beg your pardon?"

"Lives out yonder in the swamp. Sort of like the Abominal Snowman they got in China. Lots of people seen him. I figure he might come up here and steal eggs."

Michael chuckled. "Our only unwelcome guest is an occasional fox that abducts a hen. Sometimes a raccoon." He leaned his head against the handle of his pitchfork, as if listening to a whisper in the ground. "But as for Hairy Men, none that I know of."

"I believe he walks at night. Y'all ever go out to the woods at night?" Purvis checked the gauge on the tank.

"Well, Brother Andrew is our naturalist. He hikes, bird-watches. But he can't help you."

"Hold on a minute." Purvis went to the truck, turned off the valve, and returned the hose. "Now, what you mean, he can't help me?"

"An extended vow. He doesn't speak."

"What kind of shit is that? What about can he write it for me?"

"He can," said Michael, "but his vow is more about communication than vocalizing. He will listen to you for hours on end, but he speaks only to Heaven. I have an idea. Look toward the garden. See the man sitting on the bench carving?"

Purvis looked, and spotted a man in his seventies, wearing a white cloak with a brown hood that draped over him like a poncho. He held a lump of wood, its shavings covering his lap and the ground around his sandaled and socked feet.

"That's Brother Garrison," said Michael. "I think he can be of help."

"He can talk?"

"Can and will. Good day."

That beats all, Purvis thought. Nutless and tongueless. What could be more useless? And bird-watching. Purvis pictured an anemic-looking little man squatting behind a palmetto, jerking off beneath his cloak while a redbird warbled on a sweet gum limb. If a pissant like that walked up to a Hairy Man, you would know the spot from the shit brick the monk left.

As Purvis approached the bench, Brother Garrison raised his head and smiled. "Good morning, young fellow," he said.

"Morning. What you carving?"

"I think this will be Odysseus, but missing an eye. Or perhaps Adlai Stevenson with a large goiter. It all depends upon how the wood guides me." He held out his hand. "I'm Brother Garrison."

Purvis shook the hand. It was much rougher than he expected. "Driggers. My daddy carves cypress knees, too, but he don't name them. People buy them for lawn jockeys. He tried to show me how. Said carving's a good together-activity."

"Your father is a wise man. A shared hobby can forge a strong bond. The knife severs, but the carving connects. A lovely paradox, wouldn't you say?"

"I reckon."

"Will you convey my invitation to your father to visit and bring a specimen of his work?" said Garrison.

"I'll tell him," said Purvis, "but he don't like coming here. Says it gives him the fidgets."

"Me, too, sometimes. But please assure him that we are harmless, and once he learns of a kindred artist, he'll change his mind. I've never known a sculptor who did not enjoy discussing his art."

"Art? Them ugly things? They look like boogeymen to me."

"Beauty can lurk even in the grotesque, can't it? Aristotle said that beauty is that which gives pleasure to behold. Many get pleasure, I am sure, from beholding your father's sculptures."

"You know about Aristotle?"

"Greatest of pagans. Medieval thinkers called him simply the Philosopher."

"Well, I don't know if the Philosopher would go for beholding some of them warty things my old man calls his cuttings," said Purvis. "They all knotty and stringy."

"So are mine." Garrison turned to his left and pointed with his pocketknife. "There's one of mine, one of my cuttings, in the garden. See the gladiolas, the tall yellow ones? Just to the right."

"That sad-faced stump with the marble eyes, all purpled?"

"I stained it."

"Looks like Jesus hiding in some weeds."

"I suspect the Savior abides there, too," said Garrison, with a light chuckle. "Now, young Driggers, did you wish to discuss sculpture, or did you have another inquiry?"

Purvis squatted and took his cigarettes from his breast pocket. He held the pack toward the monk, who shook his head. "I bet you know all about Ockham the Razor." He lit a cigarette.

"The principle of parsimony. Entia non sunt multiplicanda praeter necessitatem."

"Do what?"

"Do not multiply entities beyond necessity."

"That ain't how I heard it," said Purvis. "I heard, 'Cut off what you don't need to get the simplest explanation, and that's the best one.' Now, if a whole bunch of people see something, which is the simplest explanation—they all dreaming, or they all saw something real?"

Brother Garrison held the wood between his knees and carved off some flecks from the top. "Under ordinary circumstances, probably the latter. But people can be mistaken, even in large numbers. Do you have a specific phenomenon in mind?"

"Okay, it's like this, Brother." Purvis sat on the bench beside Brother Garrison. He picked up a wood shaving from the ground and touched it to the tip of his cigarette. A tiny flame glowed. "I saw the Hairy Man at the edge of the water last night when I was down there fishing. He's like a ape man."

"I see." Glancing toward Brother Michael under the shed, Garrison gave a quick wave-salute with his knife. "Driggers," he said, "ours is a world of strange and splendid things, but we don't need monsters to hold our wonder. In this case, I think that when we add everything we know about nature to the evidence, Ockham's Razor may excise the ape man, leaving overactive imagination as the better explanation."

"So you ain't seen him?"

"No, and I doubt that anyone has."

"I know what I saw, and I'm going to flush him out one way or another." Purvis stood and shook the smoldering wood chip to put out the fire. "But I got to go. I'll tell my old man to come out here and look you up."

"Please do," said Garrison. "Say, why don't you take that carving in the garden to your father for his inspection? As a token of good faith, we'll say."

"If you think it's all right." Purvis walked out to the garden and picked up the carved cypress knee. It was heavier than he expected, and looked even more like Jesus up close. It had a long, gaunt face and a beard. Tears seemed to run down the nose, and an arm was curled at the side. The two monks in the garden stopped hoeing and looked toward Brother Garrison, who waved their way.

Purvis returned to the bench carrying the carving. "Is he supposed to be getting crucified?"

"I had not thought of it as Christ when I shaped it. I call him Barbarossa."

"Whatever. I got to go. Thanks for the stump." Staring out into the woods now, Purvis glimpsed the tall monk he had seen standing alone earlier. Now he saw that the monk held not a fishing pole, but a bow. The monk extended his left arm, pulled back the string with his right, and the arrow shot out. About forty yards away, a piece of paper was stuck to a tree. Purvis could make out several arrows wedged in the paper.

"Who's that out yonder, shooting a bow?" Purvis asked.

"That would be Brother Andrew," said Garrison, "our silent forest wanderer. He brings me the cypress knees."

"He the one that don't talk?"

"Never."

"Always hit what he aims at?"

"Always."

"Well, that seems to me like a pretty good way of saying something."

Purvis climbed into the truck and placed the cypress carving on the passenger's seat. If Spessard didn't want it, Purvis could find some sort of use for the ugly thing. Most things seem to find their place if you give them enough of a chance.

SEVEN

As she massaged her forehead with one hand and poured a Miller Lite into a checkerboard-etched glass with the other, Ruthie's nostrils dilated, and her lower front teeth peeked out. She had that look she got when about to bless somebody out, which always happened when they raised the issue of how Ruthie's dead husband came to marry two one-armed women in succession—even though she and Doris had promised not to bring it up on their mother's seventieth birthday.

"He thought she was Norene," Ruthie said.

Doris shook her head. "Why in the world would he want to marry her again, and when they was still married?"

"You know good and well that he was on a two-week drunk when he married Jaynelle, thinking he was marrying Norene again." Ruthie slammed down the now empty beer bottle. "Are you saying my Gamewell didn't love Norene, the one he bought that little—what kind of pistol was that, darling?"

"Walther PPK," Martha said.

"Walter PDK for?"

"You shouldn't be listening to this, Martha," Doris said. "Love ain't the point, Ruthie. Plenty men loves their wife, but don't marry them a second time while they still married."

"There won't but one Gamewell Umphlett," Ruthie said.

"That's for damn sure. Now you got me cussing in front of Martha and her just been baptized." Doris worked her hot pink lips as if she were about to spit. Her chin wart's four stubby hairs angled upward as she turned to Martha. "Let me see that cross your mama said she got you for your baptizing."

"Lost it."

"Come again?" Ruthie asked.

"Slipped off in the water."

"How come you didn't hold it?"

"She was holding her nose," Doris said. "They flip you over backwards. If you'd've been there, you'd know that. Anyway, Norene had left your Gamewell for two weeks."

"That's right," Ruthie said, "she left *him*." She pulled a Salem from the leather cigarette case Martha had made for her twelve years before at 4-H camp. "RutHie" was scorched on one side and "LOVe" on the other. "Forty dollars throwed in the creek."

A pool cue slapped against a doorjamb. "I know what y'all doing," Lula said from the carport.

"Who left that door open?" Ruthie asked. "God knows that old woman's got some ears."

"Y'all saying I chased that old Norene off." Lula stepped through the doorway, using the pool cue as a walking stick. "The good Lord knows I couldn't stand the sight of that prissy girl around him, and me knowing my daughter loved her Gamewell. But I don't mess in other people's business."

"Lord God," Doris said. Ruthie pressed the beer glass to her forehead.

"If they happy ruining their life," Lula said, "then a good mother don't hand them any more heartache. Ain't that right, Martha?"

Martha looked out the kitchen window. "Yeah, Grandma." She looked to Ruthie. "Mama, why exactly was Gamewell never around when I was a kid?"

"I still don't know why she left that whole wardrobe of special-made clothes," Doris said. She fanned herself with a license tag she had taken off her last boyfriend's Firebird. "Martha, honey, close that carport door, please. That little window unit's cooling the whole trailer court."

"Them clothes is why he thought she was still there," Ruthie said. "He spent a fortune for them one-armed blouses and dresses. My Gamewell said no woman of his was going to safety-pin her sleeve up like government cheese-eating trash."

"I don't blame you for wishing your Gamewell hadn't wasted them custom-mades," Doris said, "but they wouldn't've done you no good. You up to what now, four hundred pounds? I could've cut off the other sleeve and made sun dresses out of them. Martha, bring me a beer, shug, and you ain't got to get me no glass like you do for your mama."

"I happen to be a lady," Ruthie said.

"Ain't nothing wrong with government cheese," Lula said. "It was good cut up in little pieces on that hamburger thing that come in the box with them flat noodles. Those flowerdy dresses were pretty, though. I liked that one with them purple blossom trees Jaynelle said was like a tree they got in Florida. What's they called?"

"Jackarollers," Ruthie said.

"Jacar*and*as," Doris said.

"I wish I could see one of them," Lula said. "Y'all don't never take me nowhere. But what Ruthie's Gamewell ought to've done was go down to Charleston and sniff around that false limb store. What do they call them things?"

"Prosthetics," Ruthie and Doris said.

"This is going nowhere," Martha said.

"Ought to be some one-arm girls going in and out of there what might appreciate a whole set of clothes," said Lula. "They can't be too choosy, being crippled and all. But if your Gamewell'd found another one, he wouldn't've finally let you marry him. I wonder if he'd left you if he'd gone on a run of fat women."

"And you never would've thought," Doris said, "he'd get a second lefty right down the road at Swanky's jook joint shooting pool."

"Pinball!" Ruthie said. Her eyes were watery. "You saying my Gamewell'd marry a pool-playing woman? He might not've looked it, but he had—what do you call it?—standards."

"Look at you, welling up already," Doris said. "All I know is you can't play no pinball with one arm."

"Jaynelle could. She'd hike one leg up like this," Ruthie said, laboring to raise one leg a few inches off her wheelchair, "and push against the flipper button with her knee. I saw her do it, and I saw my Gamewell pump nine dollars' worth of quarters into that machine just to watch her hump against it. You can't blame no man for that."

"Jaynelle," Martha said. "Was she was my biological mother?" Her eyes, sharp and narrow, pointed toward Ruthie.

Ruthie dabbed a handkerchief at her eyes. "Do we have to discuss this now, honey, on your grandma's birthday? But the answer is 'yes,' and you look just like her."

"Lord, I hoped we wouldn't have to dig this grave again," Doris said. "Where did Larson run off to? Norene was your mama. That's how you come to have that pistol. Anyhow, that's not the point."

"Jaynelle was *so* her mama," Ruthie said. "I ought to know, me the one what went and got her from the bus station when she left."

"Then how come I got that picture of Norene holding her on her lap in the Tilt-A-Whirl?" Doris asked.

"I have told you and *told* you that's me in that picture. The Tilt-A-Whirl's spinning so I look blurry like Norene with all her makeup."

"Then where's your arm?"

"It's dark, for God's sake. Who the hell goes to the fair in the daytime?"

"The schoolchildren do," Lula said. "Martha brought me a candied apple one time, didn't you, shug? It broke out my eye tooth, but it was still sweet of her. Now, I want y'all to stop talking about that mess and getting Martha all upset with her just coming back home and being baptized. Just be thankful, Martha baby, you were born with all two of your arms."

Martha spun around from the window and slapped her chest. "I am a *grown* woman. I've been married and divorced and suffered more than all of you. I ought to be able to tell people who my biological mother was and why my own father treated me like a stranger. I got a *right* to know."

Doris dropped the plastic forks she was setting around the table. "I'll be dog. Who'd that sound like, Ruthie?"

"I heard it," Ruthie said.

"What?" Martha asked. "Aunt Doris, who'd I sound like?"

Ruthie spat her gum into a beer can and pulled another stick of Dentine

PURPLE JESUS

a novel

from her purse. "Who's ready for birthday cake?"

Doris stuck her head out of the door. "Where's that boy? Larson!"

"We was playing pool, then he just upped and gone," Lula said. "Something about a job. I'm going to forgot whose shot it is. And that better not be no German chocolate, Doris, like you always make. That coconut gets me all backed up. Did you make another'n for Armey's tomorrow, or we got to save some of this?"

"So this is how it's going to be?" Martha asked. "I come home after all I've been through, and this is how you treat me? Like you do Grandma?"

"Larson! I better not have to go looking for that boy," Doris said. "So when's Beulah's girl—what was her name—due?"

Ruthie blew her nose. "I believe it's Lynette. She's Beulah's youngest, I know that much. She's off living with Beulah's second husband—I reckon he's Lynette's daddy—who's just as sorry now as he ever was."

Martha opened a beer. "Y'all're just going to ignore me now, is that it?"

"How come she hadn't told you before now?" asked Doris as she looked out the door.

"She just found out herself. Her daughter was going to the hospital to get them eggs stuck in her but wasn't telling her boyfriend, who she'd been living with for three or four years, and both of them only nineteen. Well, one of them eggs took, and when she got to showing, the boyfriend got scared and run off. After a while, come to find out the boy was in jail after trying to rob a feed store or bait store or something another."

"Maybe he was getting money for the baby," Lula said.

"It was still stupid. So Beulah's sold the shop and going to get the girl— yeah, I'm pretty sure it's Lynette, or maybe Jeanette—right after Easter. So what with marking down everything and making up that bunch of corsages for Easter Sunday, she asked if Martha could help her a little. And now look at her. Not even a whole day after baptizing and her already drinking." Ruthie reached for another napkin to wipe her eyes.

"I'm going to skin that boy. Larson!" Doris yelled. "I think you'll enjoy working there a few days, Martha honey. And a beer once in a while ain't backsliding. I ain't saying I'm a saint or anything, but . . . well, yonder he comes, and running, too. Lord, is he crying? Larson, honey!"

Larson stumbled through the door sobbing and babbling.

"Take your hand out of your mouth, son," Doris said. "I can't tell what you're saying."

He took his hand out, but went on about grabbing "the rake like he said do and I done told him we didn't need no more gas, and he didn't listen even, but old lady Markham put me up in charge, but it caught on the nest and it come down when I pulled it and they come after me and they fast and bit my fumb."

"Who?" Doris asked.

"Them wast-es what the gas man was fixing to shoot with his hose, but they come down with the rake and chased me—"

"He needs some salve on it," Ruthie said. "Hey, there goes a Beasley truck driving by right now."

Doris kissed Larson's thumb. "He just needs some birthday cake, don't you, darling? That'll get your mind off it."

"Alum," Lula said. "Alum draws out the poison. I got a little hunk back in the cabinet." She disappeared down the hall.

Doris removed the top from the cake plate and cut a slice. "Darling, I've told you about messing with people working. Remember when the phone man was doing something with that little box beside the pole and you got shocked?"

Larson picked up the cake with his hand and shoved the slice into his mouth.

Lula returned with a small paper bag. "Now this is already been ground up. You wet a pinch with a little spit—careful, Lord is it sour—then mash it on the wasp bite. Draws the poison . . . Y'all *know* I can't eat no German chocolate!"

"One of y'all's going to straighten all this out for me," Martha said.

"Sweetie, let it alone for a while," Ruthie said. "The party's started."

Martha downed her beer and got another from the refrigerator as she went outside to the carport. She rolled the balls along the length of the pool table, over and over as quickly as she could grab them. As they collided and ricocheted away from each other at crazy angles, they made soothing *clack* sounds, like bones cracking.

EIGHT

If the potholes in the narrow limestone road, bisecting the rows of tin boxes at Markham's Mobile Home Village and Resort, were not real speeding deterrents, the abandoned big wheel tricycles and BI-LO shopping carts surely were. When Purvis got out of the truck to move an upended baby stroller, a short man wearing a translucent green visor and carrying a rake hurried toward him from between two trailers.

"Hey! You what's getting from that truck what nobody don't need no gas from now," the little man said. He looked around Purvis's age. "You got to ask me if you go to do things around here like that fellow what come for the tires off Miss Fairchild's trailer with a big wrench—what you call them that turns real fast with the hosepipe on them?—already twisting off them screws and I caught him." His feet snapped forward as if his knees were tied together.

Purvis thought there might be something wrong with him—maybe off in the head or something. He couldn't understand all of what he said. "Y'all need to keep this shit out of the road," Purvis said. "If somebody runs over it and tears up their car, they going to sue you." He pushed the stroller under the nearest carport. "I'm just going to the office to see Miss Markham."

"That buggy don't go there. It's Hattie Jean's with the blue trailer yonder. She puts her bags of cat food in it, what's too heavy for her to tote but saves money on, and them mean Hurley young'uns plays with. You got to buy big bags of things to save money. Or boxes." The little man took a Lifesaver, already unwrapped, from the pocket of his khaki pants, put it into his mouth, and chewed it fast. "Old Lady Markham gone to see her sister what had the grandbaby in

Pamplico, and I'm in the charge 'til she gets back, and I got more worry than running off a gas man we don't need."

Purvis thought he may have seen this man before, but he knew he wasn't Radford, the regular caretaker. Radford didn't have sense enough to run things with Miss Markham away, but this guy seemed worse.

"Where's Radford at?"

"Radford's dead and buried down yonder by the Half Moon Pond, you know, where the little brass ankle girl got bit by that whole nest of pilates and was all dead before they gotten her to the hospital. Radford, he fell outen the chinaberry tree, getting that Chester boy down from when he clumb up it after his daddy whipped him. Radford broke every bone in his body, and the Chester boy got all whipped again after all that." He spat on the ground and lumped dirt over it with two quick swipes from his brogan toe. "You got a piece of your ear gone. How you done that?"

"Dog bit it." Purvis always felt nervous talking to people who were crazy or off. They like to follow you around and hug you. They don't understand things like "I'll see you later" or "Get the hell on away from me." If you're nice to them and talk long enough, their families think you're trying to get the off person to do something you don't want to do yourself, or maybe trying to steal from them. Someone was probably looking out a trailer window right now, hoping Purvis would go a step too far so they could stick a pawnshop-bought .410 barrel out the door and be the talk of the park this week.

The little off man took a step toward Purvis.

"Listen," Purvis said as he reached his hand back to the truck door. "You know some Wrights here?"

"What kind of some rights? I know all what is for to know here and why you think Old Lady Markham put me in the charge if I didn't? Except them wast-es is giving me a time, we got to get them." Purvis glanced up, spotting, at the top edge of the nearest trailer, a paper wasp nest the size of a cabbage.

He turned back toward the little man. "I mean people with the last name of Wright," he said. "Don't some of them live here?"

"I do."

"You do what?"

"Live here, right here is where I live, not in this trailer here but over yonder. Can't you hear good?"

Purvis felt short of breath, like he was going to have one of his asthma attacks. "Okay, but does anyone here have Wright for a last name?"

"Me. My last name and I live right here, too. This here is Markham's Mobile Home and Trailer Court Resort and my name is Wright, my last name, and I live here and you don't. Now when are you going to fill up them gas tanks for the trailers? I got to get back to them wast-es."

"But you said the tanks . . ." Purvis took a deep breath. He reached into his pocket for his inhaler. Placing it to his mouth, he pressed and puffed the albuterol deep into his lungs. He counted to eight, blew out, and inhaled another puff.

"What you sucking on?" the Wright man asked. "Let me have some."

"This is medicine." Purvis, feeling relieved, put the inhaler back into his pocket. "Are you kin to Armey Wright?"

"Uncle Armey don't live here. He lives down at the river where they shot them dog-looking things at, and we going to see him for his birfday, and it ain't no trailer."

"His birthday? When?"

"That's when he was born," said Wright. "Today is Mawmaw Lula's birfday but we ain't give her the cake yet, but they said we got to eat it soon so Ruthie's girl I ain't seen in a long time can get to work, and I got to get them wast-es before they biting on somebody."

"Larson!" A woman's voice came from a couple of rows away.

"Mama calling." Wright started to walk back in-between the two trailers from where he had emerged.

"Hold up, Speedy," said Purvis. "When are you going to your Uncle Armey's?"

"Not today. On his birfday, and this is Mawmaw Lula's birfday. You reach up there that wast nest for me?"

"Floating Jesus." Purvis wondered who would send somebody so off to knock down a wasp nest. Perhaps this was how the strange little Wright had fun. At least he wasn't trying to hug Purvis. "Look, does a Martha Wright live here?"

"Larson!" the woman called again.

"Come on before Mama is mad and gets me. Look at it." Larson Wright pointed up, toward the wasp nest. Then, closing his eyes, Larson swung the heavy rake at the nest, missing wildly. The metal teeth clanged against the side of the trailer, making scratches in a layer of mildew.

"Godamighty damn, it looks like somebody's head hanging up there," Purvis said. "You stay right there. I got an idea." He pulled the propane hose back between the trailers. "When we shoot this gas at the nest, it'll kill those boogers instantly, like they were froze. Now you point this at the nest like a gun while I go back and cut it on."

"Not supposed to cuss." Larson held onto the rake with one hand and reached with his other.

"Hold it with both hands," Purvis said. "Get rid of that root rake, or I'll be cussing a assload more."

Larson threw the rake straight into the air. It hooked and stuck into the nest as if it had been slapped against a cantaloupe. "Lookit!" Larson squealed. A cloud of wasps swirled around the top of the trailer.

"Don't move!" Purvis said. "They come after you when you run. Let them settle down, then I'll ease back to the truck and flip on the valve."

Larson giggled and jumped for the rake handle.

"Keep still, you little dumb-ass!"

Larson jumped again, reached the handle, and pulled the rake and the nest down on top of Purvis.

"Larson!" the woman called.

Purvis tripped over the propane hose and landed on his back. He felt a fiery pain in his bottom lip. He slapped the nest from his stomach and felt a stab in his right ear. He scooted off the hose, then rolled up to his hands and feet, dog-scuttling for a few yards before straightening up to run, flailing at his head.

He heard a scream, and at the edge of his field of vision, alongside the limestone road, he saw Larson doing his jerky run, probably how a hog would look if it ran upright. Purvis felt another sting on his throat as he made it to the truck.

"Driggers." Beasley's voice came on the radio. "What's your twenty?"

Purvis picked up the receiver as he cranked the truck. "I'm leaving Markham's."

"Markham's? What the hell you doing there? How much you done?"

"I made a mistake. But I got most of the rest." *Whalank.* He ran over a bicycle.

"I told you I got Little League this evening, and I got to lock up the yard. Hell, just drive the truck on home."

"Ten-four."

"You sound funny. You been drinking?"

"Negatory." He looked into his side mirror. The hose dragged along behind.

By the time Purvis finished his route and got to the Rexall drugstore, his lip looked like a plum. He could say he'd been in a fight, but the earlobe, sagging like a muscadine, would be hard to pass off as a punch wound. Most of the stores on Central were already closed, even though they claimed to stay open until five o'clock, but maybe the Rexall wasn't. Purvis pulled the truck in front of the drugstore, angling in and taking up two parking spaces.

The store was open. Purvis walked in.

Lizzie Turnipseed emerged from the back of the store with a box. Purvis caught up with her just as she sat on the floor of the foot-care aisle.

"Excuse me."

"Yes, may I . . . Purvis? What in this world happened to you?" said Lizzie. "You look like somebody beat your butt. Was it DeWayne?"

Purvis clenched his fists. "Hell no. You think DeWayne could do it? No way in hell."

"Calm yourself, sweetheart. I was just asking. So who—"

"Wasps. I need some salve. What's good for wasps?"

Lizzie stood and smoothed the front of her smock with her palms. "Are you allergic? Can you breathe all right?"

He felt pressure in his throat, but he thought it was probably from the welt swelling against his larynx. "I can breathe. They just burn like a son of a bitch."

"You ought to take some antihistamine anyway. And we've got some ointment that'll help the swelling and the discomfort. Lordy, that knot on your throat looks like a goiter."

You pay all that money learning to be a pharmacist's assistant, Purvis thought, and they teach you to say "discomfort." He followed Lizzie through the aisles for a tube of Bee Beater and a pack of allergy soother tablets.

"What's that for?" Purvis asked. "That's just cold medicine."

"It's an antihistamine," said Lizzie. "Sometimes people think they have a cold when they really have an allergy. Those swellings from the wasp stings are allergic reactions, but you must not be too allergic or you'd be having trouble breathing. People can die from stings, you know."

"I get trouble breathing sometimes and have to use this." Purvis reached into his pocket and showed her his inhaler.

"That's for asthma. That's different."

"Whatever. This better not cost much. I ain't got but a ten."

At the counter, Purvis paid six dollars and thirty cents for the medicine and three Squirrel Nut Zippers. He read the label on the tube of ointment as he reached the door to leave. Someone entered, nearly bumping into him.

"Pardon me," a man said.

"Yeah, pardon you," Purvis said. He looked up to see a man of about sixty, wearing something similar to a hooded sweatshirt, and another tall, bearded man, wearing a full-length cloak.

"Oh, monks," Purvis said. "I was to y'all's place this morning, gassing up the chickens."

"Of course. I saw you speaking with Brother Garrison, our resident philosopher," the same man said. The other remained silent.

"Yeah. Look, I'd like to stay and shoot some monk shit with you, but I got to go rub up with this grease." Purvis stepped around the two men and went to the cab of the propane truck. He opened the tube and swiveled the side mirror in to smear thick layers of the ointment onto the swellings. Surprisingly, the stuff did not burn. He wiped the excess onto his shirt, opened a Squirrel Nut Zipper, and slid the caramel chunk over his fat lip into his mouth. He backed the truck away from the curb.

"Aah!" someone yelled.

Purvis hit the brakes and spun the side mirror out. Agnes, the secretary at Beasley's Gas, stood at the back bumper of the truck with a hand over her heart.

"Who's that nearly about run me over?" Agnes said, approaching the truck window. "Mr. Driggers? Mr. Beasley wouldn't like knowing one of his drivers don't check before they back up." But her mood changed when she reached the window. "Oh my Lord," she said, "what's become of your face?" She smiled, showing more gum than Purvis could take, then placed an index finger into her mouth.

"I'm sorry, Miss Agnes. I should've been more careful, like I should've been when them wasps got a hold of me."

"Bless your heart." Agnes took the finger from her mouth and pointed it at Purvis. "You know what's good for wasp bites? Tobacco. Just wet a pinch and press it on the bite. Draws the poison right out. I keep a little pouch of Half and Half in the house just in case."

"Thank you, Miss Agnes. I might have to try that." Purvis noticed a tiny drop of blood forming at the tip of Agnes's tiny finger. "I got to go now."

Agnes placed a white and tan saddle oxford onto the curb. "I'll see you tomorrow then. I think Lum's out for good this time." She turned and went into the drugstore.

Agnes was probably forty, Purvis thought, but he'd still take a tour of her old cooter if she would just keep all that gum out of sight. He could handle the eyebrows she drew on with a magic marker. He could even stand the sagging eyelids she held up with little strips of surgical tape. But all that gum looked as if somebody had popped her in the jaw when she had a mouthful of pomegranate.

He checked both side mirrors before backing onto Central. He pushed the Rexall receipt into his breast pocket, smearing the caramel-colored drool that had fallen onto his shirt from the corner of his numb, purple mouth.

NINE

"Few creatures inspire greater awe in a woodland foot traveler than the magnificent Pileated Woodpecker. His scarlet crown points extend the formidable length of this regal bird to raven proportion. This feathered lumberjack stabbing its pike at a pine trunk makes an impressive display as the planks of bark fly away as if in a storm. His hunger sated by beetles, the marvelous animal will take to swooping flight, its rhythmic wings bearing it in airy crests and troughs.

"The locals call the Pileated God Almighty, some say due to the oath provoked in many upon hearing the startling volume of its wood chops. A more likely explanation is the locals' habit of confusing the Pileated with the exceedingly shy Ivory-Billed, whose sighting is as rare as the Creator's. Indeed, some say that the Ivory-Billed is, as some say of the Creator, but a myth, only the wishful dreams of those unsatisfied with the Pileated's earthy ordinariness.

"This morn I tracked the double-rap chopping of a foraging Pileated, but he ever kept a thicket between us and remained obstructed."

—Fra. Phillip.

May 19, in the Year of Our Lord 1943.

Just after Lauds, the orange sun was only half-risen when Brother Andrew exchanged his sandals for lug-soled boots and a cloak for denim to ward off yesterday's briar vines, which had awakened to spring by growing a foot a day. The creatures of the swamp were shaking off their last winter chills to preen and prance for mates and sing their territories. Whitetail does, their fawns bulging inside, gorged on fiddleheads and slipped into gardens for early peas. Birds transported dogwood twigs and long-leaf pine straw to weave nests. Fishermen cast bucktails into the schools of the spawning striped bass they call rockfish. In another two hours, all this activity would be over—the animals in the shade awaiting dusk, the fishermen in their same clothes atop tractors or behind desks.

As some of the brothers had breakfast, and others remained in their dorm rooms in silent meditation, Andrew came upon Brother Bernard, already kneeling in the garden.

"The colors, Andrew," Bernard said without looking up. "I've been to Rome. I saw Raphael's work, Michelangelo's, all the greats. Breathtaking. No wonder they attract so many pilgrims. But they would pale among these blooms. Look at how the dew works like little prisms, drawing out the crimsons, the purples."

Andrew squatted, forming a tripod with his walking staff and the balls of his feet. The sun would be entirely up in a few minutes.

"Maybe you should have been a Buddhist, Andrew, one of those forest-dwelling monks, practicing archery. Get a handful of sutras to meditate on as you wander about the rain forest. None of the inconvenience of the hours."

A wren chattered at the edge of the trees.

"I'm joking with you, Andrew. You could smile occasionally." Bernard stood and looked toward the trees. "Yes, the best time of day. I know you're eager to get going. Bless you, brother, and your wooded ways. Don't get lost."

Andrew emerged by the creek, farther upstream than he had been in months. He knew that an old house with junk in the backyard sat directly across the creek, but the bushes and vines had grown up to block the view. Two fishermen in a Jon boat upstream drifted with the current. Little had changed since the days when Brother Phillip sat on this bank, scribbling in his journal.

An osprey circled overhead. Gauging the depth and instinctively calculating the height from which she must fall to sink deeply and rapidly enough to capture her meal, she folded, plunged, and emerged with empty talons. What liberation to submit fully to the forces of creation, though t Andrew, folding into oneself and freely releasing all support, to plummet without fear!

Andrew walked downstream and for a moment was even with the fishermen, who spoke low but excitedly and half-stood in the ungainly little boat. Something as dark and slick as an inner tube rolled in the surface, and one man slapped a paddle down onto the water.

"Bastard!"

"Get him?"

"I don't know. Where's he at?"

The boat floated out of sight just as Andrew got to the train trestle. He climbed the ramp to the tracks and walked to the middle of the trestle. Andrew leaned over and spat into the water. He was no longer in the abbey. *This is the edge of my world*, he thought. *What a metaphor. Right here I could fall off the edge of the world.*

He balanced along the smooth rail away from the trestle and toward the road, surprised at how sure-footed he felt. He picked up his pace, but then a muddy boot slipped from the rail. His hands broke the fall, but his stomach met a cross-tie, knocking the wind out of him. He turned onto his back and stretched his chest up. *At the edge of my world, I have lost my breath.* He felt a slight panic for the few seconds before the spasm in his diaphragm unclenched in tiny spurts, allowing in small bites of air, until he finally breathed a deep, satisfying chestful. Andrew turned and rested on an elbow. The heels of his palms began to sting. He looked at his hands and saw where the gravel had scraped them.

Something shone on the rocks beside his wrist. It was silver and flat, and shaped somewhat like a four-leaf clover. One leaf had a hole in it. Perhaps the object had been a pendant. He put it into a pocket as he shifted around to sit on a railroad tie. He removed the journal from inside his shirt to see if it had been damaged. It hadn't.

"At the edge of a clearing before a stand of pines, as the sun sets, a yellow-shafted flicker, marked with speckled belly and bibbed breast, scrounges about for final morsels. Known to the locals as the yellowhammer, he exists in the margin of the woodpecker realm, for he alone takes his meals from the soil as well as the trees. He has adapted his toiling to highs and lows, accustomed his meals to moths or ants, and accepted his perils on the wing from above or slithering below."

Andrew brushed himself off and started back to the dormitory.

The tips of Andrew's fingers touched the corner of his mouth. Exhaling half his breath, he released the string. The arrow met the paper target just below the black circle. Andrew placed the bow on the ground and went to fetch the arrows from where they stuck into the dead pine.

In a half hour, he had shot only three rounds of the six arrows, trying to empty his mind between each shot.

Some of his fellow brothers, he noticed, seemed to marvel at Brother Andrew's ability to be entirely present in an activity, and maybe envied the serenity it seemed to bring him. Others, Andrew was sure, regarded the practice unbecoming for a Trappist. They were embarrassed having to explain to visitors why a monk practiced weaponry. No one, however, could doubt his marksmanship.

But on this day, Andrew's aim was off. Perhaps the burn in his scraped palm distracted him when he drew the string. Maybe the index fingernail that had bent against the railroad spike altered his grip—Andrew never wore a leather tab or shooting glove, preferring the feel of the string against his three pulling fingertips, accepting the raw soreness he would feel the rest of the day. Or perhaps his frequent night wanderings had left him sleepy and unstable.

Whatever the reason, he just could not find the center.

He retrieved the arrows and paper target, picked up the journal from where he had laid it by the tree, and went to the dorm to put them away. This was his day for sweeping and mopping the cafeteria. He enjoyed the rhythms of these tasks—the swipe of the broom with the grain of the floor planks, the arcs of the mop, the dance of his hips and shoulders. He would say to himself, "I am sweeping, I am sweeping," until the "I" would fade and only the sweeping would remain.

"Andrew, just in time," said Abbot Christopher as Andrew entered the dorm. "I think the cords are tangled on these blinds. Can you reach them, please? A man of my age shouldn't risk climbing upon chairs just for a little light."

Andrew untwisted the strings where they wrapped onto a roller. He pulled, and the blinds raised.

"Thank you, son. Andrew, let me see those hands." Abbot Christopher looked at the scraped palms. "My word, nasty marks. Have you even washed them? Come with me."

In the bathroom, Abbot Christopher fumbled through the medicine cabinet as Andrew washed with soap and water. "Ah, tweezers. Now let me see those hands." Abbot Christopher took off his glasses, held Andrew's hands close to his face, and squeezed the tweezers around the first bit of gravel. "How peculiar, Andrew," he said. "You're tall and lanky, yet usually quite balanced, perhaps in more ways than one." He pulled out another bit. "More puzzling is the rock. We've hardly a pebble here and, of course, none down in the forest where you hike. Were you extending boundaries today?"

The abbot narrowed an eye at Andrew, then went back to work with the tweezers. "Say, how would you like to accompany me into town this afternoon? We're out of iodine and a few other items. It's been quite some time since you've been out, hasn't it? We'll go after the work period and be back for supper. In the meantime, favor those hands to avoid infection."

The Piggly Wiggly had few customers, and Abbot Christopher's grocery list was short: rice, dried beans, salt, flour, and tea. In the hardware store, where they went next to get light bulbs, a garden hose, and a lawnmower blade, Andrew and the abbot were the only people present, except for the two clerks.

So far, Andrew's trip into town, one of only a dozen he had made since coming to the abbey, was painless. No one stared. No one asked why they wore those hoods. No teenage boys yelled from pickup trucks, "Getting any?"

Abbot Christopher parked the Escort hatchback in front of Rexall Drugs, beside a large truck. A few yards away, loud teenage girls in high heels pranced like thin-legged foals into the Moncks Corner Ladies Shop. Andrew opened the drugstore door for Abbot Christopher, who stepped in just as a young man tried to exit.

"Pardon me," the abbot said.

"Yeah," the young man said. "Pardon monks. I went to your place this morning to guess the chickens." His lip was violet and swollen. Andrew could not decipher some of the slurred phrases.

"Of course. You were speaking with Brother Garrison, our resident philosopher."

"Hey, I like to stay soon with monks a bit, but I've got to run please." The young man rushed out the door.

"The lad seemed preoccupied," Abbot Christopher said. "Perhaps due to an aching lip. To the first aid aisle?"

"Here comes Peter Cottontail," a lady warbled as she entered the drugstore. "Ready for Easter, Lizzie?"

"Hey, Miss Agnes," said Lizzie from behind the counter. "Yeah, we're having a big family dinner. How about you? Your eggs all dyed?"

The woman stopped. She spun on her heel to face the counter. Her eyes bulged. "What did you say? What did you *ask* me?"

"Miss Agnes, I asked you if you'd colored your Easter eggs yet. What's wrong?"

Agnes placed the back of her hand over her forehead in a mock faint. "Oh my Lord! Forgive me, sweetie, I misunderstood you. Now, listen, I need me a nipple—well, lookie if it isn't Reverend Christopher. How nice to see you about town." She smoothed down a feathery tuff of her hair.

"Nice to see you, too. I hope you're having a pleasant day." The abbot's tone told Andrew he did not recognize the woman. Surely he could not have forgotten someone with such peculiar eyes—or peculiar adornments. They appeared to have tape above them.

"Speaking of eggs, Lizzie," said the woman, "I need to get out to Cainhoy tomorrow if I'm going to get a couple dozen for the hunt at the church. What brings you in, Reverend?"

"Brother Andrew suffered a slight injury to his hands, and that reminded me that we needed a few other supplies."

"Let me see that." Before Andrew knew what was happening, the woman held his palm to her face. The tape that held her eyebrows up at odd angles made her look surprised.

"Some witch hazel," she said. "That's what you need. And the ends of your fingers! They all roughed up like you been gnawing them. Some nipples will fix you up."

Agnes held Andrew's hand and pulled him to the baby supplies aisle. Abbot Christopher and Lizzie followed.

"My name's Agnes. Are you a reverend, too?"

"Brother Andrew is under a voluntary vow of silence," Abbot Christopher said.

"You mean he don't talk? Well, that's one vow I could never hold onto, but I know a whole lot of people who wish I would! Whoo! Here we are, baby bottle nipples. This is the same thing I came in for. See this little cut on my pointer finger?" She held her finger up to Andrew's face. "Best thing in this world for it is take a nipple and cut off the little rim and slip it on, and in a day or two you can't even see a mark. They come two in a pack, so you'll need two packs. You can save a nipple for another time."

"We thank you, Miss Agnes," Abbot Christopher said. "I hope to see you at the abbey soon. Now, we must run along or we'll miss dinner."

"You are very welcome. Nothing I like more in this world than helping people. I love to help." Agnes cocked her head and narrowed her eyes. "Say, Lizzie, is that little Brenda Lee on the radio? I just love her. *Ooh sweet nothin's*. My favorite's that 'Rockin' Around the Christmas Tree,' but it's the wrong time of year now. Did you ever hear if she did an Easter song?"

"I wouldn't know, Miss Agnes," Lizzie said. "I'm not sure I've heard of her."

"Would you listen to that, Reverend?" Agnes said. "These young people don't know good music, do they? I bet this tall fellow here's got a deep voice if he ever decides to open his mouth again. Well, we'd better get rung up. Oh, Lizzie, I near about forgot I need me a roll of surgical tape."

Andrew lay stiffly in bed. He could not sleep but did not feel like a midnight walk. He heard crickets, frogs, an owl once, and some distant thunder. He thought he heard cicadas, which seemed to have emerged early this year. A waxing gibbous moon sat high in a purple sky. Its phases change, Andrew thought, but the satellite cannot escape its orbital tether. It wouldn't be time to rise for another two hours.

He lay his hand upon his chest and found the flat, clover-shaped pendant he had strung onto a piece of twine. His palm smarted against the metal edges, and the tips of his fingers throbbed in the rubber nipples as if they were trying to break out.

TEN

The perfumes of flowers and the tunes of the Miracles coming from the boom box behind the counter at Beulah's Blooms and What Nots were welcome contrasts to the dull odor of laundry and antibiotic ointment, and to Ruthie's shrill calls for help getting on or off the toilet, or for Martha to fetch another bowl of ice cream and chocolate syrup. The work was soothing, too. Take an orchid or carnation, a few strands of greens, tie a white ribbon around, and stick a large pin with a faux pearl head through it. It was the only peace Martha had experienced since coming home.

For the past two hours, Beulah had been placing reduced-price tags on vases, candlesticks, clocks, picture frames, and the other gift items that crowded the shelves. When a customer came in, she would point out Martha through the door in the "office." "You remember Ruthie Umphlett's girl Martha, don't you? Umphlett, used to be Wright? I don't know what I would've done if she hadn't helped me out, what with Janice quitting to work at the plant and me having to sell this blame shop. Oh, you didn't know about that with my daughter and all?"

Beulah put a "Half Off" sticker on a pen and pencil set. "That's going to be a smart gift for graduation coming up," she said. "Well, four-thirty, I'd better be getting Agnes's bouquet ready."

Martha got a bit creative, positioning a small orchid to bend over a tiny carnation. "Crazy Agnes who used to draw on her eyebrows with a magic marker?" she asked.

"It's worse now. She tapes them up, too. I guess she thinks her eyes are drooping, and that a little transparent tape, that's not so transparent, will fix them."

"What did she order?"

Beulah pulled a lily from a refrigerated case. "Oh, she didn't order anything. She comes by right after work every day—she's the receptionist at Beasley's down the street—and gets whatever I have on special. She always says, 'And don't forget my extra baby's breath.' I think she just likes saying 'baby's breath.' Hell, I'd just give her a clump every day if she'd ask. Then again, it might just set her off. And it's not my business anyway." She picked up a little flask from under the cash register and raised it to her lips. "I don't know what she's going to do after next week."

The Miracles began "The Tears of a Clown" just as the bell on the front door jingled. "Beulah, I have had a day *of* it," Agnes said. "Lum quit again, so Mr. Beasley was in the fits all day, and then he knocked off early, leaving me to run the whole operation. What we got on special today?"

Beulah held up the lily. "I'm sorry you had it rough today, sweetie." She glanced back at Martha for an instant. "Since Easter's coming, I'm having a special on lilies the rest of the week. I already pulled out a pretty one for you."

"I just love lilies," Agnes said. "Put me some extra baby's breath around it, will you, honey? Baby's breath." Agnes narrowed her eyes and cupped a hand around her ear. "That's that old Smokey Robertson, isn't it? What's he saying right there? Always sound to me like 'just like my *Yahtzee* kid,' but that wouldn't make any sense."

Martha stretched her neck to try to see Agnes's eyes.

Beulah lit a cigarillo. "You remember Ruthie Umphlett, used to be Wright, don't you, Agnes? You probably haven't seen her much for a while. She's blowed up like a cow and stays laid up all the time. That's her Martha back there."

"Hey there, darling," Agnes said. "You got married and moved off a couple of years ago, I thought. How come you back?"

Martha wondered how Agnes knew that. "I had a sorry husband—sorry enough that coming back here was better."

"There's sure plenty of them around, you know it?" Beulah wrapped the bouquet in pink crepe paper.

"Beulah, you ought to play some women on that machine every once in a while," Agnes said. "A little Dolly or Loretta never hurt nobody."

Beulah used a tissue to wipe lipstick off the filter of a cigarillo. "You know I can't stand a woman's singing voice. Gives me the skin crawls."

"But you listen to all them high-voiced men. The other day you were playing them Bee Jays . . ."

"Bee Gees."

". . . and you always got that old Webb Pierce on there—ain't he dead?— who I like and all, but why don't you like a woman when you love a high-voiced man?"

Beulah held the cigarillo between her first two fingers low near her palm, like a man does. She took a long drag, then let the smoke wander from between her lips and drew a wisp up through her nostrils. "Agnes, I got to sell the shop."

"I believe that Smokey—he was kind of nice-looking, for a colored man, don't you think?—is dead, too. Say, Johnny Mathis had a high voice, and sang a bunch of Christmas songs. He's still alive. I wonder if he sang any Easter songs."

"You heard me, Agnes. And you heard me every day last week."

Agnes rubbed her trembling fingers over the tape on her eyelids. "You remember when I was in the hospital for that stomach condition? I swiped three rolls of that nursing bandage, but it gave my skin underneath a yellow look, like I had the liver problem." Her chin quivered. "You like my shirt my niece brought me from her trip last year?"

"You bought that from me last month, Agnes."

"It says 'Happy Easter' in Mexican. Look, this little bunny here is Peter Cottontail." A tear fell onto Peter's sequined nose.

Beulah moved to the customer side of the counter, put her hands on Agnes's tiny shoulders, and whispered, "It'll be okay, sweetie. You have to get over it."

"What?" Agnes pulled away and tried to stifle her sobs. "Get over what?"

"I mean me having to go take care of my daughter, sweetie, and, you know, that other stuff. Let me get something for you. Martha, dear, bring me one of those big green boxes from the refrigerator."

Martha looked up to see Beulah roll her eyes and mouth something that looked like "Poor thing."

Agnes turned to look out the window. "Yonder goes Heywood McNeil Senior and his Junior into Buddy's Hardware. I bet they're getting a new baseball glove for Junior, what with Little League fixing to start. Junior didn't play so good last year, but it was his first, and his stubby legs were so cute in those red hose his team wore. And there's Pearl Ard and her twins coming out of the Rexall. Any kind of weather change—cold snap, warm spell—gets the girls' asthma acting up. See those men going into the drugstore? Durned if one don't look like Reverend Christopher from the monk place, don't he?"

Martha handed Beulah the box.

"Here you go, Agnes." Beulah drew an exacto knife along the edges and removed the top. Baby's breath pushed out like springs. "Take these. I got way more than I can use. You could decorate with them."

Agnes picked up a stalk and watched the tiny white blooms of the baby's breath droop, like tired little heads.

"You know, sweetie," Beulah said, "you can grow these yourself. Anybody can."

Martha was about to return to her corsages when she heard a strange noise rise from Agnes—like a small engine choking. When she looked up, she saw spit bubbling between Agnes's teeth, just as her arm lashed out like a whip to slap the box from Beulah's hands.

The box ricocheted off two shelves. A vase etched with cherubim shattered on the floor. A ceramic chicken and her four bitties all fell from where they had marched in single file for six months. They knocked down a plastic hinged egg with tiny robed people inside, kneeling at the base of three crosses—the last of a dozen such eggs Beulah had set out three weeks before. The shop's only menorah, which had stood unsold for four years, fell until caught by its electric cord. Its colored bulbs swayed and flickered just above the baby's breath scattered across the tiles.

A bead of blood clung to the tip of Agnes's pointing finger. "You think you know something, Miss Beulah Warren, but you don't! It was a *tumor*!" Agnes took three steps toward the door. She turned back. "If we had another flower boutique like we should in this backwards town, you'd never had to worry with me no way!"

"Agnes, listen." Beulah ran out from behind the counter and took Agnes's arm. "Sweetie, I'm sorry, but you got to move on."

Agnes dug her nails into Beulah's hand and yanked her arm away. "Watch me."

Agnes left the shop and crossed Central.

Beulah took a drag from her cigarillo and inspected her hand. "Didn't even break the skin. Must be some of her blood on me."

"What the hell happened?" Martha asked, looking through the window to see Agnes across the street, standing by a big truck.

"She probably cut her finger on a staple in the box when she slapped it."

"No, I mean, what brought on that fit?"

Beulah got the flask from under the counter and took a long pull. "I know you just got baptized, but . . ." She held the flask toward Martha.

"Thank you," Martha said. The small plastic bottle was covered in cordovan grain vinyl. She remembered the stainless steel flask her father carried in his hip pocket, contoured to hug discreetly against the flesh—one of many things he kept hidden. Martha turned up the flask. Like her father's, this one held bourbon. She gave it back to Beulah, who took another sip and placed it back under the counter.

"I reckon she was upset about me closing the store," Beulah said. "But also that mess about her losing the baby. She pretends like it was something else."

"Baby?"

"I guess I can tell you. Hell, everybody knows. Say, run back to the closet and bring me that broom and dust pan." Beulah picked up the pile of baby's breath and mashed it into the waxed box. She spoke louder as Martha stepped through the office doorway. "She got pregnant a couple of years ago. Might have been about the time you left. They say it was that Holiness preacher Myron—"

"Pyron. Necessary Pyron." Martha began sweeping up the glass and ceramic shards.

"Is that his name? Well, he was asshole buddies with Sheriff Calhoun Funderburk—Agnes is Calhoun's cousin or niece or something—and instead of whipping the preacher's ass like he'd done most every other man in the county one time or another, he got old Doctor Helmly to write up a note saying Agnes had complications, life-threatening, so he could take her down to some clinic in Charleston to get it took care of."

Martha poured the shards from the dustpan into the trash can. "Are you saying Pyron raped her?"

"That depends on whether you think she could consent or not." Beulah picked up an unbroken bitty and placed in on the counter. "Sometimes she just seems a little, what? Peculiar. Other times you wonder how she can hold down her job. They say it happened during a revival, which I can believe, because half the babies born in this county were conceived at revivals, you know it? You get four or five churches' worth of those pew-jumpers out there singing and stomping around and all piled up on the creek bank, and I mean to tell you, the spirit moves them in all kinds of ways! I know what I'm talking about. But with Agnes, I think she had no idea what was going on, either with the pregnancy or the operation."

"Maybe she knew exactly what was going on," said Martha. "Seems like it's all too easy to treat peculiar people, as you put it, particularly women, like they don't matter."

"I hear you," Beulah said, returning the menorah to its spot.

"And I don't like that it was forced on her, but many a woman has or could have had a better life because of an abortion."

"God knows, honey, but don't get all worked up."

"Listen to yourself—even you're doing it right now."

The front door jingled, and in walked Buddy Wyndham, the hardware store owner.

"Beulah, you ain't closed yet, are you? Good," Buddy said. "I see you put up that 'Everything Must Go' sign. I'm sorry you've got to sell off. We're going to miss you at the Chamber for sure. But, look here, I got to get something for Junie. She's burnt *up* at me for buying that four-wheeler. What you got real pretty that might smooth things over?"

"Jesus Christ," Martha said, throwing down the broom, untying her apron, and walking out the door.

✱

Ruthie sat up in bed, holding a glass of chocolate milk in one hand and the TV remote in the other. A bag of Hydrox cookies sat on her stomach. "I don't know why I even turn on the news when there's nothing good going on noway. There's that old ugly bitch again trying to get the president kicked out of the White House. You just can't make anybody happy." She dunked a cookie into the milk. "Anyway, like I said, Beulah said she was sorry Agnes had to show her behind like she did and get you so upset. She said come in whenever you want to tomorrow. But remember, you got to get me out to Armey's."

"Why can't Doris take you out there? I never could stand that old man."

"I don't need to burden down Doris when I got you. You seen my ointment? My armpit's chafing me something fierce."

Martha picked up the tube of ointment from the floor.

Ruthie unbuttoned her shirt. "And I been itching so, I believe I got the pinworms. You need to get the flashlight and look me."

"No way in hell."

"They come crawling out at night. I'll sleep on my side so's you won't have to try to roll me over." Ruthie raised her elbow to shoulder level and, with her other hand, shifted her flap of a breast towards the center of her chest.

"Not going to happen." Martha squirted a dollop of ointment into her palm. "I've done more than I should have already, and damned if I'm shining a flashlight up your ass. Jesus Christ, you've about scratched all the skin off under there."

"You know I can't reach under there, and you shouldn't take the Lord's name in vain like that, especially when you just been baptized."

"Goddammit, how long are you going to play this game?" said Martha. "You insisted that if I moved in here, I had to get baptized. You know how close I came to turning around and never coming back? But I marched right down into that water with those self-righteous mother- and daughter- and sister- and son-fuckers. Just don't pretend it means a shit to either you or me."

"I just want you to be respectable."

"Jesus! Now button up your shirt and give me those damn cookies." Martha stepped toward the door.

"Sweetie," Ruthie called, "could you hand me that pack of Salems from off the dresser while you're over there?"

ELEVEN

The aspirins and Pepto-Bismol did little for Purvis's headache and roiling stomach. He should have stopped at the station—Clarence surely would have given him a beer on credit there. At least the wasp bites, which had kept Purvis up most of the night and driven him to drink that sloe gin, no longer throbbed. Sweet liquor always tore up his guts, but that was all the package store had for under four dollars other than beer, which just doesn't kill pain fast enough.

On the southern entrance of the driveway that ran through Markham's, the limestone gravel and most of the dirt had worn or washed away, leaving the concrete culvert exposed. Purvis slowed to ease the bump he knew would jar his head, but he risked cracking the culvert. A hazard was what it was. Old lady Markham had no excuse, rolling in all that cash. And still in the road was the bicycle he'd flattened yesterday. That's just sorry. If they thought he was about to climb down from the truck to clean up their trash, they thought wrong.

As the bicycle creaked under the front tire and then hooked to the chassis, Radford emerged from an old Airstream. Purvis stopped the truck.

"Driggers, you trying to break that pipe? Why you didn't come in the other way?"

"You supposed to be dead," Purvis said.

"What kind of 'supposed to be'?" Radford hitched his suspenders higher up on his sloping shoulder. "I'm supposed to be quit drinking. I'm supposed to be don't eat no greasy food. I'm supposed to be stay out of married women's business. None of them 'supposed to be's is done neither. What makes you say such of a thing noway?"

Purvis lit a cigarette and hung both arms out the window. "That little snap-legged Wright was going around here yesterday saying you fell outen a tree and old lady Markham put him in charge. Son of a bitch was on me like a gnat."

"Your daddy told me you was full up with the dull dumbass, but you sure ought to know not to listen to no retard shitbird like that. Rally Wadell, from across the road over yonder, runs the musher for the hash plant, fell outen the tree. They got him up from a dead sleep—he's third shift—and sent him up a tree half-asleep, and then he broke his blessed-ass neck. I look like that ugly-ass bastard? Give me a smoke."

Purvis held out the pack of cigarettes. "I know Rally, but I hadn't heard he was killed. Anyway, that retard or his mama or some damn body owes me six bucks for medicine I had to buy from after he pulled a giant wasp nest down on me."

"That's what got your lip and neck, eh?" Radford took a cigarette and broke off the filter. "What was you doing out here, what with Lum just been here?"

"Got my schedule mixed up. Say, which trailer them Wrights live in?" Purvis handed Radford a lighter.

"Green and white one with the service pole leaning up on it. But they ain't in it. Just left, gone out, I believe they said, to Armey's. He's their uncle or something. That fat one come to get them, and then had to go inside to take a shit. I had to help load her fat ass back into the van, and her about to break that little plywood ramp she shuffles up on. Like getting a cow up in the truck to take to the sale. Listen, you ain't got a bottle in there, eh?" He hiked up the suspender on his bent shoulder.

"Nuh uh. Let me ask you something. You know anything about old Armey? Everybody says he's got money hid out there."

"Everybody says all kinds of shit. This Lum's truck, ain't it? He usually keep a little something in the glove box."

Purvis mashed his earlobe and wondered if he should try to pop it like a riser bump. "I done looked. They say Armey put money in the walls or somewhere."

"How the hell I know? Alls I know is I don't doubt nothing about no Wrights, mean as they is. Shoot one another all the time. And sic a dog on you? Just as soon as look at you. Armey used to feed a passel that he took all around the country to fights. I seen it a time or two. Rake out a circle about fifteen foot and set two dogs in it and bet on which one lives. Some kind of way for a man to make a living. Maybe he got rich off them dog fights and couldn't put his illegal money in no bank."

"He ain't got no dogs out there no more."

"Why you asking me if you already know all about him?"

"Look here," said Purvis. "One of the women living in the trailer named Martha?"

"Don't know any name of Martha, but then again, I can't tell who belongs here and who don't. Might have been one or two extra ones here this morning. All I know is to make myself scarce next time that fat one's here."

Purvis cranked the truck. "I got to get on. Beasley give me an ass of a schedule today. Keep out of trouble."

"You the one'll be in trouble you run back over that pipe," Radford said as the truck pulled away. "And you dragging some shit under Beasley's truck, you dull dumbass."

The first beer had gone down in two swift gulps. Purvis drank the second one slowly and tried to enjoy it, even though his taste buds were numb. The headache, which earlier had been like a roofing hammer slamming his forehead, had spread around his entire skull like a lead hat, but less intense than before. That meant the beer was doing its job, and old Clarence was a lifesaver. Clarence didn't hand out beer on credit to just anybody. You had to be respectable.

Bullhead was a long, meandering dirt road flanked by the river and the Francis Marion National Forest. When Purvis was a boy, a dozen or more families lived along its steep ditch banks in A-frame houses, but now Bullhead was nearly deserted. Someone had bought up most of the land and lined the road with "Posted" signs. Rumor was that a developer was putting in a bunch of condos and a marina with pontoon boats. You could rent those little water scooters that you peddle like a bicycle. DeWayne said they would have a fancy restaurant like he had seen when he was in the army, where you sit at the bar and eat all the roasted peanuts you want and throw the hulls right on the floor.

What if Armey was the last holdout in selling his land to the builders? That would be a reason for him to get killed, and those killers wouldn't even know about the fortune, so it might still be there.

For now, Bullhead was just a dirt road, a mat of briars growing in its ditches, that led to the rundown clapboard house of a dead man. A fresh set of car tracks from bald tires meant Markham's Wrights must already be there. Purvis tried to remember what the odd little Wright had said the day before—maybe that today was Armey's birthday. Or did he say his grandmama's? What kind of people have a birthday party at nine o'clock in the morning? Did they think a hermit like Armey wanted them out there messing with him? Maybe they were really going out there to snoop around for that fortune. And what kind of birthday cake did they bring?

One thing was for sure—they were in for a nice surprise. Armey dead at his kitchen table, the house tore all to hell, and not a dime to be found. Or maybe they wouldn't be surprised. Maybe they put the bullet in him in the first place and now were going back to look for the money they didn't have time to find before. Or what if they did find it, and now they're taking that retard out there to frame him? Good deal: Get the cash and get shed of that annoyance, too.

Armey's front yard looked like a bulge in the road—sandy and flat. Used to be a gum leaf or pine needle hardly settled before Armey raked it up. That was back when Purvis and his cousins rode dirt bikes out here, cutting doughnuts right in front of Armey's porch to irritate the bull mastiffs penned up under the house. Their yellow teeth yanked wildly at the chain-link stapled to the bottom planks, pegged to the ground with rebar. You could not tell how many beasts—five, fifteen?—made up the snarling fury that delighted the kids so. If the fence gave way, maybe the motorbikes could outrun the dogs, but maybe they couldn't—Purvis and his cousins pretended to be unafraid, and dared each other to plant a broganned heel against a protruding snout. Sometimes Armey would step onto the porch, his cap low over his eyes, and point his index finger at the boys, snapping his thumb like a pistol hammer. They'd yell, "Crazy old bastard!" over their shoulders as they sped off to the boat landing to unhook trailer hitches, steal valve stem caps, and remove wiper blades from fishermen's trucks.

A rusty, dark red conversion van sat in Armey's yard. Women were doing something at the side of the van as somebody walked up the porch steps. Purvis stopped the truck behind the van and saw the little man from yesterday enter the house. The women fussed at each other and seemed not to notice Purvis as he walked between the vehicles.

"That ramp ain't fixed right."

"How *do* you want it? I done turned it ever which way."

"Hold my arm, baby, and how did I lose my shoe?"

"Let go my hair, Ruthie. Where did that boy go? Larson!"

Three women struggled to help another, a fat woman, out of the van. One woman, her back to Purvis, moved with such a flurry of twists and adjustments that she seemed to have many arms, like a spider. He was mesmerized by the confluence of limbs that fanned below a head of blue-black hair.

"Let me help y'all with her," Purvis said.

The dark-haired woman turned to him. He saw her face.

"Godamighty," he said, coughing. He raised his hands as if fending off a blow and side-stepped to keep his balance.

The dark-haired woman reached for him.

"Leave him go!" the fat woman called from the side door of the van. "You going to let me fall but catch him?"

"You sure spooked him, Martha," another woman said. "Is he choking?"

"I'm all right," Purvis said. He bent to place a hand on his knees, then took deep breaths from his inhaler. Martha Wright. Martha Right, right for Purvis. She'll be hurt when she finds Armey, her uncle or cousin or maybe granddaddy, dead, and she'll need a man to hug and comfort her. He'll tell her everything's okay, and she won't even have to say the same to him—she'll just sob into his loving arms.

The fat woman wiped her face with a bandana. "You going to hold that board steady or worry about him? Put your arm up under my titty here."

"Mama!" the little man shouted from the house. "Uncle Armey ain't talking at the table with them cans, I told him we's here and brought the party, just leaning like he asleep and don't look up."

"Boy, get out here and help us get your Aunt Ruthie down this ramp."

Purvis regained his breath and approached the scene. "What y'all need me to do? I can help if you show me where to grab at."

An old woman stood at the bottom of the plywood. "You ain't about to fall out again, is you?"

"No ma'am. I just needed a mouthful of my medicine. I got the asthma."

Martha lifted his arm around the fat woman's back. "Just hold her here. I'll get the other side." Her voice was like rain, not like on the roof, but the way quail must hear it, bunched in the broom straw, the drops sliding down their speckled, feathery backs.

"This your mama?" Purvis asked.

"Hard to say," Martha said. "Is she, Aunt Doris?"

"Just help her on out towards me," Doris said, thumping a cigarette to the ground.

Purvis felt the woman place her weight down onto him. Her dress, held to her by an elastic band circling her armpits, let a mass of flesh at the top of her chest press against Purvis's face. A great, flabby arm hugged his shoulders as he wondered how long he could stand there waiting for her to take a step. That's half-inch plywood, he thought. They should have three-quarter-inch for something this size. If that thing cracks and she goes tumbling, DeWayne will have to run the forklift from the rendering plant out here just to set her to her feet. What was that around his arm, a fold of back fat? Maybe it was Martha's arm reaching from the other side. He could stand there longer if need be.

The voice came from the house again. "Uncle Armey I said acting like he dead in that chair, not talking back to me when I said we's here with the party, and said it again to him sitting over, but I don't got the cake it's in the van to show him . . ."

"Mama," Doris said to the old woman, "go see what he's carrying on about. You just in the way here nohow."

Ruthie placed one dinner plate-sized foot onto the plywood. She huffed, lifted the other foot, and leaned onto Purvis, mashing his face farther into her flesh until he could not see. He wondered how they moved her when he wasn't around. Haven't they done this a time or two? The woman must get out of the house on occasion. Does Martha have to wait on her all day? This is one burden that baptizing could not wash away.

The old woman screamed from inside the house.

"What in hell is it now?" Ruthie asked. "I told you we shouldn't've come out here."

Doris leaned to peer over the hood of the van toward the house. "You think I'm all happy about it? You heard Mama carrying on. I thought she'd bust a gut. Nothing would do her except coming to see Armey. Remember a few years ago when she just had to go to Myrtle Beach for—what kind of candy was that?"

"Salt water taffy," Martha said, the words thick like cane syrup, oozing over her mother's shoulders to seep into Purvis's ear.

"Sweet," Purvis mumbled into Ruthie's breast.

"Yeah, taffy," Doris said, "and after all that she said it hurt her teeth—"

Another louder scream came from the house.

"Y'all better go see what's wrong with her," Ruthie said. "I'm about down off this board anyway, and this boy—what was your name?"

Purvis turned his face upward to speak. "Purvis."

"Purvis'll help me to the house." As Martha and Doris went to the house, Ruthie reached the ground and lifted her arm so Purvis could stand straight. "Lord God. I believe I can make it now. I'll need you a little bit when I get to the porch, but going up ain't hard like coming down. I just don't feel steady when I can't see where my feet's at."

"You owe me six dollar," Purvis said.

Ruthie stopped walking and leaned back to look Purvis full in the face. "For what? Hauling me down from the van?"

"No, ma'am, not that. For the medicine I had to get yesterday for the wasp stings from that nest your son pulled down on me."

"First off, he ain't my son, or I'd be constant wore out from blistering his ass with a switch every minute of my life. He's my sister's boy. And second, why was you, a grown normal man with a job and all, messing with wasp nests with a boy what ain't right?" She grabbed Purvis's chin and turned his head. "Looks like them wasps popped you pretty. Good for you, messing like that. What was your last name?"

"Driggers. But I don't have money to throw around on—"

"Armey's dead!" Doris called from the front door. "And the house is all tore up."

"I *told* her we shouldn't've come," Ruthie said.

An airboat roared downstream as Purvis leaned against the truck and smoked. Only Lum Hereford rode the water that fast. It was as if he was mocking Purvis. How many men can walk away from a job and then fish all day like they were rich? How many have an airboat, much less run it wide open like they're *trying* to blow the engine? This is the same Lum Hereford who hand-waxed the propane truck and changed the oil himself every two thousand miles.

The women had talked and moved about the house long enough for Purvis to finish a second cigarette. Had they found something? Purvis had surely left nothing inside. Did they see and finger the hole in Armey's back? Were they looking for the money? In that case, they were going to be there a long time. Why had nobody asked Purvis why he was here?

The screen door creaked open, and Martha floated out onto the porch, descending toward the yard like a spirit. Her arms were on the door, then one on her hip, then at her hair, then on the rail, again as if she had four or six arms—but not like a spider. This was a symbol dance, Purvis thought. He tried to remember where he had seen that picture, the one of some goddess from China or India who had a bunch of arms, and each hand made a sign, and people from over in whatever that country was could read the finger movements like a Bible. Martha was not really a boat, but maybe her arms could scoop up Purvis and save him from drowning.

She came straight toward Purvis, and as he tried to decide what shape her face was—first sort of an oval, but then changing to more like a square—he realized that his mouth was agape, lolling like an idiot's. His lip was no longer numb, but still swollen. He might still be prone to drooling, so to be safe he wiped his mouth with the tail of his striped Beasley's Gas shirt.

"You don't look Holiness," Purvis said, pushing the slobbered edge of his shirt into his belt.

Martha stopped a few feet in front of him, hooking her thumbs into the belt loops of her jeans, her hands forming a heart shape just above her crotch. "What?"

Purvis looked up at her face. She did not seem upset by the death of her kin. She had the same smirk he had seen at the baptism. "You look more Indian. You got some Cherokee or Comanche blood in you?"

"I don't think Comanches were from here, but no, I don't think I do. What did you mean?"

"Ain't nothing wrong with being Indian. My granny was part Indian, and she wasn't trashier than anybody else, except for she'd take a . . . use the bathroom in the yard sometimes."

"No, I meant when you said I don't look Holiness. Do you know me?" She leaned forward a few inches and seemed to smirk on both sides of her mouth.

Purvis felt his neck heating up just like he felt when his mother caught him in a lie. This conversation was going horribly wrong. Maybe he could save it by saying something romantic, like he has known her all his life. He *feels* like he has known her all his life. He feels like he has never known anyone else. Or, nobody could really know her, because she's so mysterious. Mysterious. That sounded like something that ought to be in a movie.

"Sure I do," Purvis finally said. "You're Martha Wright and you just got baptized and I wish you'd tell me a whole lot more about you." He rolled his inhaler in his palm.

"It's not Wright."

"Why not? I won't tell nobody."

"No, my *name* is not Wright. My mother was a Wright. But how'd you know I got baptized? Give me a cigarette."

Purvis put two cigarettes between his lips and lit them both. If she took the one he just lit, it would mean she was willing to share something with him, especially if she didn't wipe it off first. The cigarette on the swollen side of his lip nearly fell from his mouth, but he caught it in one hand and held the other cigarette toward Martha. She leaned closer and took it directly from his fingers into her mouth.

"See, I was out fishing the other night," he said. He placed his thumb, the one that had brushed Martha's lip, to his mouth, pretending to wipe something away. "I saw you and the others getting dunked by that bald-headed preacher."

"I didn't see anybody fishing."

"I was done, see. I was walking back from right along about here when I saw y'all wading out there, so I just sat down in the bushes, see, because I didn't want to disturb y'all from y'all's—what you call it?—ceremony."

Martha blew a smoke ring that twisted upright and rolled, and throbbed like a drunken hoop snake, and flattened and floated over Purvis's head. This could be another message from symbolic Martha, who was moving again. Turning to lean against the truck beside Purvis, she placed some of her arms on the fender. She searched Purvis's eyes, as if helping him remove a speck.

"Why are you out here anyway?" Martha asked. "Uncle Armey didn't use gas."

Purvis took a deep breath and held it for a second. Maybe he could get through this without the inhaler. "He was your uncle? I'm sorry he's dead."

"Great uncle. Don't be."

"See, the fire tower uses propane, and I thought this was the road. You didn't ask, but my name's Purvis. I just drive the truck sometimes. How long's he been dead?"

Martha dropped the cigarette butt to the ground and pressed it beneath her sandaled foot. A tattooed tail of a snake, or maybe a gator, touched the base of her middle toe and the body hid beneath her pant leg. "Must've been a while," she said. "He's stiff."

"No shit? You know what that's called? Rigor morphis. It don't always take, and then it might come and go. Most people don't know that. I know because my brother works at the hash plant," Purvis said. "Some people say glue factory, but it's really called the rendering facility, where they take dead horses and mules and stuff and grind them up and cook them down into something useful. I worked there once or twice. Nasty place." He thumped his cigarette toward the porch and put the inhaler back into his pocket. "I never seen a Holiness with a tattoo, and sure not one like that. Now, an Indian might have one. Anyway, it looks good on you, what I seen of it. Who you think killed him?"

Martha stepped away from the truck and stood in front of Purvis. "What makes you think somebody killed him?"

Purvis's chest tightened up like it did when he had to crawl under a house to fix a pipe, or drag out something that died. "I don't know. I just say all kinds of shit sometimes. But it seems to me like if y'all'd known he was sick with something bad, y'all would've just said he was dead instead of hollering it. Just seemed all surprised." Martha was close to him. He thought he might have smelled her hair. "My lip and ear don't usually look like this. Well, the ragged one the dog bit when I was little does, but the other one and my lip got was stung yesterday at Markham's when that retar—"

"The thing is," Martha said, "Armey's phone is out and we need to get hold of the sheriff. You got a radio in this truck, don't you? Radio in and have them call the sheriff."

"I can't. Beasley says don't use the radio for personal business."

"This is sort of an emergency, and this isn't your personal business, is it?"

"No, I got nothing to do with it, but he'll still be mad, specially since I'm not supposed to be out here noway."

"Goddamn! Didn't you just tell me you're on your way to the fucking fire tower?" She paused, as if expecting Purvis to "explain himself," as Purvis's mother always said. Martha's smirk had returned, and the rest of her face was defined by it, as if the corner of her mouth was the center of a painting.

"See, Radford said y'all was out here, and the wasp medicine was six dollars—"

"My fucking God, what are you carrying on about?" Martha leaned forward with all of her hands on her hips. "Can you at least go to a station or somewhere and call then?" She took a quarter from her pocket with one hand and passed it to another, and then to another, and held it out to him.

Purvis wondered if she was really offering it, or if she was being smart with him. A girl who cussed like that, particularly right after being baptized, is probably a straight-talker. If she was being smart, though, and he took the quarter, he would be a double-barrel dumb-ass. But the quarter would be warm from her pocket.

"I could run to Flippo's and call. Won't take but a minute." He was about to reach for the coin when she returned it to her pocket. "I'll come back and help fix up before the sheriff gets here."

"Fix up?"

"You know, just whatever needs to be done." Purvis opened the truck door. "You want to ride?"

Martha took a step back from the truck. "No thank you."

Purvis climbed onto the seat and closed the door. "I just got to find a place to turn around."

"Story of my life."

"Do what?"

She had already turned toward the house, her four or six arms drawing diamonds and hexagrams and other beautiful shapes in the air.

TWELVE

Lula slipped a peppermint into her mouth and dropped the cellophane wrapper onto the van floor. "I done called Armey twice and him not answering. He better not've forgot we coming. He's older than me, you know, and sometimes old people forgets things." She bit into the candy and removed a shard to examine. "How you reckon they get them little stripes on this here candy? Looks sort of like fan blades to me. I've always wondered that. Armey might could tell me. He reads books."

"Maybe he could tell you why you so mule-headed and eat so much candy," Doris said. "You not supposed to have sugar."

"You know when my eyes get weak I need something sweet or I get blind as a dead snake," said Lula. "Riding always does it to me. Trees and houses and all zip-zipping by and things get blurry."

"With all that cake you had yesterday," Ruthie said, "you ought to be seeing clear for a month."

"Give me that candy, Mawmaw," Larson said. He got up from the bench seat and shuffled to the front to stick his hand over the seat.

"Sit back down, boy!" Doris said. "And stay off your knees before you ruin the one good pair of pants you got. Bad enough you took the real seats out of here, Ruthie, but then didn't even put any seat belts back."

"I think it's nice," Lula said. "I ain't been in it since you fixed it up. Who'd you have do it?"

"Double Happy," Ruthie said. "He give me a good discount, too. Family."

Doris grabbed Larson's belt and yanked him back as he stuffed the candy into his mouth. "Family, hell. Every time y'all talk to Double Happy's sorry ass, it stays one step closer to me. I swear y'all see more of him now than when we were married. And all he did here is rip out the real seats and put some slapped-together benches with some old quilts tacked to them against the walls. This one's eating into my ass now."

"I got to get my wheelchair in here," Ruthie said. "There won't no room before. He knows something about customizing."

"Not but one thing he knows," Doris said, "and that's which end of a bottle to turn up."

"He cut that ramp for me."

"Ramp? A piece of scrap plywood he probably stole from some construction site. You think he could have at least painted it red to match the van."

"Maroon. This *conversion* van is maroon."

"Maroon, scarlet, pig-asshole cherry for all that matters," Doris said. "Point is, a sorry man is a sorry man. Every one of us has had a belly full of them and ought to have learned how to steer clear of them by now. Am I right, Martha?"

"Martha's Young won't sorry," Lula said. "He just had his ways, and she had hers."

Martha dug her fingernails into the steering wheel. "Jesus Christ. Do I turn onto Hard Pinch?"

"By your Uncle Blease's place," Lula said. "I think they do call that road Hard Pinch. Ruthie, what's them big old boogers Blease keeps in the field with his cows?"

"Buffaloes," Ruthie said. "And he's not 'Uncle.' He's some kind of cousin."

Lula shivered. "They give me the fidgets something fierce. Big old hunched-up things. Mangy-looking. We went and watched Blease breed one to a cow. Whoo! That was the beatingest thing I *ever* saw! Took two Hersheys and a Butterfinger to set my eyes right. You'll see them old boogers up here. I'll have to duck my head until we pass them," she said. "And Martha, sweetie, you ought not to call the Lord's name in vain like that, what with you just been baptized and all."

Martha looked into the rear-view mirror. Ruthie crimped her eyes and stared into her seek-a-word puzzle book. Doris held a loose fist to her forehead as if cooling her brow with an invisible beer bottle. With his finger, Larson explored a hole he'd found in the bench's fabric. Young had been the first train leaving all this, and Martha had jumped on, destination unknown, like a hobo. Could she hop another, one with no stops until it plunged from a trestle in Mexico at seventy miles per hour?

"The ramp's upside-down," Ruthie said. "See that orange 'down' writ on it? I swear none of y'all got sense one."

"That 'down' was on there before Double Happy ever stole it," Doris said. "It's the same difference whichever side of the board is up. Larson, where you going?"

Martha flipped the sheet of plywood over. "There. Better?"

"Who's that a-coming in a truck yonder?" Lula asked.

"Unless that truck's coming to haul me out of this conversion van, you ain't got to worry about it," Ruthie said. "Now I said I'm going to do some walking today, so come on. Martha, baby, get up under my arm and prop me."

"Somebody's getting out," Lula said.

"Do y'all *want* me to fall? Now look at it. That ramp ain't fixed right."

As the others kept on fussing, Martha tried to find a way to steady her mother without clutching a handful of flesh. She pressed her palm between Ruthie's shoulder blades, pushed the other against her side, where on anyone else she would have felt ribs, shifted the first arm down and around the massive haunches, and reached with the other, up and over the shoulder, in what looked like a grip in a wrestling throw.

From behind her, a man's voice said something about helping, and Martha turned to see him.

"Godamighty," he said, coughing and crossing his hands before his face as if wincing from a bright light. He slouched against the side of the van. Then he reached into his pants pocket and glanced back at Martha. His lip and one ear were swollen, and the other ear looked as if the lobe had been ripped off. What struck Martha most about his face, though, was the hopelessness.

Pacing back and forth in front of the stove, Lula hugged her stomach, humming like she was working up to a tune she could not quite recall. Larson put a condensed milk can to his lips and tilted back his head. Armey sat at the table as if reading something in his lap.

Lula stopped and placed her hands on her chest. "Look how dead he is. He's the deadest man I ever seen. Deader than dirt."

Doris went around the table and put her palm to Armey's head. "He's cold all right."

"Do you think he had a fever?" Lula asked. "We got to get somebody out here, not mess around feeling of his head like you knowed what to do with a dead man. You can't see he's all dead?"

"Where's that birfday cake?" Larson asked. "I told you he was sitting and not talking when I come in here and no lights." He sucked from another milk can. "That one had some in it—"

"Get your ass out of here, boy!" Doris said. She grabbed Larson by the arm and pulled him toward the back door. He managed to get another condensed milk can before she shoved him onto the back porch. "And stay out of the dirt with them good pants on. Now let's just all calm down. Martha, you call Sheriff Funderburk. That's about all we can do—just wait here until Funderburk comes and tells us what to do."

Martha tried the phone that sat on the floor by the pie safe. "It's out."

"I told you I tried to call," Lula said. "It just rung and rung. You'd think they'd make it say if it didn't work, not just ring like nobody wanted to answer. He won't but three years older than me."

Doris left for the front door. Lula paced again. "Mm-mm. What we going to do?"

"Why are you so upset?" Martha pulled a chair from the table. "Sit here and settle down." Lula slumped down into the chair. "Better?" said Martha. "Listen, he wasn't *your* brother. You saw him, what? Once a year? And you know what else? He was an evil son of a bitch."

"You shouldn't talk so ugly, shug, him dead and all."

"I'm glad he's dead. Do you have any idea what kind of slime he was?"

Lula picked up an empty condensed milk can from the table. "Some men just can't help it."

"Can't help what?"

"You reckon this cream was all he'd been eating? I drink it in my coffee, but, Lord, a can lasts me a week." She put the can flat on the table and turned it slowly like a knob. "Like I say, we've all sinned and fallen short of grace. Get me some tissue, sweetie."

"Use this." Martha drew a blue paisley bandana from her jeans pocket. "What was Armey's sin? Are you telling me you knew about him—knew what he did?"

"It's hard, Martha darling. It's hard when you love somebody."

"Grandma, *what* are you saying?"

"Let me," Ruthie panted, "see him." She stepped into the room, taking rapid breaths, with Doris behind her. Her tremendous breasts spread and rippled as she heaved at the air. "Get me," she said, panting, "a chair."

Martha pushed a dinette chair against the backs of Ruthie's knees, and Ruthie dropped to the seat. Her feet slid forward, and the chair skidded and tilted back on the slanted floor. The other women lunged away from her, but then the chair rocked forward with a thud. "This slanted," *pant*, "damn house," said Ruthie. "Wonder we," *pant*, "don't slide right out the door." *Pant*. "You sure he's dead?"

"He's dead to beat all," Lula said.

"Anybody," *pant*, "shake him?"

"I felt him," Doris said. "Cold as ice."

"Cold as godless hell," Lula said.

Ruthie fanned herself. Her neck was red and splotchy, and her face was covered in sweat. Her breathing slowed. "He ain't getting no better with us just talking about how dead he is. Somebody ought to call Funderburk is what somebody ought to do."

"Phone's out," Martha said.

Ruthie pulled her muumuu up over her knees. "Lord, I'm hot. I reckon you need to run somewhere what's got a phone, baby. You supposed to call the law when you find somebody dead if they kin or not."

"That gas truck should have a radio on it," Martha said. "Is that guy still out there?"

"You owe him six dollars, Doris," Ruthie said.

"How you mean?"

"Wasp medicine from when him and Larson got into a nest yesterday."

"Did he get my boy wasp-bit?"

"Who you think got into the wasps," said Ruthie, "Larson or a grown normal man with a job? He helped me all the way up here when the rest of y'all run off. Sweet Lord! I'm give out. Somebody ought to hand me a glass of water." Ruthie pulled a crumpled paper towel from between her breasts and wiped her face. "How come I got to be the one to find him sitting up at the table? Didn't I *say* we shouldn't come out here?"

The gas man leaned against the Beasley truck at a risky angle, as if he were testing the strength of his hip. His frame was unorganized, puppet-like, as if his skeleton was carelessly attached, joints ill-fit, ligaments insecure. He was probably about Martha's age, but his slack-jawed gaze was stuck on her like a fourteen year old, watching his first dancer at the strip joint. As Martha approached, his eyes shifted, as though he were tracking a swarm of bees around her back and sides or thought himself unworthy to look fully upon her.

He wanted Martha. Like all the other men with so much as a pulse in the groin, he wanted her, but not like the others wanted her. This one did not want simply to ease an unbearable ache, to lie upon her body and clutch her thigh and chew her neck. He wanted to sink through her body's depths, to be dragged along by its undertow, until resurfacing was impossible and the only responses were drowning or growing gills. This one would do anything she asked. He would kill for her, kill his mother and father if they turned on her, kill himself if he became a burden to her, kill her if she tired of living. He sprang erect and straightened his legs, as if someone had yanked him up by the nape of his neck. He wiped his chin with the tail of his shirt, revealing a stomach that was flat, white, and hairless, with a navel peeping out like a smooth, pale nipple.

"You don't look Holiness," he said, tucking the wet bit of shirt into his belt.

Martha stopped a few feet in front of him and tucked her thumbs into the front belt loops of her jeans. This surely was a sign.

Larson plundered the refuse of Armey's back porch as Martha crossed the yard and parted the bushes to the creek edge. It was like stepping into a different climate zone, only one that was cooler, brighter, quieter, more open, more alive. The breeze carried a few notes of a bird's song and the rumble of a distant boat. Martha considered sloughing off her clothes and lying back in the water for just one serene moment alone, but instead slid off her sandals, rolled up her jeans legs to her knees, and stepped into the creek. She looked down at the tea-colored water that rose to the neck of the dragon tattoo on her shin.

"Blood of the lamb," she said.

Unwatched, completely to herself, she closed her eyes and rotated, feeling the sun on all sides of her face. The breeze picked up, and she leaned into it, raised her arms, and turned like a weather vane. She stopped and let her arms hang in the air like a scarecrow's, or the wings of those diving birds—were they some sort of duck?—when they sun themselves on a log. How could this be the same cursed creek in which she had lain submerged in corrupt hands? Is this what the Holiness seek, and perhaps find, in their baptisms and babbling in tongues? A perfect moment?

"How about a boat ride?"

Martha glanced to the side to see a boat drifting just beyond the middle of the creek. Two men in tank tops, probably already drunk, peered out from under low-slung caps. They called out a few more times, and Martha tried to ignore them, but her moment was gone. She walked out of the water, picked up her sandals, wiped the mud and sand from her feet, and reentered the world of the dead and dying.

Doris met Martha at the kitchen door. "Look what they're doing, Martha. You think anybody listens to me?"

Lula was filling a large plastic bag with empty condensed milk cans. Ruthie leaned against the stove behind Armey and rubbed his glasses with the hem of her muumuu.

"I told them not to touch anything," Doris said. "Everybody knows you supposed to leave it alone until the police get here."

Ruthie reached over Armey to set the glasses onto his face. "I told you *sheriff*, not *police*. We're just cleaning up some, Martha baby. I couldn't stand for Funderburk or anyone to come out here, see what a mess Armey lived amongst."

"They'd think Armey was trash," Lula said, "and all the rest of us, too. Then they'd be talking about how Ruthie's Gamewell married into trash and must've trashed up hisself."

"These durn one-eyed glasses don't want to stay." Ruthie tried pressing Armey's ear to pin the glasses' arm against his head. "Beside, I tried telling your Aunt Doris that touching nothing is when somebody's been murdered, not when they died of being old and crazy and drinking nothing but canned cream. That gas boy gone to call?"

"He went to Flippo's."

"I wish you'd've told me that," Doris said. "I sure as hell could use me a beer about now."

"Why would he come back here just to bring you a beer?" Ruthie asked. "You reckon if I wedge a matchbook or something back behind this ear, them glasses would stay?"

Martha looked out the kitchen window. A speckled-back bird landed on an oak tree and scurried up, then down, the trunk. "Oh, he'll be back."

"I've about worked myself blind," Lula said. "Where's that cake? Not a one of you thought to bring it in. Martha, dear, go out and get that cake for Grandma, shug."

The slope of Armey's front porch was so steep that Martha expected Lula to pitch out of the chair and into the yard each time she rocked forward. "At least slide that chair in front of the rail so it'll stop you when you sail out," Martha said. "Everything here is off-balance."

"I'm okay, baby doll," Lula said. "I ought to know by now how to rock in a chair. You better have you some cake before your mama gets at it." Lula closed her eyes and put another forkful of cake into her mouth. She chewed with her front teeth, working the jaws in slow, elliptical motions, as if she resented having to swallow.

Boats hummed on the creek behind the house. Fishermen spat into the water and laughed with their buddies. Not far away, men and women sat at desks in offices, or on tractors in fields, or on couches in living rooms, thinking of the weekend and lacy Easter dresses and hams covered with pineapple rings. Children dreamed of pastel eggs and hollow chocolate bunnies and wind-up toys in plastic baskets. Martha scraped her sandaled foot in a wide arc across the gray and splintered two-by-fours that composed the porch, pushing a pile of dust to the edge of the rail.

"How could you know what that bastard did to me and just stand by?" Martha asked.

Lula swallowed, laying the plate onto her lap. "Martha, baby, listen. You don't know what all went on and I don't know neither. I was just a woman. A woman what grew up in a dirt-floor shack and just wanted a place where she and her children had food to eat."

"And the only way you could get the minimum, plain necessities was to pay that sort of price? Your granddaughter? Was it Mama and Doris, too?"

"Listen." Lula scratched in the cake crumbs with her fork. "We had nothing when I was a girl. *Some*times I had shoes, brogans to wear. I wore feed-sack clothes. Maybe got a cold biscuit in my pocket when we were out hoeing somebody else's dirt. You don't know what you'd do to get out of that kind of life. But when you love somebody—"

"I've heard the hard-luck story all my life as an excuse for everything imaginable, and I'll be damned if I'll listen to it again. And what the hell are you talking about, love somebody?"

Lula's fork traced lines in the cake crumbs to resemble a stick figure. "I have prayed to Lord God to make me forget things—things you don't know about. Maybe my punishment is I have to remember and live with how my love for my brother-in-law was my sin and my damnation—"

"Wait. Are you telling me you were in love with Armey?"

"He's dead and gone now, so I can turn loose of these demons."

"You were protecting him? *Him*? You turned a blind eye to what he did and then kept quiet until he was dead because you *loved* him, knowing what he did? Jesus. I don't know who's more despicable."

"You ought not to talk to your grandma like that, Martha. There's more you don't know. It was all—how do you say it?—complicated."

Martha kicked the pile of dust off the edge of the porch. "You're going to tell me everything. Those women in there won't tell me a thing. Won't even tell me who my mother was."

"Ruthie is your mother."

"What? The one thing they *will* tell me over and over is that she's not. Are you telling me *she* is my biological birth mother?"

Lula dragged the fork across the plate and decapitated the stick figure. "I watched you being born. I told you it's complicated. Ruthie and Doris would rather you worry about that so's maybe you won't ask into other things. But he's dead and gone now."

"You mean they had me think that one of Daddy's exes was my mother so they could cover up something else?"

A rumbling noise came from the dirt road. Lula leaned forward. "I wonder who that is."

"That idiot in the gas truck." Martha turned and leaned back against the rail. "Don't think you off the hook, old woman. You're going to clear up some things for me. I have a right to know."

Lula scraped the crumbs into a pile on her plate. The gas truck stopped in the yard. The driver spilled out from the cab and settled into a shaky gait toward the porch. Martha heard a train whistle and the rattling of the trestle as the Special rolled toward the county line.

THIRTEEN

The parking lot of Flippo's Landing was filled with pickup trucks and boat trailers. Although nearly all Berkeley County residents were Baptists, Methodists, Church of God, or Holiness, with the rare Presbyterian—hardly a Catholic—tradition still demanded fish on Good Friday. Locals took the day off from fields and offices to spend the day in boats or on creek banks, baiting up with crickets or jigs, which is what they normally did on any day away from work. Today they would return to their backyards earlier than usual to scale and gut messes of bream or striped bass, cooking them in large pots of peanut oil set on homemade racks of crudely fastened plumbing pipe. Beasley had instructed Purvis to be back by 3 p.m. to fill up their propane tanks, the ones these same fishermen brought in by hand, the ones they'd put under those pots to cook their Good Friday feasts.

Just as Purvis parked in the lot, Lum Hereford gunned his primered Chevette, pulling the airboat and trailer up the ramp. Lum circled back to a stop beside the propane truck.

"You didn't think this little fart-dodger was going to make it, did you?" Lum said. "I bored her out myself. Soon as I get a few dollars to paint her up—I'm thinking orange and black—I'm taking her down to the speedway and slipping her in the normal aspirated four-cylinder category. What'd you do to your face, hoss?"

Purvis had to strain to make out some of what tongue-tied Lum said. "Wasps. Yeah, I'll put a dollar or two on her at the speedway," Purvis said. "And just so you know, I'm taking good care of your truck. Anyway, I got to run into

Flippo's."

"Why's it so dirty, then? But it don't make no matter. Beasley can kiss my ass upside-down off a camel before I 'yes sir' him anymore." The hulking Lum swayed and huffed and unpacked himself from the car. "Speaking of boring things out, I left something in the floor box." He opened the truck's passenger door. "What in holified hell is that thing?"

"Cypress knee one of them monks carved and give me to show Spessard."

"What you doing out at the monks'? I was just there the other day."

"Got a little mixed-up. So, I'll catch you later. I got to use the phone and hit the road." Purvis was about to open his door when Lum lifted the carving, holding it at arm's length and studying the stringy features.

"Looks kind of like a woman's purple," Lum said.

"Do what?"

"Man in the boat." Lum ran his thumb and forefinger in an inverted V down from the top. "See how this looks like a hood like the monks wear? A woman's purple has a hood, too, but you already knew that, right?"

"Damn straight I did. Listen, I got to get into Flippo's."

"Bullshit. You ain't been close enough to study no purple. Clitoris—that's the real name. One thing I know is anatomy. Right above her cooter-hole, what's real name is vagina—now I _know_ you had to know that, right?—is the clitoris, kind of folded back under its little hood." Lum turned the carving toward Purvis. "See? Cli-_to_-ris."

"I thought it was Jesus."

Lum set the cypress back onto the seat, threw back his head, and howled a laugh. Purvis could see the tipless tongue anchored to the jaw through the gap between Lum's lower front teeth. In school, Lum would fascinate the other kids by making his heart-shaped tongue swell into two lumps with a crease in the middle. Then he'd undulate them independently in some obscene dance. The double-bumped tongue matched the rising halves of his deeply cleft chin, and with the heavy philtrum of his top lip, the thin blade of a nose, and the vertical fold in the middle of his forehead, Lum's face was bisected, as if someone had snapped a chalk line on it.

"Jesus? Ha ha!" The laughter made Lum's speech harder to understand. "The cypress knee or the clitoris? Whoo! I tell you what: That little purple pea can sure be a savior! Ha whoo!" He fell against the truck door and tried to catch his breath.

"That's a metaphor."

"Ho, lord! Okay, I think I'm all right now. What did you say?"

"You said the purple pea is a savior. That's a metaphor. But I reckon you don't know about them, eh?"

"There's a lot I do know, hoss, like something about what I left in here. I was worried I'd have to go to Beasley's to get it."

Lum lifted the top from the homemade console between the mismatched bucket seats. He removed a tray, reached into what Purvis thought must have been a secret compartment, and took out a pint bottle of bourbon and a small bag. Lum shook the plastic package, which had a cartoon drawing of a naked woman and the label "For Entertainment Only." Inside was something that looked like a rubber band with a pink thimble attached. "If you want to make her come back for seconds, buddy roe, your old pecker alone won't hardly cut it. Now ordinarily that would mean laying the tongue on that purple—that purple Jesus! Ha! I just can't get over that one." He shook his head. "Anyway, that puts me in a bind, so to speak, because of my abnormal lingual frenum. That's that little string under your tongue, except there's no *under* under mine. See?" Lum opened his mouth. His tongue humped up like buttocks.

"You've shown it to me before." Lum's only three years older than me, Purvis thought. What makes him think he can give me lessons? Then again, Lum had been married twice, so maybe he did know something about women. Purvis wanted to leave but felt cornered. After all, this was Lum's truck.

"My cheap-ass parents could have had this thing snipped when I was a young 'un, but you think they'd come off a dollar? Hell, I'm used to it now. But back to what I was telling you. You know that string under the head of your pecker? That's a frenum, too— frenum glandis—and your pecker helmet is called the glans penis. Like I told you, I know some anatomy."

"You got a regular frenum gladis, or is your glans pecker tied down, too?"

Lum's voice dropped. "Get smart with me, sonny buck, and I won't tell you where you can get one these Stim-u-Rings."

"I'm just picking on you, Lum. You know I just say all kinds of shit."

Lum dropped the package into his shirt pocket and patted it. "This is the old lady's Easter present. The one we had give out a few weeks back. I think some lube or something got down into the contacts and shorted it out. The old lady's been getting the short end the stick for a while, and her jelly's about to lose patience. But she's going to damn well believe in the Easter Bunny this year!" Lum closed the truck door.

"I got to go use Flippo's phone." Purvis stepped from the truck and toward the bait shop. Lum followed him.

"You coming to the PJ party, ain't you?" Lum asked.

"PJ party?"

"Damn, son, you *have* been working. DeWayne didn't tell you? Tonight. That's why I'm off the creek early, so I can run get the stuff. I already got the trash cans from last time—just need hosing out. I got to pick up the Kool-Aid, some sugar and fruit, and a few bags of ice. DeWayne's bringing the grain alcohol. I can't believe he hadn't told you."

"I just saw him yesterday morning. It must have slipped his mind."

"No, we just decided yesterday," Lum said. "Because of all them river dogs come back, I bet nobody hardly catches a mess of fish today. I didn't get but four bream and a warmouth and didn't even see no rockfish running. So we going to meet at the old landing just this side of the trestle and shoot some river dogs and mix up some PJ about nine or so. That'll give everybody time to get home and eat fish, then get back out here." As Purvis opened the door, Lum slapped him on the back. "Hey! When somebody asks if you want a Purple Jesus tonight, they going to mean a drink, not that other kind of purple. Ha! You wish! Goddamn, I can't get over that. Whoo-whoo! I can't wait to tell the old lady that one."

Inside, Flippo stacked cups of night crawlers in the cooler beside the beer singles. "Well, damn if it ain't old sorry-ass Driggers. What can I do you for, son?"

"I just need to borrow your phone to call Sheriff Funderburk. Armey

Wright's dead."

"You didn't tell me that," Lum said. "I thought he'd been dead."

"No. Just two or three days. He's sitting up at the kitchen table right now."

"If that don't beat all," said Flippo. "Well, you know where the phone's at. Watch out for that scorpion I saw by the register. What happened to your lip? Looks like the head of my pecker."

"Glans penis," said Lum.

As Lum and Flippo discussed how bad the fishing had been, Purvis leaned over the gallon jars of pickled foods—dills, eggs, pigs' feet, and turkey gizzards—and plastic containers of jerky—beef, venison, alligator, and buffalo—and picked up the receiver. A gospel song about lost sheep played from the radio on the shelf. The sheriff's number was scrawled on a piece of paper taped to the phone that also listed numbers for fire and rescue, McNair's Towing, and Smiley the Bail Man.

The moment Purvis finished the call and hung up the phone, he saw something purplish and snaky slide behind the shelf. "Hanging Jesus!" He jerked his hand from the phone and fell against the counter.

"See that scorpion?" Flippo asked.

Purvis took his inhaler from his pocket for two quick puffs. "No. One of them big purple lizards."

"Like I said, scorpion," Flippo said. "They spit poison. Hit your mouth nine feet away, and it gets under your tongue in your saliva glands, goes straight to your blood veins, and that's last call for you."

"One killed my granddaddy," Lum said. "Spit *through* the window of his old Fairlane."

Purvis turned for the door. "I thought a scorpion was a spider-looking kind of thing but has a stinger tail."

"No, shit-for-brains," said Flippo. "You thinking about a locust."

Lum followed Purvis outside. "So, Purv, you coming to the PJ party?"

"I might." Purvis stopped. "Listen, where'd you say you got that Stimu-ling?"

"Stim-u-*ling*! Ha! Stim-u-lingual. Purvis, you coming up with some good ones today. It's Stim-u-*Ring*, $19.99 at the Venus Parlor, or like I call it, the Penis Puller, down on Rivers Avenue. You know where the super slide used to be? Right past that on the left. Anyway, you might just have use for one when that PJ gets to working."

Purvis started for the truck again. "I got to get back to Armey's."

"What the hell for? He sure ain't needing you."

"Armey's niece, great-niece Martha, sent me here to call the sheriff. I got to get back and tell her the deputy's coming." Purvis got into the truck.

Lum squinted. "Armey's great-niece? Yeah, I remember Martha. I thought she run off and got married. Now, I'd like to try out the Stim-u-Ring on that pudendum."

"You ought not to call her that," Purvis said. "Anyhow, so that's why I had to run in here and use the phone. You know how Beasley is about the radio."

"Beasley can suck my left testicle. I'll even shave it for him."

Martha half-sat on, half-leaned against the porch rail, and the old woman in a rocking chair held a plate on her lap. Purvis walked to the house and rested his foot on the bottom step. "I called Sheriff Funderburk's office and told them Armey's sitting up dead at the table, and about the boards tore off the walls and all. He's on the way out. Well, a deputy is."

Martha glanced over her shoulder at him and then turned back around. Purvis thought he saw the smirk again. The old woman leaned the rocking chair forward. Her feet touched down at the edge of the porch. Why would she rock, Purvis wondered, in the one place where the railing is missing? If she fell, he would have to try to catch her. Maybe he should move in front of her so Martha will see he's preparing himself.

"What was your name, son?" the old woman asked. A dab of icing clung to hairs on her top lip.

"Driggers, ma'am. Purvis."

"You Willis Driggers's boy?"

"Spessard is my daddy," said Purvis. "Willis was my great uncle. I know how sad it can be to lose a great uncle."

"Willis Driggers had the prettiest tail I ever saw on a man."

"Oh God," Martha said. Her back was toward Purvis, her buttocks pressed against the top rail, forming, Purvis thought, a cross.

"Some of us girls went down to the reverse curve to wade out in the water because we'd been in the field all day and Willis and some boys—we was all teenagers, you know—had them a rope tied to a tree limb on the other side and was swinging offen it. He seen us and I reckon he thought he'd give us a show."

"You should get back inside," Martha said.

"I need me something to drink. Did we bring any tea?" said the old woman. "Anyway, he slipped off his britches and swung on the rope and flew way out into the middle of the river, and his tail just a-shining like the rapture come for us. Us girls all giggled and ran but I went to prayer meeting that night and thanked the Lord God in heaven for showing me Willis Driggers's bare behind. Some people would say that's sinful, but I don't think it is. Do you, what was your name again?"

"Nome, I don't. Purvis." He glanced at Martha, who was looking at her grandmother but not smirking.

"I mean your first name."

"Purvis is my first name, ma'am. Driggers is my last—"

"I never had no use for any of them other Driggerses. Whatever become of Willis?"

"He had a heart attack and fell out a pontoon boat and drownded."

The old woman picked some crumbs from the plate and dropped them onto her tongue. "That's a real sadness. And here Armey fell dead on Good Friday and his birthday, too."

"He didn't die today," Martha said.

"I bet y'all give Willis a pretty funeral, eh, Purvis?" the old woman asked.

"I don't hardly remember him. I was real little."

Martha's head jerked around. "But I thought you said—"

"I saw Willis Driggers's tail on August the eighth, nineteen and—"

"Larson!" Doris called through the screen door. "Martha, honey, go see if you can find that boy for me, please. Lord knows where he is, and it looks all snaky out there."

Martha turned with one hand on the rail, another hand on a chair arm, another brushing off her leg, another adjusting her belt, and maybe two more making signs in the air.

"I'll come help you," Purvis said.

"Yeah," Martha said, "I think you should." She walked ahead of Purvis more quickly than he expected. With her back swaying side to side and her neck loose, her head moved in circles like those of the Gypsy dancers Purvis had seen at the hoochie-coochie show at the fair. Maybe he was being hypnotized, pulled along into some unknown part of the woods. "Watch closely, my Purvis," Martha would say. "This body is a symbol-maker. I am creating meanings all around you. Metaphors, metaphors just for you." He would begin to understand things about himself and the world as if he were reading her—her fingers would be words, her hands sentences, her many arms that other word for a bunch of sentences together that make a box of words on a page. She would draw him close to her and whisper into his ear, "Listen, my Purvis. Listen to a secret mystery: A-ris-to-tle." He felt light-headed.

"Purvis, you okay?"

"I just need to sit a minute." They were in the backyard. He sat on an upturned washtub. "I haven't slept well lately. It's catching up to me."

Martha stood over Purvis and placed a foot onto the lip of the washtub. "What did you say earlier about the rendering plant?"

"Facility." He lit two cigarettes and held one out to Martha. She lipped it from his fingers. "DeWayne, my brother, runs the grinder. I can't hardly stand the smell in there."

"You know how to run it?"

"Well, I done it a couple times. Why? You found some of Armey's dogs dead up under the house?"

"No, just wondering."

"Cause they'll take anything. Just throw them in whole and they gone."

Martha tapped the washtub with her foot. "This junk around here is what needs to be got rid of. God knows what's under this rusty thing."

Purvis jumped up. "What? A snake?"

"I'm just saying it's a junkyard." She pointed her chin toward the back porch. "Look at all that garbage there. And inside, too. Pots and pans on the floor, old books piled up."

"Yeah."

"And that foot locker in the bedroom."

Purvis jerked his face toward her. "What foot locker?"

Martha blew a huge lung of smoke at Purvis. The sun was behind her, and Purvis could not make out her features well. Her eyes may have been closed, or her hair may have fallen into her face. Earlier she was all motion, shifting and flowing. Now she was still and hidden. What was happening between them? Had he offended the old woman? Had Martha really hypnotized him and got him to confess something?

"Purvis, you said you told the sheriff that Armey was sitting up at the kitchen table, right?"

"Didn't you tell me that before?" His chest tightened. Martha's face was all shadow. "We'd better hunt up your cousin. With him not right and all, he might be got lost or wallowing in a gator nest."

"And about the walls tore up. Did I tell you that, too?"

Purvis's throat felt like he'd been working in fiberglass insulation all day. He puffed his inhaler and held his breath and stared at Martha's feet. He held up his palm to buy a few seconds. He could say she was crazy and hearing things. That sometimes worked when people said he lied. Or he could say he had to leave, then get up and hot-foot it to the truck, and she would probably forget the whole thing even before the deputy got there. Or he could just cry into her arms and tell her he never hurt her poor great uncle and that they could look for the money together and she could wave her symbol goddess arms and lift the two of them into the sky and out of this place, this hard place where old men die alone and retards run around not knowing not to mess with wasps and otters eat up all the fish, this unforgiving world of tied-tongues and scorpions and Ockham the Rusty Razor too dull to draw blood from his swollen lip. "Your britches' legs look wet."

"I went wading, but that's not what we were talking about."

"That's a dangerous creek, you know?" said Purvis. "There's gators out there. And gars. Big old gars that'll eat a dog. Hey, you want to go to a PJ party?"

"PJ?" Martha asked. "A pajama party?"

Purvis wondered what sort of pajamas Martha wore. He had once imagined that his fantasy women slept naked.

The first time Lum quit, Purvis delivered propane to Miriam Crawford's trailer. Miriam, whom Purvis had silently admired in high school, was recently divorced, and had no curtains on her windows. Purvis had no choice but to sneak through two cornfields and a cow pasture and climb over four hog-wire fences to peek into her bedroom. That night, under a full, accommodating moon, nude Miriam lay supine atop the chenille cover with arms and legs spread like the drawing Purvis had seen by da Vinci, the one of a naked man in a circle and square in a book called *The Mystery of the Human Form*. Squared by the edges of the bed, she looked like a painting, matted and framed, tittied and split, but a marvel to behold, not a fantasy that had become flesh for the taking. All he could do was run home and call her on the telephone and hang up when she answered.

Since then, he clothed his fantasies in pajamas—blue flannel with big white buttons and a breast pocket with initials embroidered in gold. Martha's pajamas, though, would come from some faraway place overseas, probably in an Oriental country like Arabia or Egypt but not on all maps, where brandy-colored women weaved, *swish swash*, at mahogany looms, and sewed, with ivory needles at long marble tables, a material so rare and precious it does not even have a name in English.

"No, the drink PJ—Purple Jesus," Purvis said. "Grape juice and Kool-Aid and oranges and sugar and grain alcohol mixed up in a big barrel. Drink enough and it resurrects."

"I haven't had that poison since high school."

"I can come get you. We going to meet by the river just a ways down from here and shoot some river dogs."

"Shoot what?"

A voice in mid-sentence came from around the far corner of the house. ". . . don't talk nair bit right there in the bushes like he can't open his mouf." Larson emerged, jerking his kneeless duck walk. "Come look, Martha, and the gas man right there what Uncle Armey don't need none from ought to see him too when my hat hit him right on the tall head that I thowed at him and him just not talking. Thisaway come and see him." He grabbed one of Martha's arms and tugged and looked as if he was going to cry.

"Turn loose of me, goddamnit." Martha yanked her arm from Larson. He quick-stepped back the way he had come, and Martha followed for several yards before looking back at Purvis. "Well?"

He was not sure if she was asking for his answer—about tearing up walls or shooting Armey—or inviting him to see what Larson was excited about. She went around the corner, and Purvis got to his feet, no idea what he was supposed to do. He sidled to the corner and peeked around, afraid Martha might bark that he had no business following her, that he needed to crank up that hideous truck and get back down the road, that he had better never again have such evil thoughts about her. He would fall to his knees, rend his Beasley Gas shirt, and declare the purity of his mind and flesh, plead that he was under a spell and was not responsible for any thoughtless thing he had said, beg for a task to plumb his heart and earn her forgiveness, then jump like a flushed rabbit and run to the truck.

Martha stood looking into the myrtle bushes by the water as Larson chattered and pulled at the seat of his pants. As Purvis neared them, a shadow formed through the bushes, an outline of a tall figure, silent and still. Martha did not speak but just looked, her smirk softer than before, as if she had caught a friend sneaking out another friend's back door, or was picking up her brother from jail. Purvis drew closer and the shadow grew more distinct: broad shoulders, an arm extended to the side, and a tree limb or a club, a head in profile. As the head moved, breaking a plane of sunlight sifted through gums and cypresses, the face revealed itself—deep-set eyes and hair.

"Godamighty!" Purvis yelled, his left knee buckling as he stumbled back a step and bumped against a vine-covered telephone cable spool. "The Hairy Man!" He reached into his pocket for his folding hawkbill knife, the one he'd kept from the flooring job he had for a week the year before. It was razor-sharp but too large for a pants pocket, and it belonged in the belt sheath Purvis should also have kept from the job. Now his hand was stuck in his pocket, and he remembered the funny TV program he had seen in which a pygmy in Africa got a monkey to reach into a hole for some seeds, but the hole was too small for the monkey to pull out his grubby fist, and the monkey was either too stupid or too greedy to turn loose his treat and escape.

So the monkey squealed and yanked as the pygmy calmly walked up and got the monkey. Purvis couldn't remember if the pygmy wanted to eat the monkey or make him a pet, but now Purvis was the monkey, and Martha was Purvis watching the TV show, except she was not laughing. The Hairy Man was the pygmy, which was sort of funny, because the Hairy Man was tall, and the pygmy was a runt. PIG-my, runt—that was sort of funny, too.

As he was struggling for a weapon to protect Martha and himself (and, if he had to, Larson, although the Hairy Man had probably killed him by now), Purvis realized that he was making metaphors. These were not the kinds of metaphors he really needed, though. How could "I am a monkey" save him? His hand was still stuck.

"Goddamn hairy bastard! Martha! Shitting hairy Jesus." Purvis's pants pocket turned inside-out and the knife was free and he broke it open and stepped forward and Martha's arms were symboling behind her where one pulled up the tail of her shirt and another arced around from the small of her back and snapped up stiff like a plank and Purvis did not have to see to know what was in the hand. He began to wheeze.

Purvis heard a splash somewhere beyond Martha. "He's getting it now," Larson said, "over to them woods with no boat, like that one by the porch, he wouldn't been wet. Look here, this was his'n."

Martha returned the pistol to its hiding place. The Hairy Man was gone, but all Purvis cared about was that Martha had un-hid something for him, had shown him her deepest secret, had bared herself to him. He owed her his life, not because she did not put lead in him, but because she had given him her soul in that flash of cold steel. He saw in her dark eyes that she understood this, too, and demanded a task from him, a task to save his life. What could he do for her? What could he sacrifice and lay at her tattooed feet? He took three deep hits from the inhaler.

"What the fuck is your problem?" she asked. "Were you going to cut that monk?"

Purvis looked at the curved, obscene knife blade. "Monk? Mary's red ass on the rag! That was the goddammit Hairy Man that walks them woods, except I thought it was always at night." He bent at the waist and coughed.

"Lookit," Larson said, holding something out to Martha. "Like a storybook what Mama reads me, but got a string on it like a boot kind, him dropped it on the ground, and done gone, yeah, way done gone in the water now."

Martha took the book from Larson but kept her eyes on Purvis. She did not smirk. "That was a monk from right over there in the abbey. He probably took a vow of silence, so I don't know why he was here, but he was sure as hell no Hairy Man or Bigfoot or Booger Man." She glanced at the book for a moment. "Hand me that knife. I cannot *believe* you pulled this on him. What kind is it?"

"Flooring."

"It almost got your ass shot."

"I appreciate that. A sharp knife is a good thing to have."

"Let me hold that," Larson said.

"You get on back to the house," Martha said. "Go!" Larson scurried away as Martha opened the book, read a line, and flipped pages. "It's a diary."

Purvis lit two cigarettes. "Anything in there about Aristotle? Them monks like to read about Aristotle and other philosophers that lived thousands of years ago."

Martha took a cigarette from Purvis. "Here's what you're going to do. You get back to work and take this diary to that monastery."

"Okay." This is not what she requires of me, Purvis thought. Returning the book was just an errand she might just as well have given her neighbor. He would know when the true task came. All of her symbol movements had been a test to see if he was worthy of witnessing a secret moment of her, of knowing what she was capable of—of risking it all to feel the power of a woman who would control all of what he was capable. "Okay," he said again, taking the book from Martha's hand. He started toward the truck.

"And," Martha said, "come get me tonight and take me to that PJ party."

"Okay," he said over his shoulder.

"You don't know where I live!" Martha called, but Purvis was running at full speed, already beyond the corner of the house.

Purvis locked the gate to the seven-foot chain link fence that protected the two trucks and propane tanks. The other driver had left early, probably reasoning that if the boss had done so, so could he. Purvis went to the office and was about to drop his keys into the mail slot when the door opened.

"Lordy!" Agnes said. "Mr. Driggers, you liked to cause me to jump out of my skin."

"I'm sorry, Miss Agnes. Aren't you usually gone by now?"

Agnes adjusted a strip of tape that had come loose over her eye. "Most days. I just been busy busy. Mr. Beasley takes off for a long weekend and thinks the office will run itself. Someone here's got to be dedicated."

"Can't nobody say you not dedicated, Miss Agnes. Listen, you in a hurry? I need to call my brother to swing by here and pick me up. Since you haven't locked up yet, that'll save me a trip across the road."

"I don't think Mr. Beasley would mind if you drove the gas truck home for the weekend, especially if you give it a good cleaning." She flashed a gummy grin as she handed him an envelope. "Here. You forgot to get your check."

"I didn't expect I'd get a check until after I worked a full week, but thank you," Purvis said. He gestured with his chin toward the truck yard. "Now, I don't know if I can spend another minute driving that headacher, but it *would* save some trouble, and I need to get home quick as I can and wash up." He tilted his head back and tried to wink, but both eyes squinted. "I got a date."

"You? Are you pulling my leg?" Agnes touched her fingers to her lips. "I mean, no reason why a young lady wouldn't want to spend an evening with a nice young gentleman like yourself. Do I know the lady?"

"Martha Wright. No, Umphlett."

"Gamewell and Ruthie Umphlett's daughter? I just had a nice chat with her yesterday. She is a lovely young woman. Such a shame what they did to her."

"Ma'am?"

"You know, with her baby and the husband and all. Lordy."

"What baby?"

"Mr. Driggers, other people's beeswax is their beeswax, but killing one of the Lord's innocent lambs is not, like some of them say, *privacy*. It's a *life*."

"I don't exactly understand, Miss Agnes," Purvis said. He took the inhaler from his pocket and shook it. He didn't hear anything inside. "Somebody killed her baby?"

"Unborn baby. Ripped it from her womb like a cancer, then made her leave her husband and come take care of her invalid mother," Agnes said. "I don't fault Martha. She's young, and how can you disobey your mother? But I shouldn't be talking about these things when you about to court her. You just forget all about what I said and have yourself a nice evening."

"So she's married, and they made her have an abortion?" Purvis puffed on the inhaler, but it was empty. He should have brought an extra.

Agnes slapped her hands over her ears. "Oh, how I despise that ugly, ugly word. And Satan's helpers who perform them call it *family planning*, like that place down on Rivers."

"Rivers Avenue? There's an abortion house on Rivers Avenue?"

"Not for long, if the Good Lord's will is done. It's right past where that big sliding board used to be."

"You know, Miss Agnes, I believe I'll drive the truck home after all." He turned to walk away, then spun back around. "Say, you don't know whereabouts

Martha and her mama live at, do you?"

"Oh, everybody knows Gamewell Umphlett's place. He was one nice-looking man in this world. Why he had to marry those one-armed women and then that Ruthie, who's as big as, well, she's got a glandular, but she was a whole lot younger than him and real pretty in the face one time. But I shouldn't be talking like that. You know where Oakley is, don't you? It burned down last year and that Padgett boy got arrested for it. Go past them big brick gates right beside it—that's where them uppity Bonners stay even though they all crossed-eyed—to the second or maybe third house on the other side of the road, about a mile. It's the one with the cattle guard, although them Umphletts never had any cows, except for Ruthie, of course." She laughed. "Lord! Listen at me! I shouldn't talk ugly about her when you're sweet on her daughter."

"Thank you, Miss Agnes. I believe I can find it. You have a good Easter now."

"I will have a blessed one, doing the Lord's work," Agnes said. "You ought to come to church and see the pageant."

"I just might," said Purvis as he opened the gate. He wheezed slightly but smiled, knowing what he had to do, but with no idea how to do it.

FOURTEEN

"The hand still quivers against the page, the effect of a morning sight both fearsome and jubilant—fearsome, for it may signify nothing more spectacular than Dementia's tender caress of an old man's mind; and jubilant, for it may truly be an instance of The Bird made flesh.

"During a repose not ten minutes ago at the base of a massive pine with limbs and flaking trunk that tell, as mine, the story of deterioration, I considered the route for my return, when came, from above my head, a high, flat paint, like the bleat of a dented bugle. When a whack released a shower of bark by me, I expected to find a majestic Pileated probing for beetles.

"It was indeed a Pileated-shaped creature I saw, the sun's corona surrounding its profiled, crested head. Then the wondrous creature moved, and behold! (I imagine an angel's alarm.) The back of the bird appeared not as the expected black, but covered in white! The wings gloved in white! Was this The Bird? Dare I speak its Name?

"Into the sun it flew, a silhouette, then gone. The entire vision—a tenth part of a second, an eye-blink, yet an eternity in an instant.

"Did I see The Bird after sixty-three years of life, twenty-four of them walking these woods? Was my life compressed into that moment of vision and doubt? When Gabriel soon fetches me, and I gaze into his ivory eyes, will they be his auxiliaries to bear that berth?"

—Fra. Phillip.

June 2, in the Year of Our Lord 1948.

PURPLE JESUS

The dark mahogany pews of the tiny chapel stood in sharp contrast to the colorful play of sunrise light through the stained glass onto the stone tiles. Diamonds in the window distorted into trapezoids on the floor, squares to rhomboids. Perhaps the white gloves in Brother Phillip's final journal entry were only sunbeams careening off a swampy pool to rest onto a Pileated's folded wings. Would Brother Phillip have wanted to know? Which is better—the safety of knowledge or the agony of hope? Or is it the other way around?

Andrew was sacrificing the best birding part of the day, when light is concentrated, sound, and crisp. Now, he owed Brother Justin the courtesy of listening to his saw blade wail "In Christ There is no East or West." From an arced panel of steel, Brother Justin, seated in front of the gathered brothers, clamped the saw's handle between his knees and held the tip of the blade in his left hand, dragging a violin bow across the smooth edge with his right. The idiophonic notes slithered into each other as the left hand adjusted the S-shaped bends of the steel—a squat S for lows, a lengthened one for highs. A knee would jiggle for vibrato or rise up to dampen the base of the blade.

Abbot Christopher had encouraged each brother to prepare a personal expression for this Good Friday gathering. "Speak to us in your own manner," he had said. "Ring upon the changes of the crucifixion. Take us where your innovative forms lead." Justin's innovation was a pentatonic version of this tune, a modal rebirth to shock those who insist on traditionally rendered hymns. Brother Bernard, Andrew imagined, must be squirming. The mournful air would slice into Bernard's ear canal with a sharpness characteristic of the instrument itself, but the transformation to another scale would roil his stomach like turned wine. Perhaps someday he would ask Bernard if he thought Jesus never tapped a saw with Joseph's hammer.

"Amen," Abbot Christopher said as Justin returned to his pew. "A common hand tool singing Christ's praises."

Andrew remembered his afternoons as a boy in Mr. Zekie's gun shop. Tools lay on shelves, hung on pegboard hooks, and rested in old boxes. The tiny concrete-block building was a study in silvers—sharp blades and blunt hammer heads—and browns—from the smooth handles of oak and hickory. Dark bluish barrels leaned in corners. Stocks in varied moments of varnish sat beside sanding belts. Andrew liked the smells—scorched sawdust, fruity oil—but he loved the sounds. The little shop seemed built for acoustic accentuation: the hum of the band saw as he followed a forearm template, the *tot tot* of the mallet on a chisel, the rhythmic drone of the jackplane. The vibrations of the sawing and chipping ran through his arms and shoulders and into his skull as if they were a message. He would open his mouth, make an O with his lips, and feel the music of tools rolling across his tongue like unknown foreign words.

"Who's next?" asked the abbot. "Brother Andrew, have you something for us?"

Andrew sat for several seconds, his head cocked as if placing a faraway sound. Not east or west, not south or north. Andrew arose and went to the front of the room as Abbot Christopher nodded and took a seat. Andrew stood for a long time with his eyes focused beyond the chapel doors. Then he gave a quick nod and walked out.

For nearly half a minute, no one moved. Andrew had left the chapel doors open. Had that been his performance, an obscure pantomime of death (standing still), resurrection (leaving the chapel, the world), and salvation (the door open to the church)?

Abbot Christopher walked toward the door just as Andrew returned, carrying his bow. Smiling, Abbot Christopher returned to his seat. Andrew leaned the bow against the wall behind him, then stood before his audience, just as he had moments before. He slid his right foot back and his left foot forward. He raised his hands flat and upright in front of his face, as if aligning himself to a focal point. He dropped the right hand to swing and point back. He slid the left foot back and exchanged hand positions. As the slow tai chi dance continued, Andrew imagined some of the brothers telling him later how they were enthused by his appropriation of foreign culture into the Christian practice—after all, the fisherman casts a wide net. Bernard, however, was sure to provide gentle challenge—not all fish are edible.

Andrew reached for his bow. He placed the stool Justin had used back into the center and sat. He put one end of the bow onto the floor and braced it against his left instep, then put the other end into his mouth. His right hand held the bow near the upper end while his left rested upon the string. Then he opened his mouth, plucked the string, half-closed his mouth, and opened it again. *Ow oh ow* spread across the sanctuary. The sound was eerily like a human voice, struggling to form its strains into words. Andrew dilated and contracted his lips, slackened and tightened his jaw, and bit, tongued, pressed, and eased up on the bow, producing, first, an array of drones, until the hint of a melody began to emerge. The others closed their eyes and searched for the pattern, like children who stare at the greens of the grass waiting for pastels of Easter eggs to appear.

The melody pulled Andrew to his feet. He stood bending over the bow as if he were speaking through it and to the earth. He uttered no words, yet sounds flowed from his mouth. In his head, Andrew could hear the lyrics accompanying the emerging tune:

On Jordan's stormy banks I stand and cast a wishful eye . . .

More boats were on the water than usual. Andrew watched the fishermen cast, smoke cigarettes, and reel in nothing. Occasionally, he could pick up fragments of conversation: "Switch to a jig." "Looks like we'll be catching our mess from Piggly Wiggly today."

Brother Phillip, too, must have sat on this bank and wondered about men's passion for angling. Did Phillip liken their attraction to fish to his for birds? Was identifying and naming birds any less a drive than hooking fish? Phillip wrote of nothing else. He spent twenty-four years at this abbey, yet the journal mentioned no other monks, recorded no prayers, described no work, and contained no information of Phillip's past. If he were to materialize on the bank beside Andrew, would his discourse be as profound and exhilarating as his writing? Had Andrew imagined him more than he was, read more into the journal's entries than was there?

A speeding airboat startled Andrew, and he realized he had sat in the bushes longer than planned. As the airboat passed under the trestle and continued downstream, Andrew looked through the bushes and out onto the creek. The brothers' performances had pleased Andrew, and he hoped they would repeat them. He could try playing his bow with Justin's violin bow. Bowing the bow. He could not recall the Latin word for *archer*. Perhaps he could jaw-harp and bow it at the same time. He would be the world's expert, its only expert, on the—what?—jaw bow. Jaw fiddle. Cello bellow.

This was a good day. No boats were in sight now. He crept forward to get a better view of the water. Something large rolled a few feet from the mud. Andrew knew that alligators lived in Wadboo, but he had never seen one, so probably this was a bass or a carp, which can make the surface boil as if something monstrous stirred below. He looked toward the middle of the creek to try to spot the fish when he saw someone on the other shore.

She was less than forty yards away, closer than two nights before—the blue-black-haired young woman from the baptism. The woman with poise. She bent to roll her pants legs to her knees. She was back for another, although partial, immersion. What was her name?

She stepped into the water with the grace of an egret, looked down, and may have spoken. She turned slowly, fully in the moment, and when she completed the rotation, she raised her arms, leaned forward, rotated again, then stopped, with her arms out and elbows slightly bent, like an anhinga sunning its wings dry. Andrew had not brought his binoculars.

He had heard the preacher say it. What was her name?

"How about a boat ride?"

A bass boat drifted into view hardly ten yards from Andrew. He slipped behind a bush. Were they facing Andrew's side of the creek, the fishermen surely would have discovered him, but they had swiveled their seats toward the woman.

"We got plenty of room," the other fisherman said. "Food and drinks—hell, we got everthing for a party right here."

The woman ignored them.

"Maybe that's how she fishes. Eye a fish like one of them big old cranes, then reach down and snatch it up."

"Hey, honey, come on take a ride and show us how to catch something. We could use a lesson."

Andrew crouched low to hide his face as the boat drifted by. The current pulled the boat a little closer to the bank, and he could hear the men talk about the high school baseball coach fired mid-season for snapping pictures of the team in the showers.

When the boat was far enough away, Andrew removed his hood and looked across the creek. Martha! The name was Martha. Poised, avian Martha, snowy egret Martha stepped from the water and into the foliage as graceful as a song.

Oh who will come and go with me? I am bound for the promised land.

Andrew squatted for a while, transfixed by an attraction to riparian Martha that he could not fathom. His arms crossed his chest, pressing the journal to his heart. Perhaps an entry would provide some parallel experience that could help Andrew sort through this feeling.

He was well trained to recognize the monstrous, subcutaneous stirrings of lust and as well practiced in how to submerge it. This was not lust. He thought of his high school girlfriend. Lorena was a Florida farm girl who raised Paso Fino horses and loved her father's record collection of old country music. They would canoe down the Ocklawaha while she made up rhymes that she sang about them to melodies from Roy Acuff or the Delmore Brothers.

Tom and Lorena making love in a boat.

He keeps her moving, she keeps him afloat.

Andrew could recall her brown, pony-tailed hair, the tiny maroon mole on her left temple, and the webbed second and third toes she would droop over the sides of the canoe into the water. He could summon instantly the fear that paralyzed him at the farm as the cantering horse stopped for no reason and Lorena pitched forward as if already dead. He could feel the smooth mahogany of the coffin and the crisp, high collar of her white dress hiding the bruised neck. He could smell the gunpowder from her father's shotgun that killed the horse that threw her. He could see the foamy tongue flopping from the mouth of the horse that Andrew helped Lorena's father load onto the back of the truck. He could feel how the ground jarred his knees when he collapsed and wailed in great, heaving gasps, thinking of how Lorena would have objected to the execution of Skipper, her killer but favorite horse. But he could not recollect feeling what he thought was love for Lorena.

Now, Andrew found himself surprised at how cold the water was and even more surprised that it was up to his knees, then his thighs, then hips, as he leaned into the current, unable to remember deciding to do so. In up to his chest, then neck, he nearly panicked when he realized he would have to swim for the first time since coming to the abbey. He kept his eyes on the point where he last saw Martha, tried to hold the journal out of the water, and then he was halfway across the creek. After a few strokes, he could touch the bottom and walk again. Then, he was up on the other shore.

Beyond the bushes stood the house that used to be visible from the abbey's side of the creek. Trash—mostly condensed milk cans—piled up beside a rusted, sooty barrel and trailed to the house. The owner must have burned garbage in the barrel once, but gave up and just left everything beside it.

"Uncle Armey's place is what this is on his birfday," someone said. "You ain't supposed to be here from coming acrost no water and just looking. What your name?"

A little man stood only a yard away from Andrew. His khaki pants were too high on his body and were held up by wide suspenders. He held a condensed milk can and a radio aerial. Certainly, he was mentally deficient.

"That's the creek out there and you ain't supposed to left on your shoes to swim in it like it was the lake where they got them big underellas to shade Grandma and life servers, why you can't get drownded and you got a hairy face. What is your name right now?"

Andrew had gone too far. He was beyond the edge of his world. Now the creek seemed like a wall. If he made a sudden move, the little man would surely summon family members who would be fast upon him, pinning him to the ground and demanding explanation for the trespass. Would he break his vow to save his life? Would Martha plead to her people to release a poor monk?

The little man tried to insert the end of the aerial into a hole in the milk can. "I don't live here but at Markham's Mobile Home and Trailer Court Resort, but come here I done told you for Uncle Armey's birfday. Yesterday it won't his birfday, it was Mawmaw's, and he's dead right in there in that there house." He put the milk can to his nose, sniffed it, and then tossed it to the ground. "That smelled like it was rottended and you ain't said nair word this whole day here in Uncle dead Armey's yard." The little man collapsed the telescoping aerial and put it into his back pocket. He unzipped his pants, reached in, pulled out an uncircumcised penis, and ejected an arc of dark yellow urine that cut through the bushes to puddle several inches short of Andrew's feet.

"I'm going to pee on you, no-talking hairy man, right on you." The man thrust his hips forward into the myrtle bushes that separated him from Andrew. "Ow! That bush sticked my weekie you ain't suppose to be looking at, and I didn't get none on my good pants." He zipped his pants, took off his faded J.C.'s Auto Repair cap and, without warning, threw it into Andrew's face and walked away.

Andrew was sure the man had gone to fetch someone, so he turned toward the water. A fisherman tried to crank a boat that had drifted near the edge of the creek. The man turned the key, the motor groaned, and he cursed. The engine failed again, and the man cursed again.

"See him and my hat down there and still not saying to me his name from out in that water. I peed right there but none on my pants, see?" The little man was back. Andrew turned to look through the bushes. He saw her.

Martha looked puzzled. She will ask me something in a moment, Andrew thought. She will ask, "Do you know why you have come? What do you seek that was not to be found in the abbey? What do you think I can do for you?"

Her head swayed as her expression turned to a smile. Her eyes changed in an unspecified way, not of shape or color, and Andrew shifted his gaze from one eye to the other, as if something darted back and forth across her face. He began to feel like a folklore bird hypnotized by an undulating snake. Snake bird. Anhinga. A sharp, hooked word. One he would like to feel work its way through his mouth.

The boat engine cranked.

"Godamighty!" Another man on the inland side of the bushes stumbled and tried to right himself. "Hairy Man!" he yelled, struggling with something as he continued to curse. He lunged forward, holding some object as if offering it to Andrew. Martha twisted at the hip and sprung back and unfurled her arm to point at the man, and Andrew made no decision, but took two leaping steps and was near the center of the creek in seconds, muscle memory calling up the deep and elegant stroke of years before. He dashed into Cainhoy's thorny undergrowth and did not look back.

No one seemed to notice when Andrew slipped into the dormitory to change into dry clothes. His irregular schedule and muddied clothes were common occurrences for the brothers. They tread their separate, narrow paths in their distinctive gaits through their own wilderness or gardens, too busy minding their own inner compasses to take note of a brother whose silent path traced the horizon of their holy space, whose soul was tempered from testing the border of the profane, whose wild explorations required ablution in a dark stream most of them had rarely seen.

When he removed his wet shirt, Andrew realized he did not have Brother Phillip's journal. He felt nauseated at the image of the book on the creek's muddy bottom, tumbling with the current, the paper swollen, the ink pale. The words would spread, their meanings growing thin and diffuse. The leaves would lose their integrity and pull from the binding to settle among beer cans and cricket buckets and other wretched alluvia, or disintegrate to bits to make their way to the ocean and distant shores. The image seemed rather fitting for the death of the body: dispersed among the detritus of the Earth, one's molecules strewn across the pulsing banks and beaches of the world. A journal, however, though a beautiful record of the thoughts of a remarkable soul, is not flesh.

Andrew thought he would vomit. He lay on his bed and breathed slowly, waiting for the vertigo to pass. The bed softened. The air thickened and darkened and filled the room and poured into his lungs and overflowed out of the building and pulled him into a liquid world where sepia forms rushed by like diving birds. He was carried to the surface and deposited on the bank with his bow in his hand. Something leaped from the water on the other bank, and its outline stretched and rippled until wings and a crested head took shape. Andrew notched an arrow and drew the string to his lips. He blew upon the arrow, and it floated across the water to where the ivory-billed woodpecker leaned its breast into the razor point. The arrow passed through the bird's body and pinned it to a tree. Then the arrow was in Andrew's chest, and he was back in the water but also in his bed.

When he recovered, his face was sweaty and his hands shook above his head. He arose, opened the window, and took a deep breath. He was dizzy and heartily ravenous. He realized he had eaten little in several days. The lack of food and sleep, combined with the excitement, had surely gotten the best of him, and he must have fainted for a moment.

Several brothers filed by on their way to the refectory. Perfect timing! Andrew had missed the sext prayer, and now was the time for the midday meal. He put on fresh clothes and ran a comb through his hair and beard. Perhaps he had dropped the journal in the woods, not the water, and it was lying unharmed where he could find it. He recalled one of Lorena's favorite songs, one she liked so much she never altered its lyrics but sang it as it sounded on the record.

> *My old gal's a good old pal*
> *and she looks like a waterfowl*
> *when I get them deep river blues.*
> *Ain't no one to cry for me,*
> *and the fish all go out on a spree*
> *when I get them deep river blues.*

Andrew was not sure how the deep river blues felt, but he suspected that Martha, waterfowl Martha, knew them well.

FIFTEEN

Larson burst into Armey's house, extending and collapsing his radio antenna. "Policeman here with his gun and all getting out of the police car that don't flash no lights and no sireen like it supposed to. He's getting out now and coming in and there ain't no more cake, we going home now?"

Doris looked out the screen door. "That's just old Hatch Tillman. Is Funderburk too good to come out here? He looks like he's hunting for something under the house."

The deputy squatted by the car, his nightstick across his lap and his hat on his knee. "Who-oop!" he said. "Somebody! Come out here and call the dogs!"

Lula walked out onto the porch. "Them dogs's long dead, Hatch. Come on in here where Armey's at."

Tillman slid the nightstick into its loop and adjusted his service belt. He placed the wide-brimmed hat onto his head, hesitated, and then tossed it through the car window. "How'd you let it get so hot all of a sudden, Miss Wright? It was cool when I walked out the station, but dog if it didn't heat up by the time I got out here, and me with a broke air conditioner. How long's he been dead?"

"You tell me. I just got here this morning and found him like that. You can't never know when your time's coming."

"Amen."

The women sat around the cleaned table as Larson tapped the faucet with his antenna. All the pots, pans, and utensils, off the swept floor, had been placed in the pie safe and cabinets.

"Morning, ladies," Tillman said. "He's dead all right."

"As dirt," said Lula.

"I'd say about two, three days. This how y'all found him?"

"Sitting right like that," Ruthie said. "We did straighten up a little bit. You know, an old man by himself don't keep too tidy. Mostly we picked up all them cream cans."

"Cream cans?"

"Good to drink," Larson said. He took a can from his pocket and sipped from it. "All gone. Shoot that gun."

"Leave him alone, boy," Doris said.

Larson touched the pistol holster with the end of his antenna. "That one right there you got, you ought to shoot it and let me hold it now—"

Doris snatched the antenna from Larson's hand and rapped him across the ear. "Get on out of here! I'm sorry, Deputy. He's a handful." Larson went out the back door. "There was a pile of empty condensed milk cans here on the table."

"Evaporated," Ruthie said.

"I read the damn can," Doris said. "Condensed, like you put in a stir-cake. Looks like the only thing he ate."

Tillman turned a chair around backwards and straddled it. "I reckon that would be enough to kill you. Can't be much nourishment. Beside, I've heard them say you can get lead poison from it."

Lula crossed her hands over her chest. "Lord, Lord! I could've brung him something to eat. Why didn't he ask me for something to eat?"

"Hush, Mama," Ruthie said. "He was crazy all out of his head."

"We done called Rondeau's to come out here and get him," Tillman said. "In this heat, he'll be blowed up and ripe sure as . . . pardon me. Y'all do deal with Rondeau's for services, don't you?"

"I reckon so," Lula said.

"Rondeau has to do the autopsy anyway," Tillman said. "If y'all deal with Gadsden's out in Witherbee, you can call them and they'll come get him after Rondeau looks him over. They'll charge for transporting, though."

"Autopsy?" Martha asked.

"Standard procedure. Can't do anything until Monday, it being Easter and all. You know Tag Rondeau, all big up in the church."

"He's big up in the liquor store, too," Doris said.

"That's between him and the Lord. Not my job to judge." Tillman slid the chair out from under himself and stood up. "I swear, it's a fight just to try and sit regular in this leaning house. How'd this blame floor come to have such a pitch to it? Say, that ain't your daughter, is it, Ruthie?"

Ruthie sat up straight. "Yes it is. Growed up and married and divorced and baptized and come home to take care of her mama."

"Dog if she *ain't* grown up." Tillman looked around the room. "Where'd I put my hat? Whoa, what happened down the hall there, with the walls all tore up?"

"Like I said," Ruthie said. "Same reason he didn't eat nothing but canned cream—crazy out of his head." She turned. "Martha, help me up."

A car horn blew several blasts.

"I'm going to kill that boy," Doris said.

"I got to get going, anyhow," Tillman said. "Nothing else for me to do here unless I could raise the dead, and believe me, I sure as hell wouldn't still be at the sheriff's department I had that kind of talent. Am I right?"

Outside, Larson sat in the driver's seat of the squad car. "Why won't this here blowing thing sireen blow I been pushing? Make it blow on this police car like it's supposed to—"

Doris yanked him from the car.

"It's all right," Tillman said. "I know he can't help it. Listen, Rondeau'll send somebody out here directly. Just call him Monday morning about the arrangements. And Ruthie, keep an eye on that daughter of yourn, hear? A girl that pretty, somebody'll be took her off again for sure. There's my damn hat."

"Shoot that gun!" Larson said. "It's like Martha's one, but didn't shoot what she had with the no-talking water man—"

"Hush!" Doris said.

Tillman pulled at his service belt and squirmed around in the car seat. "Let me turn around here, and I'll toot the siren for him one time."

Tillman made a three-point turn and gunned the car onto the dirt road, shooting dust into the yard. The siren wailed.

Larson clapped his hands and hopped. "Hee-ow! Hee-*OW*!"

"Goddamnit!" Doris said, whacking his behind with the antenna. "He done pissed in his good pants!"

Beulah set a porcelain fisherman onto the shelf. The little barefoot man with one overall strap unhitched lay against a tree stump, his cane pole propped against his knee and his floppy hat lowered over his eyes. The dented bucket at his side was etched with "Good things come to those who BAIT." "That's better," she said. "All my whatnots I got left fit on one wall."

Martha, sliding open the glass door of the refrigerated case, stacked clear plastic boxes holding magenta-, mauve-, and violet-streaked orchid corsages marked $8.95. Faux pearl hatpins for dress bosoms stuck through some; strips of laced ribbon for wrists fastened to others. White, pink, and yellow carnations for $4.95 sat on the shelf below. "Are you sure this case is working right?"

"It was making a whiny noise this morning," Beulah said. "Thought my old man had come back."

"It doesn't seem cool enough."

"It's just got to get me through tomorrow. Hell, even if I get somebody to look at it, they'll just say they got to order a part, and that probably won't do any good. Nothing ever works right the first time, you know it?"

"I do. Maybe it just needs some Frezone, or whatever that coolant gas is called. Does Beasley's carry that? I could get somebody to come over with a quart, probably for free." The door jingled. "Speak of the devil."

Purvis stood in the middle of the store, his left hand at his mouth as if hiding his swollen lip.

"Durn if it ain't," Beulah said. "We were just talking about Beasley's, and in you come. We might can use you, eh, Martha?"

"I think so," said Martha.

"I don't," Purvis said. "I don't, I mean, didn't know . . ."

"You do work for Beasley's, don't you, what with the shirt on?" Beulah said. "I'm sorry, hon, you came in for something and we started in on you. What can we help you with? We just put out some pretty corsages."

Purvis rubbed his hand over the "Beasley's Gas" embroidered over the pocket of his shirt. "Corsage."

"It's okay, Beulah," Martha said. "Purvis's had a hard day. Right, Purvis?"

"Purvis? Purvis Driggers, Arlene's boy? Lord, I hadn't seen you since you and them other hellions used to ride your mini-bikes, knocking over rakes and shovels Buddy had leaning out front the store just for meanness. Time flies, you know it?"

"Yes'm."

"And you're friends with Martha?"

"We just met today," Martha said.

"Now how about that?"

Purvis took one step toward the counter. "See, I come in to get a flower, a corsage, for Mama, for Easter. Sunday's Easter. She likes to go to church."

"Martha just made some precious ones. She's a natural."

Martha took a box from the case. "How about a purple?"

Purvis coughed and leaned onto the counter. "Jesus." He coughed, struggled to suck in tiny amounts of air, and tried to take a hit from his empty inhaler.

"Son, you all right?" Beulah asked. "Look at you. Your whole face and neck are flushed."

Purvis bent over and coughed several times, then stretched up and exhaled slowly. "I'm all right. I got wasp-stung, and it's got me swoll up and my asthma more worser." He took the box from Martha's hand. "I'll have this one. This one is exactly what I want."

"Anything else?" Martha asked.

"Not for now, but I know how to find you."

Purvis paid Beulah but didn't move from the counter.

"We almost forgot," Martha said. "This case isn't cooling right. Can you see if it needs some of that coolant gas?"

"I don't know about that. I'm not much of a fixer, but I'll look it for you."

Purvis lay on his side and placed his face at the bottom edge of the case. "Godamighty, looks like some kind of animal under there."

"That Janice!" Beulah said. "I told her she better not try to leave that damn cat here. You reckon that's what I heard whining?"

Purvis squatted and pulled the case away from the wall. "Just a bunch of hair. Orange."

"That damn tabby!"

"It's clogged up the compressor. You got a vacuum cleaner?" Beulah brought Purvis the shop vac. "Okay," he said after a minute. "I believe it'll cool good in a little bit. Might want to keep it away from the wall awhile."

"I sure appreciate it, hon," Beulah said. "You just might be a fixer after all. What do I owe you?"

"Oh, no ma'am. That was a favor. Besides, Beasley don't do appliance work, just fills tanks."

"Then, here." Beulah took a rose from a vase. "Give it to your sweetheart."

Purvis looked at Martha. She narrowed an eye and flared her nostrils. "I already know how to find you," he said, leaving the store to stand on the sidewalk in front of the gas truck.

"Now, he was a nice boy," Beulah said. "Looked like he was fixing to hand you that rose."

They watched through the window as Agnes walked up to Purvis. She spoke, then turned to look through the store window.

"She can't see us because of the glare this time of day," Beulah said. "You think she's coming in? Poor thing might've already forgot."

Agnes turned back to Purvis as he handed the rose to her, climbed into the truck, and drove away.

"Now, wasn't that sweet?" Beulah said. "I was just saying he was a nice boy, you know it?" Beulah took out the flask and had a swallow. "Martha, darling, I just want to tell you again how thankful I am you came back today. I couldn't blame you if you hadn't, after Agnes pitched that conniption. My nerves were shot all to hell, too."

"That wasn't it."

"What's Agnes doing, pointing that rose at us? She probably thinks she's putting a whammy on the store. Lot of good that'll do with me closing up. Ha!" Beulah put a cigarillo between her lips. "Durned if she ain't smiling."

"She's gritting her teeth." Martha saw the tendons straining in Agnes's neck.

"I ought to go out and talk to her." Smoke escaped Beulah's nostrils and floated up in a V. "My God! Her hand's dripping blood!" Agnes's fist was clenched so tight, she'd squeezed right into the rose thorns and didn't even seem to feel it.

Beulah ran around the counter and to the door just as Agnes darted away. "Agnes! Agnes!" She turned back around toward Martha. "She's gone. I swear, see what happens when you try to help somebody? No use worrying over it. I can't hardly see after my own life, much less somebody else's. Say, that refrigerator case has already fogged up. Durned if that Driggers boy ain't a life saver, you know it?"

"Yes, I think I do."

As Martha parked the van in the yard, she saw Ruthie on the porch eating something. "Get him out of there before he gets snake-caught," Ruthie said, pointing toward the end of the porch. A pair of brogans stuck out by the steps.

"What's he doing here?" Martha asked.

"Said he was chasing a frog or something."

"I mean, *why* is he here?"

Ruthie spat something into her lap. "Doris and Mama went out to the Honey Hole for catfish. I don't know where they got the money. That place is high as Double Happy on somebody else's liquor. They figured you be here soon enough to help me watch him."

Martha kicked the brogans. "Come on, Larson. Let's get you something to eat. I think we got some of that cake left."

"I done eat it all, and the sweetening gone off it what Mawmaw eat by itself, because her eyes quit, and I can't eat fish what ain't picked."

Ruthie hacked. "Damn if this ain't some boney little bream in this world. Doris fried it up and brought it to us so's she wouldn't feel too bad about leaving him here, I reckon. She left clothes and his pillow, so you got to make a pallet for him to sleep on. I wonder who give her these little minnows? Anyway, you got to pick them bones for him to eat it. Did you get him out yet?"

Martha reached down and pulled Larson out by the belt. He got up immediately, ran up the steps, and sat beside Ruthie. "I'm going out, too," Martha said.

"How you mean? You can't leave me with him and me can't get up and chase him around. If I could, you think I'd be eating cold fish here where Doris helped me to get to the porch and not propped up at the Honey Hole, too? If you go somewhere, you taking his off ass, too."

"I will. You can sit here by yourself."

"Fine. But I need my cigarettes before you go." Ruthie spat another bone. "Now, pick him some fish. Larson, if you swallow a bone, you eat a piece of that light bread quick, hear? God knows she might miss one."

"That's right. I miss a whole lot," said Martha.

"And run inside and get me the salt, baby. These hush puppies need some help."

PART II

"For nothing else either is or shall be except Being,
since Fate has tied it down to be a whole and motionless;
therefore all things that mortals have established,
believing in their truth, are just a name:
Becoming and Perishing, Being and Not-Being,
and change of position, and alteration of bright color."
—Parmenides

SIXTEEN

"I follow distinctive, rapid drumming through the brown wintry wood to find well-wrought rows of holes drilled high on a gum trunk. My suspicions are confirmed when I espy the dappled fellow at his diligent, solitary work: a yellow-bellied sapsucker. He is an uncommon breed, although perhaps seen more often than recognized, similar as he is to the flicker or the red-cockaded. But the sight of his neck, the red throat, betrays him."

Purvis sat in the gas truck in his yard, holding the book, and wondered why a monk would swim across a creek to stare at two regular people and a retard, then jump back into the water. And why would he tote this book around? Monks are supposed to read the Bible and Aristotle and Ockham the Razor. This book was like the diary they made you do in fourth grade, but this one was by a grown woods-walking monk fifty years ago who had nothing better to do than write pansy words like "wrought" and "espy" and chase a redneck sapsucker. Redneck sapsucker—now that was a metaphor!

"What'd you say?" Spessard stuck his head into the passenger's window.

"I said that was . . . nothing. Why you espying on me?"

"I was hollering supper was ready, but you kept sitting out here so long, I thought you fell asleep. You reading the damn Bible?"

"No sir, just a book I found."

Spessard reached through the window. "What's this?"

"Cypress knee," said Purvis.

"Like I don't know that. Where'd you get it?"

"Monk."

"When'd he start carving?"

"Not Monkey Tillman. A real Cainhoy monk." Purvis wrapped the leather strip around the book and slid it inside the console. The soft cover *did* make it look like a Bible, and it had olden-days words, Bible sorts of words, in it.

"What's it supposed to be?" Spessard asked.

"Something about chasing woodpeckers."

"Woodpeckers? I'm not talking about the damn book," said Spessard. "Boy, I keep threatening I'm going to turn you out, and how you going to root out a living when you can't hold one thought steady between your ears? A job, like you don't exactly have, takes focus. A woman, like you don't nowhere near have, takes focus. A skill, like, hell, I don't even got to say it. Carving is a skill. I was talking about what this here stump was."

"I might have things you don't know about," said Purvis. "I might have a charm or a genie or a fairy goddess dancing and leading me through enchanted woods like in some story you never heard and wouldn't understand. She just might be. She's that way." Purvis squinted his eyes and pinched the bridge of his nose. "Anyway, the stump, I thought it was Jesus. The monk said it was Bobby Rose."

"Listen at you. Work two days in a row and you can't talk straight. So what you doing with this stump?"

"He sent it to you."

"That's what I'm talking about all over again. It's like I have to wrench answers out of you, like you're putting your brain to a use it wouldn't never meant for. Now, try to trail your answer out. What did the goddammit monk send me the stump for?"

"Do I know what a monk is thinking?" Purvis rubbed his thumbs against his temples. "It's like this. He was carving. I said *you* carved. He said, 'Here, take this to your daddy. I said 'all right.' Is that focused enough? Now, you want the ugly thing or not?"

"You need to heave that ass down off your shoulders, boy, and don't call a piece of handiwork like this ugly. Some men use their hands for something other than pocket pool. This carving here is what they call stylized. It ain't supposed to look exactly like anything, but just sort of like something. Any of this getting into your blunt head, or am I just farting in the dark?"

"You don't know what I been dealing with. It's all just happening. Things coming at me. Moving and patterns and like singing and I got somewhere I got to go."

"I know what you'll be dealing with if you don't prop yourself up at that table and go at them fish. Your mama with the royal red ass is what. Then see if you get another mouthful of groceries out of her kitchen." Spessard held the carving up to his face. "Bobby Rose the roofer? No, but he do look a little like old J.C., what I've seen of him."

Fish bones and green onion tops were piled on a spread-out newspaper in the middle of the table. Spessard finished a slice of chocolate pie. Purvis spun a hush puppy on the table, trying to make it stand like a toy top. Arlene counted the fish on the platter.

"Eight bream left. Son, don't you want one more? And stop playing with that hush puppy and eat it."

"I had enough," said Purvis. "And you put bell peppers in the hush puppies again that I can't stand. Anyway, I got to get going."

"Maybe DeWayne and Sylvie can eat these tomorrow."

"They not coming over?"

"Sylvie's bad off again," said Arlene. "DeWayne said she hadn't been out the bed since yesterday and hadn't eat hardly a bite. Mm-mm, they have a time of it. At least she's got somebody to look after her."

Spessard dropped his fork onto the table. "And you don't?"

"I might catch a stroke tomorrow and don't know that you'd pick me up off the floor."

The hush puppy rolled in a half-circle and stopped on the edge of the table. "Touchdown," Purvis said. "Then he ain't using his truck tonight. I'm getting me a shower, then heading over there."

"Take these bream with you," Arlene said. She wrapped a sheet of aluminum foil over the plate of fish. "They say fish is the best thing you can eat, healthwise. DeWayne'll pick some for Sylvie."

Spessard refilled his glass with milk. "To have and to hold, to pick fish and up off the floor."

The dusk air along Snipe Hunt Road washed into the truck more coolly than Purvis expected, but not strong enough to blow out the propane smell. When he got into DeWayne's Pup, he'd feel better, and wouldn't have to worry whether Martha had a high tolerance for chemical odors. Maybe, with her six or eight arms, she could fan away the fumes, or charm them to turn sweet and plait into a rope of aromas, then stretch out of the cab window and up to the open sky like snakes out of baskets for those diaper-wearing flute players in Oriental countries. She would climb the rope fast, hands over hands, until all he could see was a spot, and then she'd come sliding back down with the rope in one hand and around one ankle, all the other hands filled with beautiful, unknown fruits and shiny candy. And then she would say, "Take hold of me, you redneck sapsucker, and I will pull you up to a magical land where you never have to work or have a headache." Up they would fly, and Purvis would not be afraid of falling.

He checked his face in the rearview mirror. The swellings on his lip and neck had eased, but shaving had been tricky. He peeled back a patch of tissue paper from the scab on his neck, removing two pieces from his lip. He licked his finger and rubbed away tiny crumbs of dried blood. At least the drooling had stopped. Tilting the side mirror to check his ear, he saw that his lobe had shrunk to the size of a marble but sagged like a blue earbob. He tried to milk it by pressing and pulling down with his thumb and forefinger, but it just hurt and turned darker.

DeWayne was bent under the hood of the Pup as the propane truck stopped in the red cedar mulch driveway. DeWayne looked over his shoulder, his hands on the Isuzu's grille.

"That's going to leave a rut in my cedar chips that I just spread Sunday," said DeWayne. "You know what a sonofabitching bag costs?"

"I don't spend my money on sawdust, especially when it smells like hog piss."

"It smells like cedar is supposed to smell. Keeps fleas out, too. Put some of that in your closet, and you never get moths eating your wool sweaters."

"When you ever had a wool sweater? And what you need to keep fleas off of? You got sheep up under the trailer?" Purvis lit a cigarette. "Mama sent a plate of fish. Said Sylvie's bad off."

"That truck got a toolbox on it? Tuning it up and me with no timing light." DeWayne dropped a wrench onto a sheet of plywood halfway under the engine. "Just set that plate on the truck somewhere until we go in. I'll eat some directly, but Sylvie won't be able to."

"What if you pick it for her?" said Purvis, dropping the plate on the truck bed.

"She can't keep anything down. Sips some Gatorade every now and then," said DeWayne. "Not asleep and not awake neither. Up just enough to moan. Wet the bed this morning. At least that meant she got some fluid through her. I got her cleaned up and went to work but came back at dinner."

Purvis spat and rolled cedar chips over it with his penny loafer. "Lum had some tools on here, but he cleaned everything off. So, you probably not going to the PJ party, huh?"

"Goddogit. I'll just have to guesstimate," DeWayne said from under the hood. "Naw, I got to stay around here. That reminds me. I picked up the jugs of grain alcohol on the way home today. I'll call Lum to swing by and get them."

"I can take them. I'll just take your truck. Won't even have to unload them."

"It's just a few gallon jugs."

"Be easier for you, though."

"Why can't you just *ask* to borrow the Isuzu?" said DeWayne.

"Here I am, trying to do you a favor," said Purvis, "and you're giving me a shitting time of it. Now, if you don't want me to drive the truck over there for you . . ."

DeWayne leaned against back the grille. "Okay. I know you're up to something. You can borrow my truck if you want to. Just don't even think about taking it to Armey Wright's to look for buried treasure and leaving my tire tracks in his yard for me to get arrested when I got an invalid wife to see after."

Purvis dropped his cigarette butt and covered it with cedar chips. "Why would I do that? Besides, bunch of Wrights already been out there and made me call Funderburk. If they hadn't found it already, Funderburk and Hatch probably got it for themself by now."

"Made you call? Cornholing Jesus! You mean you already been out there again? And don't put your cigarettes in my cedar."

Purvis picked up the butt and thumped it into the grass. "It's like this. Remember we talked about Martha Wright, I mean, Umphlett? I told her about the PJ party."

"I knew it," said DeWayne. "You got a date and want my Isuzu because she's too prissy to crawl up in a propane truck. Or you're too prissy to have a girl who *would* crawl up in it."

"You just don't know. She's just that. Everything about her. How she moves. She looks at me—a look that could worm a dog. And her mouth. Lips like corn."

"What?"

Purvis turned his head slightly as he stared toward the tress. "Like mutton corn. Her eyes like an okra stem when you cut off the pod. And she's swerving. All her arms curving in waves. Flowing one, two, three, four—"

"Jesus' splintered ass. You talking out your thin head. And I'm supposed to let you drive my truck?"

"Talk's like rain—like hard rain coming down when the sun shining. And the wind that comes when she walks? You wish Sylvie could walk like that."

"You about got it right. I wish she could walk at all." DeWayne turned and bent under the hood again. "Now, back that gas tank off this driveway if you taking this Pup."

The Pup's unfamiliar sound, a soft hum like a distant train, told Purvis that DeWayne's plug job had done the trick. It caused a rumble deep in his chest that soothed him, even as it threatened to work into his throat and choke him. Some other things seem good for you and bad for you, too: salt, liquor, hard work, reefers, bananas. Some things seem to draw you, but then could hurt you: snakes, fuzzy caterpillars, straight razors, decks of cards, pokeweed heavy with dark berries.

He passed the remains of the Oakley plantation, once the largest clapboard building in the county and the envy of everyone who drove by. That much wood, though, was hardly more than a tinderbox in a Low Country thunderstorm, and a lightning bolt finally leveled it, despite the dozen lightning rods that reached like steeples to heaven.

Purvis wondered if other people saw the world like this. Most people he knew were so sure of themselves, so confident. They saw things one way. Do it. Don't do it. Good. Bad. The Bonners who lived down that long driveway beyond the brick gates he was passing never worried whether someone else was so big that you might disappear into her—so big you feel pulled down a road of her, covered over by arching tree arms that close in to hug you as you move away from everything you were, and nobody can get you then, but still the tree arms mash you to chicken-size, then scorpion-size, then to just a tiny darkness, like a tough-skinned berry floating first in someone else, then spread out in her. She is the world, and you no longer have to be anything but a part of her.

What is it like, never to worry about this sort of thing, never knowing, *knowing* that, despite your worries and thinking, you *can* change your mind and you *will* move? Maybe like watching yourself from someone else's body, toward an undeniable end.

Rattling over the cattle guard, the pickup spanned a ditch matted in green briars that, in a few months, would sag with blackberries. In front of an asbestos-sided house sat a red van parked on a narrow, short limestone driveway. Purvis stopped behind the van and wondered if he should blow the horn. If he went to the door, Martha would probably invite him in to sit in the den on a chair with a knitted shawl over it. He would have to talk to her mama to get the fat woman's approval, or maybe just for Martha to show him off as she stood behind her mama and smiled pleasingly, while Purvis told jokes about one-legged men in bars and did his card trick about the face cards all going to a hotel and seeming to get mixed up but right where they should be when he turned the cards over. But if Martha and her mama are Holiness, they might not let cards in the house. Martha might ask if he wanted a glass of tea, and then he would have to wonder if he should show his politeness and say "no," or show his gratitude and say "yes." Maybe Holiness are like the church Laverne Bobo goes to, which sends the boys out on bicycle trips and does not allow tea or coffee or Co-Colas, only 7-Ups. If Martha offered him a 7-Up, he should probably take it.

Prissy girls do not like to be called out by a horn, and will say things like, "What do you think I am, your field hand, jumping in the back of your truck to go pull up burrs for a dollar a row?" Martha was not prissy, but she was not one who would come when called. She would sit until her fat mama finally had enough and rocked herself from her special fat people chair or rode her electric scooter chair to the window and said, "Now who'd come up here in a little pickup truck and not decent enough to walk up to the door?"

So Purvis stepped out of the pickup and walked along the far side of the van, hoping the extra time would give Martha the chance to notice him and meet him outside. In the carport at the side of the house were two old couches, several bed-frames leaning against the wall, a freezer, and a claw-foot bathtub. The house was badly in need of a paint job. If Martha and her fat mama went away for a weekend, and Purvis knew they were gone and had some extra money for paint and could borrow that tall ladder from Sim Fosdick, the window-maker, Purvis could surprise them with a new-looking house when they got back from Folly Beach or South of the Border or wherever Wrights and Umphletts go. He would have to keep a hush on it so Spessard would not find out. "You can't get your thumb out of your narrow ass long enough to earn a dollar," Spessard would say, "but you can paint a whole somebody else's house for free?"

Purvis would have to be prepared with just the right thing to say if Spessard found out. Maybe, "You don't ever have to worry about where my thumb is no more, because I'm gone from here." Or, "It's not somebody else's. Martha's fat mama give it to us to stay in when we get married tomorrow." Or, "Now I got a woman *and* a skill. How's that for focus, you old bastard?" Spessard would proceed to whip Purvis's ass, but Purvis would take it like a man.

"How come you where's the gas truck"—Purvis jumped, but the voice didn't pause—"what was to Markham's Mobile Home and Trailer Court Resort and to Uncle Armey's, where the sheriff police blowed the siren, but got a little truck now, and we riding in too, Aunt Ruthie's not. I'm'll be in the back and you and Martha in the front to the creek, but Mama and Mawmaw's at the Honey Hole and Aunt Ruthie here."

Purvis stared at Larson. The little snap-kneed man wore a welder's cap, a blue and brown plaid shirt buttoned to his throat, olive work pants with dirt on the knees, and slip-on sneakers. "You're like a gnat," said Purvis. "A gnat-man is what you are. And what in the hell makes you think your aggravating ass is going anywhere—"

Coming down the steps, her tight-jeaned thighs moving like wings, Martha lit a cigarette and slid the butane lighter into her pocket. Her lipstick was the color of an eggplant, a vegetable Purvis had never eaten but certainly was highly nutritious. She wore boots Purvis could see were not exactly western-style, but the sort he supposed a woman would think made her look nice, and would be good in a fight. Her flowing yellow shirt was untucked and silky, forming Vs in the front and back—the kind of shirt he thought a woman might wear to an outdoor wedding performed by a hippy preacher who, instead of preaching sermons, played guitar and wrote songs about Jesus the weed-smoker. The loose collar was embroidered with fleur-de-lis. Purvis had seen the design on Whip Noble's handkerchief. Whip belonged to the Masons.

"Whose truck?" Martha asked. When she blew smoke from the corner of her mouth, it spiraled behind her, picking up light as if fish scales had been thrown into it. Her hips worked in their gliding way, like they were breathing, as she came through the yard.

"DeWayne's, my brother's, you know, at the hash plant, except he's home because of his invalidic wife what's real bad off." Purvis tried to prop a foot on the front bumper of the van, but could not find a lip or crevice big enough. "It's not a bad little truck, what with being Jap."

"Can we all three fit in it?"

Purvis felt the back of his throat go dry and prickly, the way it did when he loaded hay bales. "No, it don't seat but just two. He'll have to stay here. What's he doing here anyway? Don't he live at Markham's?"

"Markham's Mobile Home and Trailer Court Resort," Larson said. "I live right there and done told you this is Aunt Ruthie's house, with the water hose bathtub, and I can ride in there in the back, done it in Uncle Bondo's truck, didn't I ride the back of Uncle Bondo's truck, Martha, you in the front?"

"You did, Larson," Martha said. "Now go on and get in the back of that truck there." She turned to see Purvis pinching the bridge of his nose. "We're stuck with him tonight. That's just how it is. You be nice to him, hear me?"

Purvis rubbed his forehead and took two deep breaths. "Okay, but, I mean, damn, I know he's retarded and all and can't help it, but don't he get on your nerves?"

"Who the hell don't?"

"Just tell him not to mess with those jugs of grain back there. Like I don't have enough worries to add a drunk-up retard I got to fish out of the creek."

Night fell quickly as the Isuzu spun along Gander Pull Road.

"I'm falling!" Larson shouted.

Purvis jerked around and took his foot from the accelerator.

"He's not falling," Martha said. Purvis faced the road and accelerated.

"I'm flying!" Larson shouted.

Purvis jerked around again.

"He's just having fun," Martha said. "Don't worry about him."

"Everybody at the landing's going to hear that crazy shit he's yelling," Purvis said. "I know he's your uncle—"

"Cousin."

"Cousin, but that's sort of embarrassing." Purvis hummed to soothe the slight nausea—the one that started when he opened the truck door for Martha and held her arms as she slid in. "See, some of the guys like to make fun of me, the ones who are a couple of years older, like DeWayne. If I'm hauling around a hollering retard . . ."

"I'm falling!"

". . . they'll pick at me all night about it." He heard a click and turned to see Martha unsnapping her safety belt and twisting in the seat to face him. Although hardly any light fell into the cab of the truck, her lips seemed brighter, and her shirt was now more orange than yellow. She reached out a hand and ran a finger across his swollen lip.

"Don't worry about those assholes," she said. "I'll watch out for you."

"I'm flying!"

Martha raised up onto her knee. "When those bastards start on you, remember this." She put her hands on his face, hooked fingers under his chin and across his scalp, and spread his eye with her thumbs. "This is a sign." She leaned against him and pressed her tongue to his naked eye.

"Flyyyiiing!"

SEVENTEEN

The only boaters who used what the young people called the Landing were those with boats that could be toted to the water, like canoes or ten-foot Jon boats. The concrete ramp had crumbled away at just about the time Flippo expanded his and began to charge two dollars to use it. The official story was that tremors caused by Hurricane Hugo had pushed the cracked and aging ramp to its limits, and a decade later, the county's budget was still too overdrawn from disaster relief to replace it. But some frog-giggers and gator-poachers still claimed they'd seen a crew—the same crew that sank the pilings for Flippo's dock—pounding on the old ramp. Even before the Landing fell into disuse, dirt-digger youth found use in its wide, unlit turnaround at the end of the macadam road, and the sandy patch of "beach" by the branch—an ideal spot for a bonfire, target practice on beer-can pyramids, and drawers-only swimming sprints across the creek and back before luring a reptile.

Cars and trucks flanked the narrow road, leaving just enough room for a vehicle to pass between. In the middle of the turnaround, shapes and shadows crossed before the fire. Purvis rolled down the window. The wet night air conducted both the musky smell of swamp and the sound of wailing guitars, the Allman Brothers' "Revival" blaring from speakers stacked on a flatbed.

"Looks like every poor-ass peckerwood in the county is here for a cheap drunk tonight," Purvis said.

"Poor in more than just money, I bet," Martha said. "You won't be able to park at the end."

"There'll be a spot saved for me—well, for this truck. We got the good in the back. Lum and the boys probably done mixed up the sweets and now just waiting for the sour."

Dozens in their teens and early twenties leaned against fenders or sat on hoods, while others milled about the turnaround, oblivious to the Isuzu's approach. A band of underage girls, standing dangerously close to the fire, raising their arms, and snapping their spines in a convulsive dance, would likely be passed out drunk within the hour.

Purvis blew the horn to part the crowd. Someone yelled, "It's Driggers!" and another, "It's the good!" The assemblage cheered, drowning out the music before settling into murmurs of "About time" and "Grab them jugs." Sitters and leaners slid from their vehicles, the dancers forgot their spasms, and Lum and the other party elders left their posts to rush the Pup. Purvis sat high and grinned. Flashlights lit up the truck bed. Larson, startled, leapt to his feet, then bent to look through the back glass.

"It's okay!" Martha yelled back to Larson. He seemed to speak, but Martha couldn't hear him. "Hurry up and park so I can calm him down."

Purvis hooked the pickup toward the fire, then backed in beside Lum's Chevette just as the truck backfired. The conclave cheered again. As Martha got out of the truck, hands removed the jugs of grain alcohol and poured them into two large, yellow, plastic garbage cans.

"Where you been, hoss?" Lum said, leaning one arm against Purvis's door and holding a boat paddle with the other. "What'd you do with DeWayne?"

"Sylvie's bad off."

Lum turned toward the cans. "Here, Tunk!" He tossed the paddle. "Mix it up and tell Harlan to turn off the music a minute." He stuck his head into the window and whispered, "That's that Umphlett girl, ain't it? Man, nothing I like better than a sticking-way-out gluteus maximus. When she stepped out just then, it looked like two cathead biscuits *made* for some sopping. You better get some of that jelly *tonight*, hoss, before somebody else sticks a spoon in the jar."

"He's choking!" Martha yelled. "Give me a flashlight!"

Purvis jumped from the cab, bumping the door into Lum's chest. He climbed into the truck bed where Larson, making a hacking sound, bent over the side, while Martha tried to steady his head. People gathered around and lights flashed onto Larson's face. He was covered with grease and crumbs.

"Fishbone," Purvis said. "I, um, some fish got put back here, and he must've eat it." He felt his chest tighten.

"Light bread!" Tunk DuPree yelled. "Anybody got any bread? We got a fishbone choking! Fishbone!"

"What?" a skinny teenager said from a few yards away.

"Not you, pecker-breath," said Tunk DuPree. "A real fishbone."

"Fuck that bread shit," Martha said as Larson hacked. "We got to reach in there."

"Here," said Mitch Bodiford. He produced a large folding knife with numerous attachments. "This has a hook remover on it. Try sticking it down in there."

"Jesus, you stupid ass," Martha said.

"How about the corkscrew?" Mitch said. "This is an *imported* knife and got it *all*."

"I can get it," Purvis said. "Make him get still." He took the flashlight and held it close to Larson's mouth.

Martha rolled Larson over and lay the back of his head against the side of the truck. She moved close to Larson's ear and rubbed his forehead. In a timbre dark and deep as a man's, she slowly spoke, "Listen, sweetie. It's just a fishbone stuck in your throat. Now hold still while we get it out." Purvis watched her lips open and close, stretch and swell, darken and lighten. He tipped the light toward her just as her tongue peeked out at the word "throat." "Purvis has to reach in and get the bone. He won't hurt you."

Three or four of her palms petted Larson's chubby chest and shoulders like she would a cat. Two or three others touched Purvis on his knee and elbow. Her voice was like many people calling from another room, the sound thickened by traveling through walls and picture frames, to sound like wood. "My Purvis will save you," she was saying. "He is a remover of not-needed things. He will make you whole, as he will me, when he does what he must do for me. Then I will lift him in my dancing arms and take him to where his breath comes easy and his head never aches. He knows the signs and symbols of things; he knows the metaphors. He is my Aristotle."

The flashlight slipped from Purvis's grasp and hit Larson's chin.

"Aaannkh!" Larson wailed, but he did not move.

"Focus, damnit," Martha said. "Can you see it?"

"Yes, focus," Purvis said. "I should be able to reach it." A thread-like half-inch bone was imbedded in the soft palette. "It's right by that little hanging lump."

"Uvula," Lum said.

"I got two of them," said Massy Deere. "Look." She opened her mouth and let several bystanders examine her throat.

Purvis took a deep breath. His chest had slackened, and he felt calmer than he had all day. "Just don't let him bite me." He placed an index and middle finger into Larson's mouth. "Focus." Larson's teeth scraped against Purvis's knuckles as he pushed his fingers toward the throat.

"Damn, he ain't gagged a bit," Lum said. "My old lady should take a lesson. You hear what I said, Tunk?"

Purvis felt the bone on the tip of his middle finger. He drew back and raised the finger, pushing the bone up to the nail of his index finger and clamping it securely. He pulled, and the bone followed the hand out of the mouth.

"Ockham the Razor," he said.

Martha drew Larson's head to her chest and stroked his hair. "You're okay now, baby," she said.

"Get me more fish," Larson said.

"Hush," Martha said, humming "The Wind Cries Mary."

"Crisis over," Lum said. "Martha Umphlett. Ain't you a beaut? I hadn't seen you since hatchet was hammer. You ready for some PJ? How about you, Purvis—a little of that Purple Jesus? Whoo ha ha!" He walked away, climbed onto the flatbed, and hollered, "Who's ready for some PJ?" Even though it sounded like *Peugeot* the way he said it, tied-tongued and slurring, the group cried out. Lum held up his hands to hush the crowd. "Here's the deal. You got to use one those cups Tunk's got. Two bucks gets you a cup, and you can dip it as many times as you want. We write your name on it so you don't try to give it to nobody else. You lose the cup, another two bucks gets you another one. Everybody got it?"

Harlan Lisenby climbed up beside Lum and said, "Everybody look here!" He pulled up his shirt to reveal "Jesus" painted in large indigo letters across his chest. "Did it myself, in honor of my baptizing."

"You done showed us all, you afflicted fucker," Lum said.

"Somebody loan me two dollars," Donald Bunch shouted.

"Better loan him six or eight," Johnson Rondeau said. "One cupful and he'll be drunk-up and losing cups all night."

"Kiss my ripe ass," Donald said.

Though the nearly full moon was most often just a faint orange glow veiled by clouds, at times it broke through and illuminated the crowd swelling along the creek basin. Cars and trucks jammed the road, blocking each other, and many sank into the musky shoulder, where they'd later rely upon young hunters eager to prove the strength of their winches. Dancing farmgirls, stepping like foals, ringed the fire, knowing well how their faceless silhouettes entranced the boys, perched behind them on tailgates. Arguments over football teams, race car drivers, bird dogs, and rock bands escalated to cursing, then melted to laughter. Romances started, sending brave pairs to the swamp for privacy and the more timid to back seats, while an equal number of bonds were severed, keeping subgroups in continuous flux. All partook abundantly of the sweet and fruity purple concoction. Many needed new cups.

At the fringe of the gathering, at the edge of the water, Purvis and Martha sat on upturned buckets she'd borrowed from the back of Dewey Spoade's father's paint truck. Martha found Orion's belt in the cloudy sky and looked east, but could not locate the Seven Sisters. She remembered the story of how they were chased by Orion until transformed by Zeus into stars to escape. One of the sisters—what was her name?—cannot be seen with the naked eye, and the legend said that she hid her face in shame from marrying a mortal. On this night, veiled by clouds, they all were ashamed.

Larson knelt a few yards away and dug up rocks to throw into the water. Farther downstream, Martha saw the creek flanked by a couple dozen young men and half as many young women. Most had small-caliber rifles, several had shotguns, and the rest held flashlights. Light washed across their faces, some of which Martha recognized. Most were her and Purvis's age: Sonny Boy Dangerfield, Pookey Villeponteaux, Fayro Mazyck, Earthine Cheatwood, the Limehouse twins of the famous breasts, Chevrolet and Candy Rouge (who got married in tenth grade and had three children before graduating), and Half-Ass Singletary, who passed as a girl until ninth grade, when his mini-skirt betrayed a hard-on after Florence Cribb asked "Helen" for a tampon. Had Martha's peers refused to grow up while she was away? If she had remained, instead of leaving a few years back, would nights shooting .22s into a creek and drinking sugared-up alcohol have been her brightest moments, too?

"Damn if I didn't walk right out of the house without a rifle," Purvis said. "I'm a durn good shot, you know."

"Forget that adolescent shit," Martha said. "I brought you over here because we have something important to talk about."

"I'm a fast runner, too. About the fastest white boy at school. I got a trophy from the track meet relay race when I was fourteen. I mean to tell you, I could fly."

"That might be exactly what you have to do," said Martha. "Now listen. The FBI came to Armey's this afternoon after you left."

Larson crawled to Martha's side and held up something in his hand. "This a good rock like them ones in Miss Emry's yard with no grass, that all smooth and taste salty sometimes, but this one fat . . ."

"Hush a minute, sweetie," Martha said.

". . . you can have it in your pocketbook. I'm giving it to you because it's a girl kind of rock and I won't chunk it but give it to you—"

"Okay, thank you, Larson," she said. "Thank you for the pretty rock. Now go find some more for us." He crawled off as Martha rubbed the rock between her hands.

Purvis rocked on his bucket. "Who called the FBI? Don't nobody need them. Armey drank all that cream with the lead, right? I can tell them about it. They might not know about the lead sealer in the bottom of the can." He began to breathe in fast gulps.

"Settle down, Purvis. You don't mean to say you killed Armey, do you?"

Purvis sucked on his inhaler. "No! No, hell no. Did they say that? Oh, goddamn Jesus' rotted ass!"

"They did not say that. But they looked all around the house, and somehow they know you were at Armey's the other day."

"Did they find a cigarette butt? Because I smoked a couple with you today right there in the front yard. Remember?" He puffed again on the inhaler, then lit a cigarette.

"Just calm yourself." Martha took the cigarette from Purvis and placed it between her lips. She took a slow drag, let the smoke out of her mouth, inhaled it into her nose, and blew it out again through rounded lips, just as a cloud moved and the moon peeked out. The smoke spiraled forward, then curled up, like a rope that changed from yellow to orange to red to purple. She placed the cigarette back into his mouth, letting her fingers press against his lips for a moment. She held Larson's rock in the same hand, her ring finger and pinky clamping it against her palm, and she noticed that the rock had an edge. Pulling her hand away from Purvis's face, she examined the object in the moonlight. "You know what this is, Purvis?"

Purvis looked at the dark, almond-shaped thing in Martha's hand. Her other hands cupped and waved in arcs behind it, then laced together to form a bowl, gathering and throwing moonlight onto the charm Martha offered him. "I think it's some kind of seafood," said Purvis, "like an oyster."

"Yes, a mollusk. This one's a mussel—a freshwater mussel. Have you ever eaten one?"

"Muscle?" Purvis wondered if this was a metaphor. "No, but one time I ate twenty-seven bream, all of them as big as your hand." He was breathing regularly now. The wet night air soothed his lungs, and he could smell many things in it—the fire, the grape juice and oranges of the PJ, and a human scent like sweat. He even thought he smelled the ocean. Maybe creeks and rivers could draw the ocean backwards through their currents. Maybe the moon had something to do with it. He knew that the moon pulled the tides.

"I want to show you something, Purvis." She removed the hawk-bill knife from her back pocket, thumbed it open, and held the point to the mussel. With a flick, the bivalve opened in her hand. "Look. M-u-s-s-e-l. What does that look like to you?"

"A boat?"

"Inside."

Martha lit her butane lighter and held the blue flame near the mussel. Purvis bent to see a soft, jelly-like mass spread within the symmetrical shell. At the top of the hinge, in the crotch of two lip-like flaps, rose a meaty bulb—a tiny knot of flesh.

"Purple Jesuuuus!" someone yelled just yards away.

"Godamighty!" Purvis said, falling backwards off his bucket.

"Let's pop some river dogs, you stump-grubbers! Get it!" the same voice yelled. Larson put his hands over his ears.

"That has to be the loudest person I have ever heard," Martha said.

Purvis screwed the top of the bucket into the ground and sat. "Son-of-a-bitching wild-ass Monkey Tillman."

"I know him. Hatch Tillman the deputy's son."

"Yeah. Always showing off, getting people to bet on him doing crazy-ass daredevil shit, acting like he ain't scared of a damn thing. One time he bet some of us he'd swim the creek with dog food rubbed all over him to chum the gators. I wish like hell he would've got eat."

"I remember some of his escapades," Martha said. "I think I recognize half these wretched shit-asses here. A couple of them were baptized with me the other night. They're too afraid or embarrassed to speak to me. Hell, I probably ran into you sometime or other." Martha spat between her feet. "Anyway, that don't matter now. We need to finish our conversation."

"You were going to tell me about them FBIs." Purvis was having trouble keeping a tight hold on the conversation. He might be accused of murder, Martha had shown him a cooter-looking seafood, flashlights were running the creek for otters, and now the crowd grew quiet as a guitar began to play. Everything was coming at him.

"Purvis, this mussel reminds me of a jacaranda tree—they grow in Florida." Martha leaned to whisper into Purvis's ear as the guitar grew closer. "Ever seen one?"

"Jacaranda," Purvis said. "Ja-ca-ran-da." He liked the way it felt in his mouth, as if it rolled down his tongue to pop through his teeth.

"Jacaranda trees line all the roads, and have beautiful purple blossoms that float to the ground like feathers. It has a seed pod, hinged like this shell, that spreads open like a broken heart. The nut inside is like skin, the color of a nipple, and you want to eat it, but it's poison, like love gone sour. They grow right among the fruit trees—oranges, peaches, cherries, bananas, and some you have never seen, purple and round and bigger than cantaloupes. They're called love melons. Most people down there don't even work—just build little bungalows out of driftwood and live off the fruit in their yards. The gators down there sleep on the sand dunes in people's yards, but never attack. Nobody teases or races them. People slice their tails into round steaks like filet mignons, wrap them in bacon and broil them in butter and lemons. Some of the sweetest meat you ever put into your mouth. The rivers are salty—they call them sea rivers—and sailfish as big as horses, with fins like palm trees, school in them like rockfish. You can hook one on a wedge of love melon and eat off that sailfish for a whole year. The people down there build smokehouses for sailfish like they do here for hogs."

Purvis reeled from the images of fruit and fish, feeling queasy, as if he were drinking cream on a Tilt-A-Whirl. Martha sounded like the caller at the fair—Do you want to go *faster*?—and Purvis heard music and tried to hold on until the ride ended.

"And my Purvis, oh my forever Purvis, the jacaranda jacaranda has a nut enclosed in its most beautiful pod, between its hinges, my love oh my love. It too looks like a boat, the jacaranda jacaranda, and you open it to find its rider inside, like this one in my hand, in my hand my love. The flesh oh the flesh."

The cascade of notes swelling in the dark began to gel into a melody, and Purvis knew it wasn't carnival-ride music, and not a guitar either, but a mandolin, its high notes balancing Martha's deep whisper. And the whisper got smoother, until it seemed she was singing her symbols to Purvis, opening and closing the mussel like a castanet in rhythm to her song.

"Purple and sweet and salty, wedged between those lips, my love, oh my always Purvis, like the hump of fat you love in the fork of a T-bone, oh a T-bone, we are alone, in the jacaranda jacaranda, where it is so sweet, oh so sweet, it is poison, but you must eat, my forevermore Purvis, and bind us in the wedge of love."

Purvis grabbed her hand, thrust his face to the mussel and, with his teeth, ripped out the flesh with the ferocity of a starving man. He threw his head back as the meat worked its way down his throat like a snake, like a puff adder spreading through him. He closed his eyes, as sated as if he'd consumed an entire ham, and felt as if he was floating in a warm, clean, salty ocean with purple flowers swirling around him.

"Purvis, we have to get Armey."

EIGHTEEN

Brother Andrew crouched just outside the perimeter of the soft light falling from the trestle's mercury vapor lamps. Spring was throbbing in late, and its thick air, spiriting rock music and laughter from upstream, made the party sound closer than it was. These were the sounds of young people cavorting by the water, risking premature marriages, in a ceremony not far removed in its basic ritualistic elements from a tent revival. Someone had even just yelled "Jesus!" Perhaps the disturbance would drive the birds closer to Andrew, but on a night this cloudy, they might appear as no more than vague shapes.

All afternoon, Andrew had been restless. Unable to concentrate on sweeping the halls, he'd found himself in a corner or doorway, uncertain why he was there. When the abbot asked if he was okay, Andrew had stared at the man's face in confusion, puzzling out the features until he recognized him.

"Are you not of the world today, Brother?" asked Bernard later, raking in the garden. Andrew had spun so quickly to see who had spoken that Bernard, startled, had stepped away.

"You are not yourself today, Brother. My advice, which you will undoubtedly ignore, is to get more rest. Rein in your wanderings. Get some sleep. And focus upon your duties. You do remember your duties, don't you, Brother Andrew?"

Andrew left Bernard and tried to settle his anxiety with archery. His fingertips grew slick as he notched the arrow. His shoulder clicked when he drew the string, as if falling from its joint. His breathing would not steady. The target would not remain still. The bow's smooth wood and tight cord, worn and stained by his hands, turned unfamiliar in his grip. Andrew kept the bow and quiver of arrows with him the rest of the day, holding the bow across his lap at supper,and draping it over his shoulder at vespers. He rolled an arrow between his flattened palms at Compline. He held the weapon out of the water as he swam the creek and searched the far bank for the journal. Now, in the moist earth near the train trestle, the balls of Andrew's squatting feet marked two points of a triangle, while the one tip of the bow formed the third.

Something rolled in the water two yards from the bank, within the mercury vapor lamp's penumbra. A head emerged and rotated 180 degrees: an otter. The eyes-forward face gave the animal an odd, uncomfortably human semblance. Andrew wondered if this was the real reason the fishermen hated these beasts so—they remind us at once of what we are and what we are not. Andrew was not sure why he had brought his bow, but at the moment, he felt a disturbing and powerful urge to send an arrow into the aquatic beast.

The moment the otter submerged, the noise from the party stopped. A clicking of notes began, first dimly, then louder. Clusters of tones crowded and scattered and moved from key to key, shifting among modes, but slowly defining a theme. A guitar? Two guitars? Banjos? A melody line of single notes, then a rush of chords. Andrew could not determine if he was listening to a psychotic confusion or a work of unique complexity. He moved downstream and kept behind bushes.

The trees and shrubs on this stretch of the creek were especially thick, so Andrew had little fear of being seen. Soon, he stopped just about forty yards upstream from where, across the creek, a group of people pointed flashlights into the water and onto the opposite bank. The music had settled into a controlled performance of astonishing sensitivity. The revelers grew silent, perhaps also recognizing the quality of the musicianship. A flashlight swung to the side, lighting up a small man with a small instrument—a mandolin, which Andrew had not heard in years. Amazingly, the man was playing solo, but he had developed a way to make the eight strings of the mandolin sound like three times as many. The melody arced back and built upon itself like a fugue, partial chords stacked within; the tempo transformed from a march to 7/8, then to a waltz, and finally, subtly, back to 4/4, the key modulating from major to minor, letting the melody soften and darken, yet wring from its very melancholia something deeply life-affirming.

This dirt-digger, feed sack-stacker, or slaughterhouse-mopper, thought Andrew, was a virtuoso condemned to play to unsophisticated ears. If only someone would put into those exquisite fingers a violin, which tuned the same as a mandolin, a new Paganini would emerge. The bright disks from the flashlights skated across the water, but Andrew nevertheless wanted to get nearer, hoping the musician would continue to play.

Andrew moved farther downstream. A band of foliage only a yard deep concealed him. He snuck along, his steps as slow and measured as tai chi, and tried to focus upon the music. As he squatted in the darkness, he could smell the dead leaves steeping in the swamp puddles behind him, see the beams of light casting before him, and feel the wet air stiffen around him, but those sensations were in the remote background. Concentrating on the music, in the world but not of the world, Andrew was as deeply focused as he'd ever been in any of his sessions of meditation or prayer.

As the song developed and spiraled, bulging to climax, something flipped and splashed near the water's edge, and the bow felt like flesh in Andrew's hand.

✳

The earthy taste of the raw mussel remained in Purvis's mouth as he listened to the beautiful music. He opened his eyes to see Martha, her eyes turned toward him and away from him at the same time, drawing his thoughts to her, bending them up the river. It made him slightly dizzy. Over Martha's shoulder, he saw flashlights skimming the water. One turned itself to the otter-hunting band, illuminating the mandolin player.

"Moment," Purvis said, smiling.

"I didn't mean right this second, but we need to get Armey tonight," said Martha.

"No, Hunkerpiller."

Purvis had suspected the identity of the musician earlier. Moment Hunkerpiller was four feet tall, shorter even than Larson, and everyone called him a midget. Most people assumed he was retarded, and many thought him mute, but Purvis once had an educational conversation with him about catfish. Moment said chicken livers were best, because the catfish, being a "benthic creature," is naturally attracted to bait that "mimics the aroma of offal." Purvis knew, therefore, that Moment could speak, but he was not sure about being retarded. Retarded people sometimes make up their own words, and Moment seemed to do that. Some people debated whether Moment, whose eyes were always closed or nearly so, was blind. Purvis had no opinion.

"Moment Hunkerpiller's playing," said Purvis. "Let's go listen, then we can get Armey."

The song changed, becoming slow and sad but prettier, reminding Purvis of a church song or something you might hear in a dentist's office. When he listened to Iron Maiden or Metallica, he knew what the song said, because they sang the words. A song like Moment's also spoke, but without words, in ways Purvis could not quite hold onto. The song was speaking, and he was getting a message, but he could not speak back to the mandolin.

A flashlight shone upon Moment's hands, the right one moving up and down in a figure eight pattern while the left hardly moved on the frets, or moved too fast to follow. He rocked from side to side, just as he did when he walked, as if he was trying to settle his torso into his pelvis. These movements were a way to speak, too, Purvis thought. A murmur squeezed from Moment's lips, and the beam rose to his face to glimmer in the tears coursing down his cheeks and dripping off his chin. Tears welled up in Purvis's eyes, and he leaned to whisper into Martha's ear, but then didn't know what to say just as something splashed in the water.

"River goddamn d—!" Monkey yelled, clipping off the last word. "What the post-holing fuck is he doing?"

The otter rolled and submerged and surfaced and slapped the water with its tail and barked and squealed. Flashlights swerved about, trying to keep up with the struggling otter.

"Maybe a gator's got him, Monk," Pookey said.

"Maybe he's got the gator," Half Ass said.

"Let's just shoot and try to hit one of them," Sonny Boy said.

"It's an arrow!" said Fayro. "An arrow in that fish-eating bastard!"

"Ain't nobody got no bow and arrow out here," Pookey said.

"Don't knock me in that water, Donald!" Jodie Craven said. "I can't get these bandages on my burnt foot wet."

"It *is* an arrow," said a Limehouse twin. "I seen the tail feathers sticking up."

"Shit on all that," Monkey said. "Look at the Hairy Man across yonder!"

A flashlight caught the outline of something, perhaps with a face, in the bushes. Monkey, shouldering his rifle, said "Get it," and fired.

"Monk!" Purvis yelled.

As Monkey ejected the cartridge of the bolt-action rifle, Martha's knees bent, her hips rocked forward, and her arm swung to the small of her back and out like a spring to place the nose of her pistol under the point of Monkey Tillman's jaw.

"Don't," Martha said.

Monkey froze, straining to look through the corner of his eye. Martha pivoted to point the gun at the creek, fired, and spun back to push the gun against Monkey's ear.

"Goddow," Pookey said. "She killed the otter."

"What about the gator?" Half Ass asked.

"Well, I'm double-dicked if that ain't Martha Umphlett," Monkey said. "Hadn't seen you since we went riding that night in my old Cougar. We had some fun then, didn't we? Get it? Hold up—it's not Umphlett anymore, is it? Is your husband here? I'd be honored to meet the man of fortune that tamed you."

"Swim across and see if you hit him," Martha said.

Monkey turned his head a few degrees to sight along Martha's arm and over her shoulder. "Old Purvo Driggs. A pair to behold. You used to be taller, Purvo. What happened? You stumped up? Bohannis Pigott said to me the other day—he said, 'Joe, I saw old Purvo Driggs at the courthouse, and that son of a bitch shrunk.'"

"What you mean 'Joe'?" Fayro asked. "Why's Bohannis calling you 'Joe'?"

"They been calling me 'Joe' since 1987," Monkey said, sucking at his teeth.

Martha retracted the gun several inches, then slammed the muzzle into Monkey's ear. He grunted, the Limehouse twins gasped, and most of the others snickered.

"Go," Martha said.

"But, Martha, *you* bulls-eyed that river dog—"

"Not the fucking otter. See if you hit the man across the creek."

"Martha, please." Monkey held his rifle by the barrel and let the butt swing down to rest on his boot. He turned his head a couple of inches to see Martha better. He also saw the crowd drawn by the shots. "That Hairy Man ain't a man. He's a two-legged night crawler, an ape man, a demon *freak*. And if I missed him, he's liable to be waiting over there angry. If I hit him, he's sure as shit furious. Get it?"

"I say you're the one who ain't a man. Purvis, didn't you tell me Monkey wasn't scared of anything?"

Purvis trembled all over, but he was not afraid. He was watching Martha act out her greatest symbol yet, and now she drew him right in, a symbol inside the symbol. "That's what he always said, didn't he, Pookey?" said Purvis. "Didn't he, Sonny Boy?"

The two looked down and nodded. Dropping to his knees, Monkey held up his hands. "But that thing's not natural!" He began to sob. "Oh, God, Martha, God, it's a monster! It looks like a man but ain't a man. Please don't make me go. Oh, God. Please don't shoot me." He fell forward, ass in the air and face in the mud.

Moment began to play a lilting, comical song as Monkey cried, and the others seemed aghast, astonished at Martha's ultimatum, and embarrassed and even more astonished at fearless Monkey's terrified breakdown.

Purvis snatched a flashlight from a Limehouse twin and leapt into the creek. He bent to the water, splashing inelegant strokes, as those on the bank called his name, probably wondering whether to summon him back or cheer him on. Arising on the opposite bank, he walked through the bushes, calling, "Hey! Anybody! Whoever's here! I want to help you!" He walked about and called for ten minutes, but saw no one, natural or unnatural. He searched the swamp floor for blood, found what looked like a drop on a gum leaf, and stuffed it into his pocket.

When Purvis returned, he unfolded the leaf and held the flashlight close as the crowd gathered around to inspect it, but either no blood had been there or the creek had washed it away.

"Hell, might not've been nobody or nothing over yonder no way," said Sonny Boy. "The dark'll sure enough play a trick on you. Ain't that right, Pookey?"

"Damn straight," said Pookey. "Say, Purvis, remember when you swore you saw a soldier on a horse ride through Strawberry Chapel that night? *Through* it, you said, holding up a sword."

Sonny Boy leaned in close to Purvis, cutting his eye back at Martha. "Say something to her, man. The bitch is a sure enough loose wheel."

Purvis whispered to Sonny Boy, "Metaphor."

Martha took Purvis by the hand and led him to the fire to warm up. Someone handed him a cup of PJ. The stereo started up and cranked out Robert Earl Keen's "The Road Goes On Forever." Purvis joined in the collective whooping and cup-raising. A few people tried to balance enough to dance, others staggered off to stretch across hoods, but most teetered around the fire, unsure what to say about what had happened, hoping someone would interpret it. Monkey Tillman sat on the flatbed, finished a cup of PJ in one gulp, and jumped down to approach the crowd.

"Hey, you grit-grinders," Monkey said, "y'all know old Armey Wright's dead? My old man told me. Let's head up the creek to his house and hunt that money he hid in the walls. I'll race you, Purvis. Get it?"

Purvis took three quick paces and threw a right cross that snapped Monkey's jaw with a sharp *clack*. Monkey collapsed like a dropped marionette. Sonny

Boy and Pookey draped his arms over their shoulders and carried him, his head drooping, into the darkness with his legs dragging behind.

"Got it," Purvis said. His fist pumped against his thigh.

"Just not old Monk's night, eh?" Lum said. "Or is it 'Joe'? All right, y'all better dip it while you can. Jesus is about all purpled out and now he's in the pink. Whoo! Y'all hear what I said? Purpled out and in the pink!"

"I don't get it," Tunk said.

"You sure as hell don't," Lum said. "I know Purvis does, or maybe *later*, right? Whoo ha ha!"

"I had something to say to you, Lum," Purvis said. "But I can't recall. Damn, it's right on the tip of my tongue. But you probably don't know what that's like, huh, Lum?"

"Ha!" Tunk laughed. "Now I get *that* one!"

"Shut the fuck up, rectal sphincter," Lum said, throwing a plastic cup at Tunk. "Martha! Here." Lum dunked a half-gallon milk jug into the PJ, capped it, and handed it to Martha. "You might need a little hair of the dog tomorrow. Or maybe hair of the Hairy Man."

"Thanks," Martha said.

"Now let's go get him," Purvis said to Martha. "I can do it, anything." Purvis was not sure what Martha had meant earlier about getting Armey, but he would do it.

"Shit, where's Larson?" Martha asked. She'd lost track of him in all the excitement. "Larson! Larson!" She spun around, eyes wide.

Others called and lumbered about the turnaround, but they were too drunk to see much of anything in the dark. "Here he is," someone finally called from beside the Isuzu, and Martha and Purvis and the rest of the search party gathered around the back of the truck, where Larson lay asleep, surrounded by plastic cups.

"He's wasted," said Harlan Lisenbee, tracing his flashlight around Larson. "Another PJ casualty. Say, here's my cup. And here's one says *Donald Bunch*."

"Now crawl up my crusty goddamn ass, Johnson!" Donald said. "I *told* you I hadn't lost it."

Purvis reached behind the seat and grabbed a heavy plastic tarp. "This so he won't get cold." He climbed into the truck bed and, with the annoying effort that comes from maneuvering an inert body, tipped and rolled Larson until the tarp covered him like a sleeping bag.

"That's sweet," Martha said, "but let's go."

Music blared, dancers stumbled, arguments started, and Purvis stood by the truck door for a moment, mumbling to himself. "Ja-ca-ran-da. A-ri-sto-tle. Pur-ple Je-sus."

When Andrew returned to the abbey, Bernard was waiting, leaning against a statue of St. Francis. "Rather cool tonight, Brother. Wise of you to take your cloak, but little good it does if you do not wear it."

Andrew stepped toward the dormitory, but Bernard grabbed his arm. "I followed you tonight, Andrew. I'm not even sure why. I guess I worry that your soul is as restless as your feet. I also suspect that you knew I was trailing you. I returned once I saw you cross the borders of the abbey."

Bernard removed his hand from Andrew's arm. He rubbed his fingers together and held them to his face before grabbing Andrew's arm again, holding it up to catch a bit of light.

"Dear God, Andrew, you're bleeding. Let's get you inside. I'll awaken the abbot."

Andrew's free arm snapped out like a spring, his long fingers digging into Bernard's neck. Bernard gagged, his eyes bulged with shock, and Andrew released him.

Bernard stepped back and coughed. "Okay, then. No abbot."

An hour later, his shoulder bandaged where the bullet had grazed him, Andrew lay in bed, his unstrung bow beside him, and meditated on mandolin music and how true an aim can be when the shooter knows the target.

NINETEEN

Whenever Purvis drove over the Tail Race Canal bridge at night on the way to Moncks Corner, his usual preparation was to inhale a squirt of albuterol, roll down his window, and hang his head out, staring at the no-pass lines to keep his bearings. He would murmur, "Dear Lord, don't let me run off, don't let me run off," followed immediately by, "Why in hell am I talking to myself in the dark of night like a fool?" then another "Dear Lord, don't let me run off." Over the whine of the tires, he would hear his mother's voice, from back when Purvis was small, reciting the story each time they crossed the bridge of Uncle Tubal's drowning.

"Me and your Daddy, just before we were married, were right behind him on the way to the fair," Arlene would say. "Tubal didn't like for anybody to ride with him, and he didn't like to ride with nobody else, so Tubal's girlfriend Spicy was riding with us. I was telling your Daddy that I couldn't wait to get me one of them candy apples when we saw Tubal drive right off the bridge. The rail just bent over like it was made of pasteboard. Spicy was crying as they winched him and his old Dodge out of the water, and she said, 'That son of a bitch not letting nobody ride with him finally paid off.' Ever since that, I can't cross this bridge without closing my eyes, and I haven't had a c-a-n-d-y a-p-p-l-e since."

Tonight, though, Purvis knew no fear. The night folded around him like loving arms made of mirrors. Shadows and images multiplied into geometric patterns as if he were driving through a kaleidoscope, like the one he made at vacation Bible school from a paper towel roll and tin foil and plastic beads. The bridge came into sight and reflected and doubled and widened so much that he could not have run off the side even if he yanked the wheel toward the canal. And even if he somehow plunged over the edge, the arms of Martha would catch him and cradle him, rocking him safely back onto the road and into the rush of necessary things.

"Pull onto Old Canal Road," Martha said. "I got something to tell you."

The side of Purvis's neck quivered, and his swollen wasp stings throbbed briefly. Was Martha offering sex? No one lived on Old Canal Road, so it would be a perfect spot to seal their love, a pact before they began their mission. They would, of course, have to manage some way to position themselves in the tiny cab of the Pup. The bed of the truck was too hard, and besides, the little Wright fellow was back there and would sure as hell wake up just when the grinding started. Martha could sit on Purvis's lap, but the steering wheel would jab into her back, and she might just get flustered and call it off. Women were like that— the least little hassle, and the whole thing turns not worth it. Purvis would have to get out and go around to her side and slide in the seat as she straddled him. He would leave the headlights on to make sure he didn't trip over anything in the wore-out road, because that might make her laugh and lose the mood, which is something else that happens to women and why men have to hurry. Maybe she would get out and do a hooch dance in the headlights, the way Massy Deere had done for him at the last PJ party just before she threw up all over the hood of Spessard's Cutlass Supreme, which Spessard hadn't known Purvis had borrowed.

Purvis went to the end of Old Canal Road and turned the truck around to face out. If another vehicle came down the road, he would flash his lights, giving the *occupied* sign.

Martha twisted toward Purvis. Her face was visible in some way that did not require light. "Purvis, you care about me, don't you?"

"I care about you."

"You need to understand what we're about to do."

"I've done it before," said Purvis. "Not a whole lot, you know, but enough to know where things go." If only he had had time to run down to North Charleston and pick up a Stim-u-Ling.

"Jesus Christ." Martha took a deep breath and exhaled slowly. "Listen. *That* might come later, if you do exactly as I say. Are you ready to do that?" Her voice sounded like bells.

"Yes. Yes."

"You could be in serious trouble, and that might implicate me, too. Do you want to implicate me?"

Martha's face rippled like waves, the words floating from her mouth. Her hair lifted around her head like crawling vines, and Purvis could not speak. *Implicate* was such a beautiful word when Martha sang it to him.

"We must dispose of Armey's body, his body, oh my love. We must get it, get it from Rondeau's, Rondeau's, and our love will grow and grow like a jacaranda tree so high so high, oh Purvis of mine. What will we do with it, do with it, do you know, do you know, oh my Purvis, my Purvis, implicate me?" The truck was rocking. The truck was a boat, and Martha, holding Purvis's arms, pumped them slowly like paddles. They were moving toward the salty ocean, and sailfish swam alongside them as Purvis threw them oranges. One of Martha's hands, purple flowers entwined in her fingers, lay upon his shoulder, then shook hard.

"Purvis! Focus!"

"The hash plant," Purvis said.

"Perfect. You're a genius. Are you sure you can get in there?" Now she was only a mouth, and her tongue, like an arm, spoke with symbols.

"I can do anything."

"We have to get him out of Rondeau's," said Martha.

"I know how. First we got to go to my place."

The mouth was against his eye, tonguing the sign again. It felt like the jacaranda mussel.

The Isuzu crawled to a stop at the edge of the road two hundred yards from

Purvis's house. "I'll be right back fast," Purvis said. "Aristotle said that the soul is all the body can do. That's right." He drank a swallow of Purple Jesus from a Gatorade bottle and trotted into the darkness.

A couple of minutes later, Martha heard a noise from the back of the truck. If Larson was awake, she would have to take him home first. If she did, Ruthie might still be up, and she'd be suspicious about Martha's leaving again so soon.

The door opened. It had only been Purvis. "Did you get everything?" Martha said.

Purvis cranked the truck. "Tool box, shop apron—"

"You sure your father won't miss it? It can't come back."

"Hell no. He's got a stack of them aprons. Still gets them and a whole lot of other shit he ain't supposed to get from the plant."

"Garbage bags?"

"Big ones," said Purvis. "Industrial strength. That's some of what else he ain't supposed to get."

Martha said something about watching their step, but the words sounded to Purvis like they were coming from a distance, carried by wind.

Softly and tenderly, Martha is calling,

Calling, oh Purvis, come home.

They drove back toward town, flying over the beautiful kaleidoscope bridge.

Everyone in Moncks Corner had at least one snapshot of the Dead End sign on the corner in front of Rondeau's Funeral Home. They kept it in a wallet or purse, to flash on the road when an unsuspecting waitress asks, "Y'all on vacation?" A picture of a grinning Tag Rondeau standing under the sign graced a page in the Chamber of Commerce's brochure, with the caption, "Tagmill Rondeau, Respected Businessman and Coroner." The dead-end street was hardly more than a driveway, running past the funeral home for fifty yards and stopping at the old tobacco warehouse converted into the First Baptist Youth Athletic Center. Inside were a half basketball court and weight-training area with a Nautilus machine and workout benches, which the Baptist youths would sneak to at night to do what they called "premarital sets."

Some of those youths had been at the PJ party and would soon weave their way to the Center, but at midnight, Purvis and Martha found no cars parked along the road, except for Rondeau's tow truck and two hearses in the garage. Purvis backed around to a set of double doors.

"How's our boy doing back there?" Purvis asked.

"Still out cold. You think there might be an alarm system here?"

"Alarm? Whoever breaks into a funeral parlor? This is history."

Setting the toolbox before the double doors, Purvis shined a flashlight onto the knobs. "I ain't believing this," he said. He took a coping saw from the toolbox and removed the thin blade. "It's like they didn't want anybody breaking the lock, so they made it easy." He slid the blade between the doors, jiggled for several seconds, clamped his knuckles—not his fingertips—to a knob, and turned. "We're in."

Inside, Purvis searched the walls with the flashlight. "This is our night. Not a window in the room. We can turn on the lights and nobody'll ever know we're here."

"Let's be safe and turn on only one—just enough to find the old bastard," said Martha. She found a switch and turned on a lamp hanging directly over a stainless steel table.

"Damn! Lucky again," said Purvis. "You got the one right over the old man. That is him, ain't it?"

"I think there're only two in here. Let's just get to it."

Armey lay naked on the table. His glasses and clothes, green coveralls and everything, were wadded on the shelf below him. Purvis put a finger to Armey's bad eye. "Looks like a marble, don't it?" As Purvis looped the apron over his neck and tied it around his back, he scanned the rest of the old man's body. "Now, that's something I didn't know—that your hair, down, you know, there, gets gray. That's just pukeable ugly, especially it not circlecized. Want me to cover it up? You probably don't want to see your uncle's, you know, glandis penis."

"I've seen it before," said Martha.

"I know that. You were married and all, so I know you've seen . . . Wait, you don't mean *his*, do you?"

"We're wasting time, Purvis. You sure you know how to do this?"

Purvis searched the items on the shelf below Armey. "This'll do." He found a sock and laid it over Armey's bluish penis. "I believe in respecting the dead," said Purvis. He opened the tool box. "My old man's got chisels and saws and every damn thing in here. He's carved a whole lot of people. I mean wood people, not *up*. These tools ought to be able to undo a thing as well as make one." He lifted Armey's shoulder from the table and peeked at the back of his neck. "Besides, I've helped clean and butcher deer. You pretty much cut around the joints, give them a snap, then slice through the leaders. Might need to saw through a bone or two. Good thing is we won't need to clean and dress him. That means gut him, at least one of them does. Might be cleaning is gutting and dressing is skinning, or the other ways around, but we won't need to skin him neither. I bet that'd be hard, what with a human not having a hide like deer do."

"Just get to it." Martha felt her stomach churn. Just nerves. She could get through this. This was no worse than putting a bullet into him.

"I figure we can put the legs in one bag," Purvis said, "and the arms in another, or a leg and an arm together. The head and body might can go in the same one together, but I got plenty bags either way. That white eye of his, the blind one, is something, ain't it? Hell, now they're both blind. Can I have my knife back now?"

Martha opened the hawkbill and handed it to Purvis. Without warning, Purvis spread Armey's legs and sliced into the groin. The knife drew along so smoothly that Martha nearly thought Purvis was tracing a line with a pen, as she imagined slaughterhouse workers might do on a hanging side of beef. Purvis rolled the body to its side and drew the knife along the edge of the buttock. "Get me a bag," he said.

Shaking open a bag, Martha heard a pop. She turned back to see Purvis holding up Armey's leg like a trophy fish. "Wa'n't much keeping him together," he said. "We might can get all his scrawny limbs into one bag. No use wasting them."

Purvis slipped the leg into the bag and went back to work. Martha, watching in silence, admired the astounding economy with which he executed his task. He pressed in the blade and ringed the joints without ever removing his hand from the knife. A deft twist extracted the ball joint from its socket. The flesh on both sides of each split was flat and even, like a grocery store ham. Looking at the table, Martha was disappointed to see only a few purple drops of blood, not the pool she'd expected.

Purvis carved the final arm from the shoulder and dropped it into the bag.

"You do that pretty well," Martha said. "Focused."

"I'm mostly a blunt tool," said Purvis, "but sometimes I can be sharpened up. Ockham the Razor."

"What the hell are you talking about?"

"This philosopher, Ockham the Razor, said cut out what you don't need, and that'll make things truer," said Purvis. "He lived thousands of years ago, like Aristotle. I don't know if they ever came across each other, but that would've been some wicked shit."

"This Ockham said get rid of dead weight, eh?" said Martha.

"Yeah, dead weight, except this old monk said something about purse money and don't multiply titties beyond . . ." Purvis looked up and squinted his eyes, as if trying to focus on an insect upon the ceiling. He tapped the tip of the knife against his lip. "Hell, I can't recall what it was beyond. I just know what my cousin—you remember him, Legare?—told me, and he's like a professor at a college."

"What about the head?"

"Whose head?"

"Armey's fucking head!" Martha yelled. She laced her fingers behind her neck and blew a long gust of air at the ceiling. "Let's finish up and get out of here. Now, are you going to cut off his head?"

As Martha's elbows multiplied and fanned around her head like a turkey tail, a shudder ran through her breasts. Purvis thought of how his Uncle Stafford's gobbler would spread his tail and shake when you got close to the turkey pen. A ripple would run through the bird, and its raised feathers would whir like a lawnmower cranking. Perhaps the signs were getting deeper—arms around her head, limbs in a bag at her feet—and he needed more training in reading them. Armey had all those books at his house and probably knew how to read symbols. But there he lay, deader than Aristotle and not whole.

"Purvis, focus again on what you're doing," said Martha.

"What you're doing."

"Give me it," Martha said. Collapsing her arms back to two, she stepped toward Purvis and took his knife. She put her hand to Armey's chin and tilted his head. The throat offered itself up, the larynx as round as a hickory nut. "I should have done this fifteen years ago," she said as she pushed the blade into the far side two inches below the point of the jaw. It passed through the larynx and out the near side to *ping* against the table. She retraced the slice, deeper, through tissue, clearing the neck bone. She stabbed the point into Armey's chest as if standing it in a block of cheese at an hors d'oeuvre bar, and then, laying one hand upon his forehead and sliding the other to the base of the skull, jerked hard, separating the vertebrae. With one more pass of the knife, the head left the body. Blood leaked from both sides of the neck, collecting into an indigo circle the size of a coffee cup saucer.

"That's better," Martha said.

Purvis, his heart racing like an engine, marveled at the entire performance. His father was right, he realized, about how carving can bring people closer. Martha must know it, too, or why else would she have taken the knife and cut? It was more, though, than just something that needed doing together—it was another symboling dance. Her arms and legs and ass and tongue and pistol could talk a book, and she played Purvis's knife like a mandolin. He wanted to speak back to her in symbols, but maybe it didn't work that way. In a love like theirs, maybe one person gives the symbols and the other receives. The one who receives has to be ready every moment to catch them, like flickering lightning bugs.

"Open the bag." Martha held Armey's head, upside-down in one hand, by the bottom jaw, her fingers hooking behind the teeth. The image was spectacular, and Purvis thought he would cry. Martha looked like an armored warrior woman goddess from way back in Rome or Egypt who had just killed a sea monster and made the waters safe again. She started to place the head into the garbage bag, but Purvis reached down and grabbed a new one.

"I reckon it deserves its own bag," he said. Martha dropped it in, and Purvis tied the drawstrings. He rubbed his hands around the bag, as if guessing its contents.

"Here," Martha said, handing Purvis his knife. "You can have it back now."

"I think it's sharper than ever." He wiped it on the apron and slid it into his pocket.

They put the torso into another bag and loaded the dismembered body into the back of the truck, next to Larson, still asleep. The sky, clear now, was full of stars, navigational signs for those who could read them.

TWENTY

"You know what time it is?" DeWayne said, standing in his doorway in just his underwear. "Sylvie had a bad night and me got to drag my ass up early in the morning."

"You got to go with us to the hash plant," Purvis said. "I got something in the back of your truck we got to dispose."

"Fuck that. I'll take it tomorrow."

"It's got to be now."

"What the hell for?"

"Armey."

"How you mean for Armey? You said he was . . ." Then DeWayne spotted one of the bags in the back of the truck. He dropped his head and rubbed his face with both hands. "I ain't believing. Jesus on a pine plank. A human man body. This ain't real."

"What's real is the FBI on it," said Purvis. "Martha said they were asking all kind of questions about me—"

"That bitch out there in my truck? She's hauled you into some crucial shit and now you hauling me into it."

"You don't know how it is." Wiping his eyes, Purvis began to talk fast. "It's all coming at me like needles of light and me trying to catch them, but they stick to me, pulling me into a drowning place—"

"What's coming at you?"

"Her symbols, and then it tastes like metal, like lead or copper, just when my head goes under. But then she's like the boat for me, and her arms fanning and shining in her symboling dance, and I'm trying to read it, trying to read it all," said Purvis. "I got to do it and then do this other thing for her, and we'll fly off or like up a beanstalk, and then things'll go away from me and from her and me just a redneck sapsucker, and you don't know a shit I'm talking about but you got to help or I'll—"

"Fuck it." DeWayne exhaled a heavy blast and turned to the side. "One punch."

"Bullshit."

"Just one punch and I'll get dressed and drive the Isuzu and you two follow me in the propane truck. He covered up?"

"Three bags."

"Baby Jesus in a biscuit. You cut up the son of a bitch?"

"Carved."

DeWayne held his fists in a boxing stance. "Rally's dead," he said, "and I don't know who's working graveyard tonight. I'll pull in and take care of it while y'all wait out front. Got it?" He dipped his right shoulder and pantomimed an uppercut. "Now, one punch."

"Just watch out where that wasp got my lip."

The fist connected to Purvis's wasp-stung ear, spurting blood and puss out onto his neck and DeWayne's knuckles. "Screw a guinea," Purvis said, choking a little. "I been trying to pop that bad boy."

"Does it hurt?" Martha asked. "Grown men."

"Not much," Purvis said. "I wish he'd've busted my goddamn nose and taken the edge off this hash stink. Or maybe if I had more of that PJ, that would dead it out. And it's just a brother thing." He sat up high in the seat, peering toward the rendering plant's front door. "He's coming out finally."

DeWayne crossed the parking lot into the shadows, where they sat in the propane truck. "He's a new guy," DeWayne said through Purvis's window. "Dude named Winky. Worried about he'll lose his job. Somehow we hadn't crossed shifts so he don't know me."

"What's for him to get in trouble for?" Purvis asked. "What'd you tell him it was?"

"I said you were this fellow I know and let a couple his daddy's hogs die he was in charge of, and want to make it look like the hogs broke through the fence. He gets the fidgets and starts to sweating and carrying on about 'I got to keep account of every time the grinder runs' and 'I don't need suspicion.' And I say 'Goddog, I'll just load them in and they gone. We do it all the time,' and he says 'I don't know who *we* is but this old boy ain't one of *we*' and I say—"

"How much does he want?" Martha asked.

"Fifty dollars," said DeWayne.

"Shit on *we*," Purvis said.

"Here," Martha said. She took a roll of bills from her pocket and handed DeWayne a twenty. "Tell him take it or leave it." DeWayne went back inside.

"What if he don't take it?" Purvis asked.

"Let's just see."

In a few seconds, DeWayne and Winky emerged. Climbing into the Isuzu, Winky drove around the back of the building, while DeWayne came to the propane truck.

"He said he's got do it hisself," said DeWayne.

"Why you not back there with him?" Purvis asked.

"Ain't nothing to it," said DeWayne. "Just put the shit in the front-end loader, drop it into the grinder, and it eats it up, bones and all. Ain't like we're cooking and separating like a normal job."

"What the fuck?" cried Winky, running around the corner of the building. "There's a man in there!"

"Godamighty!" said Purvis as he and Martha jumped from the truck. "He must've opened them damn bags!" The three ran to the building.

"What you trying to do to me?" Winky yelled. "Twenty dollars my ass!"

Winky led them inside. And there, eight feet off the ground, in the pan of the front-end loader, Larson sat up, his arms in the air. "I'm flying! I'm flying!" he said.

"Wrong bag," said Purvis.

"Get him down!" Martha yelled.

DeWayne climbed into the loader and lowered the pan.

"I'm falling! Woo hee!" Larson yelled.

Unwrapping the rest of the tarp from Larson, Purvis and Martha sat him on the tailgate. Purvis put the garbage bags into the loader, and DeWayne drove it into the building. Winky, wheezing, leaned against the truck fender.

"Take a squirt of this," said Purvis, offering his inhaler.

Winky took a puff. "Hate this damn job. Smells like hell. And me with a bad heart."

"We all got a bad heart," Purvis said. He tapped his cigarette pack, and out popped a joint. "See if this'll help."

"I believe it will," Winky said, lighting up.

"Way high," Larson said. "Fly me again way high, woo, and give me a suck on that little something the gas man won't give me I asked him for."

"Hush, sweetie," Martha said.

DeWayne returned. "Hogs gone. Let's head out."

"Hogs hell," Winky said. "What y'all had in them bags?"

"Like you said," Purvis said, "a man."

Winky coughed, and slowly released smoke through his nose. "Twenty dollars my ass."

Purvis looked out the propane truck window. "I know some constellation names," he said. "Yonder's the Big Dipper, which is pretty easy, but did you know its real name is Roman or Egyptian that means the Big Bear? The two stars at the front edge of the pot point to the Little Dipper, that's really called the Little Bear, and the tip of its handle is the North Star." He sighted along his arm like a rifle, his other hand on the wheel. "That's what everybody uses to navigate. I don't see them right now, but there's a line of three that lots of dumb-asses think's a dipper, but it's Orion the Hunter. He's my favorite, but he must be down below the trees now. The three is his magic belt, and with a sword hanging off it. There's a half-circle up above—that's his bow he hunts with. Plenty animals up there for him to shoot at—a lion, a bull, a swan, might be a river dog."

"This here's that water man don't talk book," Larson said, scrunching in the space behind the seats. He had opened the console and held the journal. "Read it, Martha, the water man throwed down and swam."

Martha took the journal. "You were supposed to take this back."

"I will," Purvis said. "But I got to reading some of it and forgot. Some dude, name of Fra Phillip, wrote it like fifty years ago, so the dates say he put in it. About birds—woodpeckers, mostly." He nodded. "One of them, he just called The Bird with a big T and B, and wouldn't say the name, like it was a devil. That's something I never been, scared of a bird. I can see somebody scared of snakes or spiders or scorpions, being poison and all. But a bird? A dog, now, I ain't too crazy for. Armey had some bad dogs. He used to fight them."

"Read it the water man story," Larson said.

"Hush, Larson," Martha said. "Purvis, you're especially talkative."

"I am? I reckon I *am* a little nervous." He lit two cigarettes and gave one to Martha. "I wish I hadn't given that guy my last doob."

"It was the sharp thing to do," said Martha. "Besides, you're tired."

"Sharp." He smiled for a second, then ground his jaw and wrinkled his brow. He pinched the bridge of his nose. "I know what to do, think I do, but it's just all here, all around, coming at me."

"What is?"

"All of it, and me in the midst, just got to go, but with nothing to go on or where."

"I might have something to go on," said Martha. "Stop here. I don't want to wake her."

Purvis stopped and cut off the truck in front of the cattle guard. "You do, you are. Something to go on," he said. "Like I said, I'm a sharp tool some of the time, but mostly a blunt one, good for bamming, not for clear-seeing."

"Where we at?" Larson asked. "Aunt Ruthie's and you live here too house, and I'm staying. Spending on a pallet, not in a truck for sleeping no more."

"Hush," Martha said. "Purvis, I told you about Florida."

"Jacaranda." He looked into Martha's face. The features began to shift across her face in a wave. "Jacaranda."

"Yes. Keep thinking about it. I'll take care of us."

"Jacky Randy," Larson said.

Purvis jerked his head around and growled at Larson, "Don't say that."

"Your name, the gas man, Jacky Randy."

Martha opened the door. "Pick me up at the flower shop tomorrow at five," she said. "Let's go, Larson."

Grunting, Larson tried to climb over the console. He slipped and fell to his stomach, his heel snapping up to kick Purvis in the ear.

"Goddammit!" Purvis rubbed his ear. "Both of them sore now."

Martha helped Larson crawl from the cab. He placed his foot onto the cattle guard and balked. "I can't walk that no ground but holes to the ditch and fall in it."

Martha nudged him. "You can do it."

"I'm falling!"

Then Purvis came out of the truck and, in one smooth motion, swept Larson up, carrying him across the metal pipes.

"I'm flying!" said Larson.

"That ought to be easy for a gnat man," Purvis said, plopping Larson down onto his feet.

"Everybody needs toting sometimes," Martha said.

"Some needs it all the time," said Purvis.

Half an hour before the other monks would rise, Andrew squatted by Wadboo Branch. The clouds had cleared away, and only the occasional frog song broke the silence. Placing the end of the bow into his mouth, bracing the other tip along a crease in a cypress knee, Andrew plucked the string, producing a big, fuzzy note that slid blue and dropped a step as he opened his jaw. Notes grew clear, resonating among the trees, and skimmed along the water, forming one tune, then another. The melodies alternated, then entwined, then merged into something indistinguishable, and Andrew heard singing in his head, a voice that may have been his own.

> *On Jordan's stormy banks I stand*
> *with my old gal, a good old pal*
> *and cast a wishful eye*
> *at her, looking like a waterfowl*
> *in Canaan's fair and happy land,*
> *where I get them deep river blues*
> *and my possessions lie . . .*

TWENTY-ONE

Purvis awoke with the steering wheel pressed against his chest and forehead. Reaching up to wipe his eyes, he bumped his thumb against the blinker. He snapped upright and, by instinct, turned the key, but when he did not smell pot, he realized he had not passed out beside the road again while at work. The sun was rising, and in front of the propane truck was a large window painted black with "Venus P" in pink, balloon-like letters. To the right of the window was a door with an iron grate, and then another window, blacked out, with "arlor" in the same fat letters. Written smaller underneath was, "Lounge XXX Adults Only Videos Magazines Toys for Ladies and Not Quite Ladies Private Peek-a-Boo 24 Hours Couples Welcome." Purvis could tell that the building was once a gas station, and he wondered how it could have room enough to be a lounge, which he knew was another name for a bar with big padded chairs.

His neck ached, and when he stretched his back, he felt the journal slide into his lap. The open page had a dent in the middle, right where Purvis had drooled in his sleep, upon the words "wondrous work of the Pileated." He remembered sitting in the truck, trying to read by the dim light of the street lamp. At one point, a car parked near him, and a man walked briskly inside, returning in a few minutes with a paper bag. Later, a boy of about sixteen, surely not an adult, rode up on a moped. Purvis expected to see the kid thrown out by a bouncer, which would have been worth a good laugh, but instead the boy remained inside for about twenty minutes, and when he came out, he circled the truck twice on his moped before shooting Purvis the bird and scooting away.

Now, a man with a clipboard, emerging from the Venus Parlor, leaned against the window, half-covering the "P." Lighting a cigarette, he spat straight ahead, as if aiming at the truck bumper. Purvis nodded at him, but instead of returning a friendly sign, the man produced a pencil from behind his ear, like magic, and moved it down his clipboard, like a storeowner checking on things.

Purvis decided he'd waited long enough. His money was as good as anybody's, and he had as much business in there as a moped boy at four in the morning. Wiping his chin with his shirtsleeve, he got out of the truck. "Morning," he said. The man did not respond. "What all you got in there?"

The man leaned his head back against the window and blew a smoke ring. "All manner of sex-related items whose sale is within my Constitutional rights, and further, legal by ordinance of the City of North Charleston. Now you can get back in that gas truck—I got to say, that's a new one—and do your evangelizing somewhere else."

Purvis felt queasy. He didn't know what the man meant, and was further confused by something that looked like a silver cross dangling from the man's ear. Instead of a shirt, the man wore a leather vest, exposing a tattoo on his shoulder of a naked woman, hog-tied and blindfolded. "Do what?"

"The regulars are probably gearing up over at the clinic now. They'll swap out their placards and be here in a few hours. You could just join in behind them, or do your denominations not mix, huh? They do drive better vehicles, after all. Maybe a higher class of righteousness."

"Listen, man, I don't know what that was you saying," Purvis said. His chest tightened, and he badly had to pee. "I just come here to buy something a fellow said y'all had that was good for women, and I sat out here because I never been to a joint like this or, like it says, lounge, and then I fell asleep thinking about if it was going to be a scary place, and then now you start talking at me in some kind of symbols and I'm just *not good at getting symbols*! *Aris-fucking-stotle*!" Pinching the bridge of his nose, he wondered if he should take a swing at the guy.

The man stepped toward the door. "Hey, settle down," he said. "You're saying you're not one of those religious freaks? What am I supposed to think, when you come towards me with a Bible?"

Purvis had not realized he was still holding the monk's journal. He puffed on his inhaler. "Not a Bible." He took another puff. "About birds." He took several deep breaths, humming as he exhaled.

"Well it looks like a goddamn Bible," the man said. "You all right? Do you have a heart condition? Don't come in here dying on me."

Purvis exhaled slowly through pressed lips, as if concentrating his breath toward a distant flame. "My heart is on fire. But I don't mean like having a heart attack pain or like heartburn. I mean like a metaphor. You know about metaphors?"

The man hid the pencil behind his ear. "Hell, I practically make a living in metaphors. Come take a look."

"I might be come to just the right place then," said Purvis. "And you don't have to be embarrassed about thinking this here was a Bible. My old man thought it was, too, because of it being soft leather. It got a little wet, but not too bad. It was writ by a monk, which is kind of like a preacher, but not like symbol talk what you'd think a preacher'd write. It's mostly woodpeckers. But why you so worried about Bibles, what with you got a cross on an earring?"

"Cross, hell!" The man pulled his hair away from his ear and leaned toward Purvis to show him the miniature dagger. "Come on inside now. I guarantee I got what you're looking for."

"I hope so. Right now I'm looking for a place to drain my crane."

"The head's outside around back." The man reached into his back pocket and retrieved a key attached to a wooden carving of a naked woman.

"Damn," Purvis said, cupping the little woman in his palm. "She's a far sight from a cypress knee monster."

The Venus Parlor was brighter inside than Purvis expected. In addition to the long, exposed fluorescent bulbs buzzing overhead, an array of lamps—some multicolored, some flashing—was perched among the videotapes and peculiar items on the shelves. An entire wall displayed inflatable dolls of every hair tone and skin shade. Another wall sported dildos of unlikely shapes and unnatural colors. The far end of the room had a row of what looked like dressing rooms, while near the entry was the counter, where the man tried to get reception on a tiny television sitting atop a refrigerator, which had a glass door revealing beer and wine. Three stools lined the front of the counter. Purvis took a seat and pushed against the counter, spinning himself around a full turn. "Lounge open?"

"Always open—that is, if you drink Miller in the bottle or white wine from a gallon jug," said the man.

"Miller."

"Two-fitty."

Purvis did not complain about the price. He had to play it smart and befriend the man. "Name's Driggers."

"How come you in a Moncks Corner gas truck in the pre-dawn, Driggers?"

"Boss is getting long-eyed," said Purvis, "maybe open a branch over on Spruill Avenue. I'm down here checking out some property. What was your name again?"

"Wasn't any *again*." He slapped the top of the television. "Crank. Now, what interests you this morning? Movies, peek-a-boo booth, how about a doll? That Asian number there's got a hand-pump operated mouth that'll melt a trailer hitch. Only work the mouth does, no bitching and whining about why you're running off so soon. Perfect woman, my friend."

Purvis moved closer to the doll shelves. An inflated woman hung by her back from the ceiling. Her arms with fingerless hands, and legs with toeless feet, pointed down toward Purvis as if she was dropping like a spider. The arms, slightly bent to catch a man, would raise him up to someplace far above the ceiling and the roof, where she would wrap you in her thread and bite you to turn you into a spider-person, and then you would have a different life and forget all about this one. Purvis thought her wide eyes and O mouth gave her a look of surprise that you could also decide meant she was pleased or impressed when you were making love to her—the doll, that is, not the spider anymore—but he had trouble believing you could crawl on her without getting scraped by the seams running along her inner thighs.

Also, she would probably make crinkling sounds as you moved against her, or maybe squeaks like when you chew on a rubber band. Either would be hard to ignore, and too much of a reminder you had sunk to such sorriness that you would try to hump a balloon. Someone had tied to her an anklet made of green-and red-plaited twine. It would make a real woman look hard-lived and slutty, but somehow had the opposite effect on the naked balloon spider-woman, and Purvis now felt more at ease in the Venus Parlor.

Below the balloon-woman sat boxed women that had never been blown up, some that said they had bendable legs and others that talked. Some promised to look just like Sunny Quivers or Minerva Parts or other famous porn stars pictured on the boxes. The small boxes, which Purvis figured must have plain balloon-women folded up tight inside, had pictures of unknown girls on them and started at $19.95. The big boxes with the stars probably had solid dolls that you had to put together with an Allen wrench, and went up to $299. This may be a time when you really do get what you pay for, but Purvis doubted that he could get a straight answer from Crank.

On the back wall of what had once been the gas station's three-bay garage were dildos, feathered objects and, hanging from hooks, black patent leather peacemakers with rhinestones and straps, maybe where fan belts and air filters had hung before.

"Got to be something of interest back there, Driggers," Crank said. "Pleasure enhancement for tastes you never even knew you had. You ought to try out that Orchid Clamp. Never worry again about timing out."

"Might could use something like that," Purvis said, although he had no idea what Crank meant. "I was thinking about one of them Stick-a-Dings, you know?"

"A what?"

"Something like that. Might be Still-a-Thing or Sting-a-Ring or Streak-a-Lean for all the hell I know. Lum Hereford said here's where he gets them. You know Lum, don't you? Actually Columbus, but goes by Lum. That truck's usually his'n."

"Don't know any Lum or Columbus or Magellan or Vasco de Leon," said Crank, "but I believe what you need is hanging on the third row from the right, about two foot from the top. Stim-u-Ring." He watched Purvis scan the shelf. "No, over. Now up. Right there. Why can't you see it? You're looking *right* at it."

"I got her." The package was green cellophane, not clear like Lum's, but it had the same cartoon of a naked woman. The little thimble was light blue instead of pink, but Purvis thought that probably wouldn't make any difference. These things get used in the dark anyway. Taking the package from its hook, he pressed the cellophane tightly around the gadget inside for a better look. Did the man wear it, or did the woman somehow strap it to herself? The cartoon naked woman was no help at all.

Purvis returned to the bar and had a swallow of his beer. "Lot of times I don't see things right away."

"I wouldn't've guessed," said Crank, curling a rolling paper and shaking into it what looked like crumpled-up pine straw from a small brown envelope.

These skin shops have special permits to sell this sex stuff you can't buy just anywhere, Purvis thought, so maybe that let them get around weed laws, too.

"You can burn a doob in here?" Purvis asked. "Hey, y'all need some part-time help?" He snorted a laugh that died quickly when he saw Crank's frown.

"Listen, boy, that shit's for punks and ginks and poor black boys and crackers that probably deserve cell time before they fuck up worse," said Crank. "One thing I do not do and have not done is break the law. You believe that, son? True as the Glock under this counter which I *will* demonstrate in the lot out back if you're interested. You can ask me, do I agree with every federal and state law and every local statute?" Crank leaned across the bar, his bottom teeth overlapping his top. "Of course I do not. But I do believe in citizenship and the lawful exercise there*of* by God of all the rights and privileges there*in* granted by the Constitution of these United States. You cannot pick and choose, my young friend, cannot pick and choose."

"I'm twenty-four," Purvis said. He figured Crank to be about the same age, so why could Crank call him *young man*?

Crank stood up from the bar, licking the rolling paper to finish its formation. "Then you are of age to support the effort to save this nation, son. This *cigarette* here is made with natural, organically grown tobacco, with no additives, produced by independent American farmers. Tobacco in and of itself is not harmful. It's all the carcinogens that the big corporations put into it when they process it."

Purvis finished his beer and, with the Stim-u-Ring, tapped out a waltz rhythm against the bar. Crank was making him feel nervous and somehow guilty, but inspired, too. "I just smoke them all, Crank," he said. "I don't know about natural or not. But I would like to try one of them organical sticks." As the Stim-u-Ring flapped against the Formica, he noticed the price: $23.95.

"Be my guest, son," Crank said, handing the cigarette to Purvis while thumbing another rolling paper from the cardboard package. "Smoke. Look around you. That says it all, doesn't it? It's all smoke. Smoke on the water. Smoke gets in your eyes. I told you I deal in metaphors. Another Miller?"

Purvis nodded at Crank, trying to understand what wisdom had been handed him. "Where there's smoke, there's fire," he said.

"You're catching on," Crank said with a wink.

Purvis lit the homemade cigarette. It didn't pull well, but it tasted like hunting squirrels on a fall afternoon just after rain. Or maybe shooting otters. Metaphor.

"Godamighty! I get it." Purvis released the smoke from his mouth, then drew it into his nostrils and back out his mouth. "Smoke. You're smoke." He drank half the beer. "Know what I am? A redneck sapsucker. Now we talking."

"I was talking. I'm not sure what you're doing now." Crank began rolling another cigarette. "Now you know that Stim-u-Ring is not a prophylactic, don't you? If it's prophylactics you need, we got the best. Not that truck stop bathroom wall-dispenser shit. Only thing those cheap wraps are good for is a trip to the clinic for a clap treatment, or make a daddy of you. That, or a visit to the pregnancy terminal to have them snatch the little bastard out. No sir, we got the reliable ones, and you don't know you're wearing them. Natural sheep casings. You can't even get them in Rexall."

"Do I look like I can't identify a prophylactic?" Purvis surprised himself with his sudden and inexplicable irritation. "Did I *ask* you for a prophylactic? Do you think I don't know what you're talking about?"

"Settle down, son." Crank leaned his head back as if sizing up Purvis.

"Sometimes the symbols buzz all around me like wasps and I can't soothe them still for a read. Sometimes I get the message but forget it after a while. Sometimes I need just a little reminder." Purvis crushed out the cigarette between the breasts of a ceramic naked woman that he took to be an ashtray. "Now I come down here, number one, to purchase this Stim-u-Ring. I will pay you for it, finish my beer," Purvis said, drinking the rest in a gulp, "and then I head out for my number one mission. Actually, that would make my purchasing the Stim-u-Ring number two, but I just happened to say it first. And I have decided I kind of like that organical cigarette after all."

"Here, then, have another one." Crank reached slowly over the bar and slid the cigarette into Purvis's shirt pocket, then picked up the Stim-u-Ring and turned to the cash register. "With the two beers plus tax, it's thirty dollars and sixty-nine cent."

"Lum said his gizmo was $19.95."

"He got the small. You do need the large, don't you?"

"Hell yeah, *son*." Purvis unfolded his paycheck from his shirt pocket. The cigarette popped out and onto the bar. He put it behind his ear. "Let me hold your pen."

"What are you doing?"

"I'm signing this check over to you," said Purvis, "then you give me the change. How long you been in business?"

"A third-party check? Come on, man."

"That's my paycheck. Remember the propane truck? The same Beasley like on the check."

Crank held the check up over his head as if to gauge its thickness. "This what you make a week?"

"Not a whole week. I'm temporary."

"I've been burned too many times doing favors for poor-ass peckerwoods," said Crank.

"I told you—redneck sapsucker."

"Let me see your license." Crank looked at Purvis's driver's license, jotted something onto the check, opened the register, tucked the check under a tray, and gave Purvis change. "Have cash next time you come back."

"I'll have the cash," Purvis said, opening the front door, "but might not be a next time."

TWENTY-TWO

The morning was full upon him as Purvis ringed another block. He hated to backtrack, but North Charleston's concrete medians and multi-lane roads he could never seem to get across sent him circling and backing and making three rights when he couldn't get a good left. This town could run you like a yard dog wired to a clothesline. Add to that the wasted gas, and you'd think nobody would ever lay tire in such an aggravating place, but it had some stuff you could not get anywhere else. When you know what you want and want it bad enough, you'll put up with signs that point the wrong way and one-way roads that you cannot turn off from until you pass the place that has it.

The clinic was only five doors from the Venus Parlor, but by the time he found his way to the small lot behind the dull, concrete-block building, Purvis worried that too much activity might jeopardize his task. Already, cars were parked on the street in front of the clinic. Purvis glanced down the alley and saw several people walking about, taking things into and out of their cars. When he saw the big squares of cardboard with wooden slats attached, he figured these people must be the freaks Crank talked about earlier. Purvis was not sure if they were going to be marching for or against abortion, and he did not know, regardless of how they marched, whether they would approve of his mission or not. The good thing was that they would draw attention to the front while he did his job in the back.

Purvis angled further into the lot and away from the clinic so he could get the hose to the building and crank up and zip out the back end of the lot if he had to run. Turning to step down from the cab, he felt something jab into his lower left side—the naked woman bathroom key fob. Purvis would need to run it back to Crank when he left, which was a shame, because the carving was grand to behold. The wood, more than the nakedness, gave the woman her beauty.

Purvis did not know what kind of wood it was made from, but the grain started reddish tan, darkening through six or eight curving strips to black, then shifting back to reddish tan. It reminded him of the lamps at the asthma doctor's office, made from glass vases filled with wavy bands of colored sand that from a few feet away looked not grainy, but smooth. This layered wood, a rainbow of wood colors, must come from a place far away, maybe Florida. Could the smooth little woman be fashioned from a Jacaranda? Purvis could call her Jackie.

He untwisted the screw from her head, removed the key ring, and slipped it into his pocket. He set Jackie's heels into the heater vent on the dash and leaned her against the windshield.

Detaching the hose at the back of the truck, Purvis reeled off a few feet. The only people in sight were the freaks clumped together at the head of the alley. They looked as if they were holding hands. He walked to the back of the building, dragging the hose along, and stopped by a window with a wooden frame so rotten that it looked held up only by the dirt dauber cells around the edges. Purvis pushed on the window, but it did not open, so he lay the hose down and took his hawkbill knife from his pocket.

Stepping back, he stretched forward to chip at a dirt dauber cell, a two-inch tube of gray earth. Purvis crouched and turned his face away—partly from fear that dirt daubers might really be wasps who attack those who disturb their nests, and partly from a dim memory of his grandmother (or some other old woman in work boots) telling him to hide his face from being recognized by the haints that inhabit burrows and cracks and the gaps between sills in the crawlspaces beneath concrete block-raised houses.

The cell crumbled, releasing dried bits of insect bodies. Purvis did the same to another cell, blowing the dirt and bug parts from the window ledge, and then worked the knife blade under the window. With a few jiggles, it opened. Purvis found a malt liquor can on the ground, propped open the window with it, and inserted the hose through.

Purvis returned to the truck and turned on the valve.

"Mr. Driggers?"

Purvis wheeled around to see Agnes, folding her hands to her chest and gumming a huge grin.

"Well, praise the Lord's holy name. You have come to the rally to do His work!" she said. "I saw that truck and I said, 'That looks like a Beasley truck sure enough,' and I told Brother Bone, 'I'm going to see if that ain't Mr. Driggers.' Then I remembered as I was coming down the alley that we were talking about all this yesterday . . ." Agnes's eyes followed the hose. "What are you . . ?" Then she looked at Purvis, and her forehead tightened, stretching the tape holding up her eyebrows. She looked back at the building, then turned again to Purvis. Her eyes widened as she reached out and clenched the front of his shirt, as if trying to rip out handfuls. "Oh, Lordy," she whispered, "you *are* doing His work." She smoothed down his shirt with her flat palms. "I'll go keep the others up front. You just do the job."

"Sister Agnes!" a voice called from the alley.

Agnes and Purvis turned to see Reverend Pyron approaching. "I'll tend to him," she said to Purvis. She ran, holding down her skirt hem.

"Who's that, Agnes?" Pyron asked. "You switching gas businesses?"

Agnes stopped him a few yards from the back of the building, still within earshot of Purvis. "That's a Beasley truck, Reverend," she said. "That young man works for us sometimes, and I'd plumb forgot we serve a few customers in North Charleston."

"That's good and all, but we getting ready to start, and I was looking to see if I could bum a cigarette off him," said Pyron. "I must've dropped mine when Polly had me crawl under the car this morning. Nothing would do her but me hunting up a clicking noise. Got grease all over my shirt from it and she wouldn't let me change."

"I don't believe he smokes, Reverend, and like you said, we need to get—"

"Look here, son," Pyron called. "You got a smoke I can bum off you?" He took a step toward Purvis. "I'm hard bad for a smoke."

Purvis ran toward Agnes and Pyron. "I can do you better." He reached into his shirt pocket. "I was saving this for something special, and you're it today."

Pyron's round head pivoted side to side as he examined the hand-rolled cigarette. "I don't know what you're thinking, son, but that's one of them marijuana joints that you are offering to a man of God. Do I look that ignorant?"

"Maybe so," Purvis said, "because this isn't marijuana. It's organical tobacco, what a fellow rolled for me just a while ago. Tastes a little funny, but it's a smoke. Good for you, too. Besides, it's all I got."

"Sure enough?"

"Sure as Jesus loves the little children."

"Amen."

Agnes stepped down the alley, tugging at Pyron's rolled-up sleeve. "We got to move now, Reverend. The clinic's about to open."

"All right, then," Pyron said, walking away with Agnes. "Time for the Lord's work. You're welcome to come out on the street and join us, son."

Purvis ran to the back of the truck. The propane had pumped into the building the whole time, and he worried that too much—a quarter tank?—was inside the building and seeping out the doors and windows. He turned off the valve and began rewinding the hose when he heard a slight, familiar, metallic *click*.

The massive *BOOM* blasted his ears and the tremor jarred his legs. Fire, bright yellow with a blue outline, flashed in the alley and receded just as fast. Purvis saw Agnes and Pyron tumble against the wall across the alley from the clinic. No one screamed or spoke. Nearby, a car blew its horn. Somewhere— a block away?—something—a woodpecker?—rapped a telephone pole. A low rumble slowly raised in pitch—probably an airplane taking off from the Charleston airport. He had never flown in a plane, but he imagined it would be tight and thick inside. The low ceiling and the curved walls that have you leaning the whole ride, and the compressed air they have to pump in to keep the plane above the clouds—it would make him feel bound and breathless, much worse than the propane truck did.

Martha had flown, surely. When he told Martha about what he had just done, she would take him away. Maybe she'd want to fly, and she'd soothe him in the narrow maw of the plane.

People from the street suddenly appeared in the alley, yelling. "Reverend! Sister Agnes!"

Purvis ran to them, even though it might be better if he headed for the truck and got on his way out. He found Pyron on his back, motionless, staring up as if watching something hover overhead. The front of his shirt was burnt off, and the smoking skin on his chest and stomach looked like fried squash. His nipples were gone. Blood ran from a horizontal split on his chin down his jowls, collecting in his ears. A crusty hole was where his nose had been. His right arm bent at the elbow, and his hand pointed up. The fingers were fused together around a Zippo lighter, still lit.

"Damn straight you hard bad for a smoke," Purvis said. "You wishing it *was* a joint now, huh?" He snapped the Zippo closed.

"Reverend! Can you hear me?" a man shouted. A woman with her hands on her head squatted by Pyron, then stood and turned around as if searching for her unruly child, then repeated the sequence, all the while saying, "Necessary? Necessary?" Purvis wondered what she meant. Maybe he could explain to her that hardly anything's necessary. Living and dying are, but how you do either is not.

Another woman, sobbing, put her arms around the panicking woman. "Pray with me, Polly," she said, and they began to mumble what sounded to Purvis like "lama lama lacka lacka." Others knelt beside Agnes, some praying, some wailing irrepressibly, and some not knowing what to do other than call her name as if trying to awaken her.

Agnes, dazed, sat leaning against the wall. Most of her hair was gone, leaving charred clumps dotting a scalp that smoldered, Purvis thought, like the ground after one of those controlled burns the rangers do in the government woods. She pressed one hand to her ear while the other picked at her eyebrow. She was trying to remove the hospital tape that had melted into her blistered skin. "I got to change my tape," she said. "I believe it's been discolored."

Purvis worked his thumbnail under a corner of the tape and pulled down, removing the tape and a layer of skin, leaving a pink patch above Agnes's eye that oozed beads of clear liquid. When he peeled the tape from the other eye, a thicker piece of skin came off her eyebrow and continued to stretch away in a thin strip until it released, with a snap, and hit Purvis on the lip. The strip dangled before him. An eyelid jiggled at the end. Purvis felt nauseated and nearly tossed the thing away, but then rolled up both strips and dropped them into his shirt pocket. Maybe a doctor could stick them back on later.

"Thank you, Mr. Driggers," Agnes said. Her gums were redder than ever. "Now we need to excuse ourselves from this place." She adjusted her skirt over her knees and tried to stand, only to fall over, catching herself with her elbow on Pyron's chest. A hollow hum, perhaps a groan, escaped from his nose hole.

"Maybe we ought to wait for the ambulance, Miss Agnes," Purvis said. "It'll be here real soon."

She held out her hand, and Purvis helped her to her feet. She stretched up on her toes, and Purvis closed his eyes and held his breath as he bent for her to whisper into his ear. "The *authorities* will be here real soon, too," she said.

"The FBIs?"

Johnson Rondeau took a swallow of coffee. "That's a sight and a smell, ain't it, Donnie? Sister Honey Jo's sure got her work cut out for her."

"Like she done for my foot?" asked Jodie Craven. "Look at it. Looks like fried bologna."

The propane truck sped up Rivers Avenue as Purvis tried to distract himself from the smell of Agnes's burned flesh and hair. She was the ugliest sight he had ever seen. The scorched and mottled skin that had begun to curl up made part of her look like a sycamore trunk. The blisters on the rest of her face had grown in just the last few minutes, and some of them had ruptured and oozed droplets of a thick, transparent liquid. Agnes ran her fingers over her cheeks and across her lips. She pressed the raw patches left from removing the tape, but gave no sign that she noticed the puffed and crusted contours of her skin or felt any pain. She did not wince, even when she dragged a fingernail across the lidless eyeball, as if removing a speck.

Purvis could look away when he found the burned face and singed hair too nauseating, but he could do little about the smell. The pounding in his head, concentrated between his eyebrows, was sharper and more rapid than his propane-induced attacks had ever been. The rendering facility produced similar odors, but not this powerful. Purvis recalled a spring day when he was ten and DeWayne was twelve, and they set fire to an old Ford pickup that had long sat, without tires, with the chassis in the dirt in the back corner of their grandfather's unplanted field. The boys didn't know that a cat had deposited her kittens on the engine block. The smell of the burning hair and flesh sickened Purvis then, and he could not sleep, in part because of the fear that the screaming kittens might pace through his dreams, but mostly because the odor would not leave him.

Agnes's smell was like that, and it grew progressively stronger. Was Agnes still cooking? She talked nonstop, between coughs, breaking Purvis's concentration.

"A godless world that could allow so many innocents, tender little lambs, brought to slaughter," she was saying.

"Ja-ca-ran-da, A-ri-sto-tle . . ."

"You, avenging angel, have saved hundreds, thousands, from never knowing the glory of God's creation."

"Pur-ple Je-sus, ja-ca—"

"What *are* you saying?"

"Me? Nothing, just humming, sort of." The smell hit him harder, and he gagged. He leaned to hold his head partially out the window and pressed the heel of his palm between his eyes. "This headache—I swear that godamighty's pecking and going to break through this time."

"I think maybe we ought to roll up the windows, eh, Mr. Driggers? And you shouldn't take the Lord's name in vain," said Agnes. "Anyway, the rush of air may be responsible for your headache, and I am satisfied that it has affected my vision. I feel that one eye is clouded over. Not to mention what the wind is doing to my hair. I must look a sight." She coughed and reached for the side mirror.

"No!" Purvis lunged and grabbed her hand. "Can't do that. You know, safety. Company policy says the mirrors have to be set for the driver's optimalest range of sight. You ought to know that, Miss Agnes. And I was talking about a bird in my head, not the Lord."

"Company policy also says no personal use of the vehicles and no passengers, which are worse violations than me tilting the mirror for five seconds." She wiped her lidless eye with the back of her free left wrist. "I don't know about a bird in your head, but I believe you have the Lord in your heart. Say, that's a pretty little lady on the dashboard."

"That's Jackie," said Purvis. "Miss Agnes, I believe you ought to get to a hospital. If we don't hurry, I'm going to be needing one, too. Tri-County's right up here, and they treated me fine last year when I fell off the four-wheeler and broke my collarbone and my survival knife doubled back some way or other and stabbed me through my leg. They patched me up real good, though. I was stove up a couple of weeks, but hell, I had a blade that long in me."

Purvis gagged, again, opened his mouth wide, and hacked as if something was stuck in his throat. He forced up a hocker and spat it out the window. He felt a little better. "Doctor said it come an eighth-inch from slicing my femortal artery and would've bled me to death in three and a half minutes. And my heart's full up right now."

"I thank the good Lord you recovered so well, Brother Driggers, but I do not need medical attention. The explosion was a shock, all right, and it threw me to the ground, but it's not the first time I've taken a little spill," said Agnes. "You know, the more the precious Lord fills your heart, the more you can fill it with. I bet a doll baby dress would fit little Jackie." Agnes stuck out her tongue and dragged her fingernails down it. She coughed. "Just drop me off at the house. I know you know where I live. Everybody knows where I live. Shoot, I got plenty work to do. Eggs to dye, baskets to make."

She touched Purvis's arm with her free hand, and he let go. She reached out the window and angled the mirror inward. Purvis leaned back to catch Agnes's reaction, and what he saw was confusion.

She adjusted the mirror repeatedly, as if searching for herself somewhere else in the truck cab. Then, suddenly, the expression in the mirror changed to horrified recognition, the eyes and the mouth forming three well-spaced circles.

Placing her other hand upon the mirror, she pulled hard, lifting herself a few inches off the seat. The mouth gaped wider and the throat swelled and arched, and then Agnes screamed, as if finally sensing the intense heat of the flames.

Purvis jumped and yanked the steering wheel. The tires scraped against the concrete median. He jerked the truck back into the lane. Agnes screamed again, this time deeper and longer and leveling into a moan of hard suffering and hopelessness.

"They can fix you right up at the hospital, Miss Agnes. I promise," said Purvis. "You'll be looking better than ever once they do some skin grasps. They'll cut patches from somewheres else off your body like your back or thigh where nobody's liable to see it and stitch them on those crisped up places and they blend in just like you were sewing a quilt. Hell, people'll say, 'Best thing ever happened to Agnes was getting all burnt up at the fetus-puller. She's looking nine or eleven year younger. I need to find me one of them explosions and get a new face.'"

Agnes shrieked again. Purvis felt a searing pain between his eyes. If only Martha was there to lay a cool hand on his head. She could reach inside, like those faith-healers in China or somewhere he saw on a TV program about amazing people. Folks with incurable ailments travel for thousands of miles to have those hoodoo men stick their fingers under the sick people's skin and pull out tumors, and rotted organs, and not leave even a scar. Purvis figured it was probably a con game like everything else, but Martha was no con. Her fingers would ease into his head as the skin and bone split and spread like a mussel. She would pull that woodpecker out by the beak and pop her wrist to snap his damn neck while another hand would close Purvis's head and wipe away the crease so nothing else could ever get in. Then she would rock Purvis to sleep with two arms while two or three others went to work on Agnes's roasted face.

Martha sang a lullaby to him that sounded like mandolins, and her voice and his and Agnes's all passed in and out of each other to tell the story of love and fire and water. "Ja-ca-ran-da, Pur-ple Je-sus, A-ri-sto-tle, god-a-migh-ty . . ."

✳

Spit bubbles formed around her lips as Agnes murmured "poo poo poo" in the hospital parking lot.

"We need to get you inside now, Miss Agnes. You might be steady getting worser sitting here. You know how you take something out the microwave and it's still cooking inside?"

Agnes turned from the mirror to face Purvis. "Is it staying?" A few minutes ago, she had demanded the tape that Purvis had removed from her earlier and, finding the detached eyelid, tried to tuck it somehow into the socket. "They're probably used to burn victims in there, but I just cannot be seen by anyone with an eye that won't shut."

"I think you got it this time," Purvis said. "Now, please, let's go in."

"Cut off the truck and leave it here. Hospitals always have the authorities roaming around."

"You still mean the FBI? Maybe they following me. But, hell, I don't know who I'm hiding from. All your church people saw me and the Beasley truck."

"They will *not* witness against you, Mr. Driggers. They're scared people who would have stayed home if somebody'd said the place was going to get blown up, but now that it's done, they're thanking the Good Lord for every cinder. Even Reverend Pyron, if the Lord has deemed he should live, will answer with silence if asked anything by the authorities. Say, you hear any ambulance sireens?"

"Nome."

"Does that mean he's dead?" said Agnes. "Maybe they don't turn on the sireen for dead people."

"They might," said Purvis. "I don't believe the ambulance people can call them dead. They have to haul them in and have a real doctor call it."

Agnes wiped her mouth and dabbed the tears from her cheeks with her sleeve. "I'm as presentable now as I'm going to get. I would appreciate your strong arm for support, but once we get inside the emergency room and I find a seat, you need to slip out."

The people in the emergency room sat in silence. Most stared at the floor;

some watched the cartoons on the thirteen-inch TV bolted high in the corner. Except for a man who clutched one hand in the other against his chest, perhaps to ease the ache of a broken finger, none showed signs of illness or injury and just as well could have been biding time in the customer convenience room at Mingo's Discount Tire and Shocks, where Purvis worked for a day until he got careless with a pneumatic wrench and cost a co-worker a toe. Three of the TV-watchers turned to stare at Agnes without expression. A little girl, walking across the back row of connected chairs, scooted between her mother's ankles to hide. In a few seconds, all went back to what they were doing. The nurse behind the sliding window with the empty cigarette holder between her lips was writing something, and didn't look up.

"Just help me to the nurse counter," Agnes said. "I'll be all right then." She tapped on the glass. The nurse held up a finger to hold them off while she traced an oval with a pencil on her seek-a-word. Then, she slid open the window.

"May I—oh!" said the nurse. The amber-colored cigarette holder whistled as she spoke. "You've been burned!"

"Just a little bit," said Agnes. She coughed, harder than before. "May I see a doctor, please?"

The nurse wedged the pencil behind her ear and tucked the cigarette holder into a fold in her paper hat. "I'll get someone with you right away."

"I love me a seek-a-word," Agnes said. "I do mine in ink."

The nurse pushed a button and then left her desk. In seconds, she returned with an orderly, who loaded Agnes into a wheelchair. "Go," Agnes said to Purvis as the orderly backed her through double doors.

On the TV, a little cartoon dog repeatedly outwitted a big dog. Purvis was thinking that, in the end, the big one would probably find out there was a bunch of little dogs instead of just one, when the nurse tapped on her window. Purvis turned to see her curling her finger at him.

"You Mr. Pigott?" the nurse asked.

"Nome."

"Brother?"

"Yes'm, but he's not a Pigott neither."

She put the cigarette holder between her lips and mimed a long drag. "Are you Miss Pigott's relation? The lady you came in here with—are you related to her?"

"I be dog. She's a Pigott? I just know her by Miss Agnes. We're not relations," said Purvis. "She just asked me to bring her in, you know, her being burnt. She going to die?"

"Lord knows I'm not a doctor, but her condition looks pretty grave to me. She'll need to remain here some time. Will you wait for a prognosis?"

"Me? No, I'm fine. I was just heading out," said Purvis. "But let me ask you something. Could she still be cooking inside? Seemed like she got to stinking more and more on the way over here."

The nurse retrieved the pencil from behind her ear and glanced at her seek-a-word. "I'm not allowed to dispense medical advice," she said, "even when I know good and well it's the gospel truth. Policy." She stuck the pencil eraser into the cigarette holder and spoke through her teeth. "Lord, not 'juniper.' I despise a 'j' word. I try to spy a 'j' and the little hook disappears. *That's* one thing the doctors can't answer."

Purvis realized his headache had diminished, and his lungs felt open and full for the first time in days. Maybe the sterile white walls and floor tiles and the antiseptic smell of the hospital had a cleansing effect upon him. He watched the big dog get to the North Pole, only to find the little dog already there. "Well maybe you can answer this, if it's not policy," said Purvis. "A woman with six or eight arms won't show them to nobody but her one true love, right? And she can float her one true love across any sea and rise above the earth like sliding up a rope and she is all the body can do, right?"

The nurse did not look up from her desk. Though Purvis could hear his voice, he didn't feel his mouth moving. He couldn't tell if he was speaking inside or outside his head, but the words continued to come, like singing, like an entire choir of his voices posing questions with beautiful sounds. The light around him was bright and all colors at once.

"And everything just coming at me in flocks, flocks of peckerwoods and sapsuckers and godamighties straight like arrows, then sucking up my air and inside my head chiseling, and them FBIs, and if I'm not her own true love to float in her eight or however many arms away out of this dead man's slanted house of a world, they'll bust through my skull, and me trying to stop being dull and be sharp and focus."

"Through them doors and to the right," the nurse said.

The choir stopped, and the room was white again. "Ma'am?"

"The bathroom. You asked where it was at."

A crowd of innocent-looking little dogs watched as the big dog suffered a breakdown, bouncing around the screen, his tongue hanging out and his eyes crossed. "Like I thought," Purvis said.

TWENTY-THREE

The first blades of sunrise slid through the cypresses to settle on the creek surface, smooth and gray like a cool, liquid metal, a dark mercury. As he stepped into the water, the cold ran up from his foot, throbbing into his ear. He worked his jaw to ease the ache. The tide was out—six hours behind the beach tide here—so the creek's edge was nearer the steep floor of the channel, and the water reached his knees in only three steps. He faced downstream toward the harbor, where he could see the horizon, the edge of the world.

The slow tai chi moves hardly made a sound in the water as he stepped forward and back, then turned, raising and lowering his legs. He improvised his own moves and mixed them with poses he had seen in ancient Hindu and Buddhist art by spreading out his arms and rotating, bowing slightly to the four directions. He formed mudras with his hands that he learned during his year of travel in Asia, spent studying the carvings on ancient temples in India, chanting with Buddhist bhikkhus in Thailand, and meditating in a Japanese dojo. He imagined that he was the Buddha, fresh from reaching enlightenment, preaching his first sermon to his fellow monks. He worked in signs: a flat palm, the Abhaya mudra for no fear; hands laid across one another—the sign for teaching; an OK, the Gyan mudra for a new start; a grasped finger, for the Vajra symbol of the elements; and the complicated Pushan, meaning ebb and flow.

Concentrating on his location, he soon came to consider it emblematic of all locations, a focal point for space itself. I am mindful of my place. I am here at the edge of vegetation, he thought. I am at the edge of water, yet I transcend all boundaries, even as I must be placed by them. I am at the edge of human, at the horizon of God. I move within and without, in but not of. All around, and we do not see it.

He would pass on to the brothers a great truth, one that cannot be spoken, one that was hidden in Brother Phillip's words, the very words that passed the truth down to Andrew. This would need a symbol, perhaps one Brother Phillip could only suggest. The Tao that can be spoken is not the true Tao. Andrew pressed his hands into the prayer position, brought the heels of his palms to his lips, and pointed his fingers out like a beak. His new pose would concentrate all that could not be said and pass it into and through the tip of the beak: the Pose of the Woodpecker.

"I don't know what it is, buddy roe, but it sure is pretty! Whoa ho!" Two fishermen pointed at Andrew from a bass boat drifting only twenty yards away.

Andrew leaped to the creek bank, turning in the air and reaching down, landing in a half-crouch in a motion both silent and beautiful. The bow was in his hand, the arrow notched between his index and middle fingers and against his cheek as he exhaled. The rest of his body went motionless. He parted his lips and ran his tongue along the cock feather. This is the taste of nature, he thought, and what is nature but challenge? I am here, on the edge of flight, on the edge of blood.

The bass boat cranked and sped away, the fishermen shouting curses. Soon, the noise was gone, leaving Andrew alone in the swamp with the deep river blues.

Lula placed the tip of her fork in her grits and tried to write "Peter Cottontail," but most of the letters folded into blobs. She thought printing might work better than cursive, and it did make "Peter" recognizable, but his last name was hopeless. "Give me a couple more of them aspirin, shug," she said. "I don't know what's got into my head."

"I think I do," Martha said.

"Ain't no secret," said Ruthie. "And don't get her no more aspirin. She's done had four and she'll puke up the whole house with any more. Take a Goody's."

Lula dragged her fork across her grits to make a crosshatch pattern. "Number one . . ."

"Here we go," Doris said.

". . . I had me a just little bit of wine, it being Good Friday and all, kind of like a Communion. Number two, I can't stand them Goody's powders. If you want to see me pyoosh, that'll durn well do it. And number three, if my own daughter would've wokened me up instead of left me outside in the car all night for some booger to get me, I wouldn't had to've sleep all scrunched up like a bitty in a egg and then wokened not knowing where I was at—how come nobody come to see about me when I hollered?—and then with the headache and hip-ache, not to mention might be got the pleurisy from outside in the cold. And number four, how come none of y'all's got Larson up to eat his breakfast? I swanee, this is one sorry bunch in this world."

Doris sipped her coffee, lit a cigarette, and then had a long swallow of Diet Chek Cola. "Number one, no church has that much wine in its cabinet for communion. And then you started on the sloe gin fizzes. Number two—what was number two? Oh—you *chewed* them aspirin a while ago, and you can't swallow a Goody's?"

"It's them little wax paper packages," Lula said. "I don't see how nobody can put wax paper in they mouth."

"Then pour it in a damn spoon." Doris snapped the pull tab off her Diet Chek Cola can and slid her cigarette filter into it. "Number three, you were passed out dead to the world in the car, and I sure as shit wasn't about to tote you. And, by the way, I put a blanket on you." She held the cigarette by the pull tab and took a drag. "And four, won't hurt that boy to sleep a little. Martha said they were out late. Right, Martha?"

"We were," said Martha.

"Not as late as y'all," Ruthie said.

"Tell that old woman right there about it," Doris said. "I'd pick up my pocketbook, and Miss Communion here would give me a 'Just let me finish my drink,' and damn if another'n wouldn't show up in her hand like a miracle. She must've had some kind of secret barfly sign going on with the bartender."

Martha took a jug from the refrigerator. "Come on out on the porch with me, Grandma. Fresh air will help that headache."

"I'm glad *some*body here cares something for me," Lula said. "My daughters treat me like you know what in the road."

Martha poured the purple liquid from the jug into a tall glass. "Drink this, Grandma. It'll help your headache."

"I sure need it. Need it all day long with Doris on me like a snapping cooter. You heard how she is." Lula took the glass from Martha and had a swallow. "Mmm, tastes like fruit punch."

"With a few vitamins. Drink it all." Martha sipped her coffee and leaned back in her chair. "Well, she does have a tough time of it. Larson's a handful."

"He sure is, honey. I ought to know, raising him as much as Doris has. I try to cut her some slack, but I don't know who's the biggest handful, Larson or her." Lula had another long swallow. "Great dow, that is good and sweet. Don't get me wrong—we love him and all, and I reckon the Lord give him to us for a reason, but I wouldn't wish that on nobody. No sir."

Martha filled Lula's glass. "I'm about to run over to Beulah's this morning and spend one more day helping her out."

"I expect it'll be busy in there with tomorrow Easter," Lula said. "I about forgot. She's closing up the store."

"That's right. I guess I'll be looking for something else," said Martha. "Anyway, I'm going by the Health Department on Monday for some tests. How's your head?"

"I believe it's a little better. What'd you say about the Health Department?"

"Listen." Martha leaned toward Lula. "I'm not telling anybody but you. This is between us, okay?"

"You know I'm not a gossip, shug."

"Good." She poured more into Lula's glass. "I've decided to have a baby."

"You what? A baby? Are you and that Driggers boy getting married? Lord!"

"Shh. No, I'm not getting married, but maybe him for the father. I just know I want a baby, but I want to be extra sure that everything checks out with my health," she said. "I figured that even though retardation runs in Mama's side of the family, Daddy's side is safe and ought to cancel it out. If my baby had something was wrong with it, I don't know what I'd do. I just don't think I would want it to go through life like that. And I couldn't live with the guilt."

Lula drank a gulp. "You ought to . . . ought to not talk like that, shug."

"I can't help it, Grandma. That's the way it is. Oh, did you see Hatch Tillman last night?" She poured more into the glass.

"Hatch come out to Armey's, didn't he? Or was that Funderbird, Funderburk?"

"Hatch did, but I ran into him later with the FBI man, and he said he was taking the FBI man to the Honey Hole."

"I was at the Honey Hole last night," said Lula. "Catfish. I eat me a pile of it."

Martha lit a cigarette. "They must've gone somewhere else, then. See, the FBI man is running some tests on Armey's body. Those FBI men can tell you every single thing about you. What you ate, how many times you had a cold, if you're the criminal type—"

"Oh, dear Lord," Lula said. "Oh Lord, shug, you don't need no baby. They nothing but trouble, regular or afflicted. You just forget, forget that. You too young. Forget about a baby. Lord God, I feel kind of dizzy."

"I think you're sounding much better. That punch must be doing the job. Drink up," said Martha. "Like I said, the Health Department checked Daddy's medical records, and he was fine. My father was fine."

"You mean Gamewell? Whew, it's getting warm out here. Give me another more, another full, a cupful."

"Yes, Gamewell, my father. Because of him, I can have a baby and not worry about anything. What were you saying about my father?"

"Your father," said Lula.

"My father," said Martha.

"He's dead now. Dead and gone."

"And you loved him, didn't you?"

Lula belched and began to cry. "I loved him. And now he's dead."

"You loved Armey."

"I loved Armey, oh Lord, I loved him." Lula found a handkerchief somewhere in her skirt pocket and wiped her eyes.

"You loved Armey. And he was my father."

"Yes, he was. He was your father, a long time ago. It wasn't nothing. It was a long time ago. Oh, blessed Lord. You too young. Your mama was too young."

Martha took Lula's wrist. "Jesus Christ. Who was my grandfather? Who was Ruthie's father?"

"A long time ago, shug. There's lots of things that's long ago, that's gone ago. Happens to everybody."

"Was Armey Ruthie's father?" Martha squeezed Lula's wrist. "Was he?"

Lula sobbed. "I loved him, baby. Everything was a long time ago. I *loved* him and did anything for love. He was just a man, but love makes it all right."

"Jesus goddammit. Just like I thought." Martha let it swell inside her mind like a gourd, crowding all the cracked remains of her irrelevant past. She thumped her cigarette into the yard, grabbed the old woman's other wrist, and brought the hands together as if in prayer. "Norene and Jaynelle—all that talk was just to keep me confused, so I wouldn't get suspicious about Armey, wasn't it?"

"They was good girls. We're good people. It wasn't nothing. Nothing for shame. I never hurt you, baby—"

Martha yanked her grandmother toward her, scooting the chair a few inches across the porch. "So help me, I will break your goddamn arms off at the shoulders. Answer me."

"Yes."

Martha dropped the old woman's hands into her lap and went inside. She got her pocketbook from her bedroom and came back down the hall as a commotion started in the kitchen.

"And all over my good couch," Ruthie said.

"He ain't wet the bed since he was a boy," Doris said. "He must be sick.

Larson, baby, how you feeling?"

"My head knocking like on a door to get in," said Larson, "not the screen one the other one that's loud, and like I got to burp big, it don't come out, just keep pushing, and I'm falling."

"Get the slip cover off, Doris, before it seeps into the cushion," Ruthie said. "I don't want to smell piss every time I sit on it."

"You see me getting it," Doris said. "It just needs a run in the washing machine. Ain't like it's silk. Larson, baby, slip off them wet PJs."

"PJ," Larson said, pulling his shirt over his head. "PJ PJ Jacky Randy Jacky Randy. I'm . . ."

"I'm gone," said Martha.

". . . flying," said Larson, standing naked.

"Have a good day, baby," Ruthie said.

"Say 'hey' to Beulah for me," Doris said.

Lula sobbed and drank from the jug as Martha walked off the porch and into the conversion van. As Doris yelled something from the doorway, Martha pulled onto the road and did not slow down.

Somewhere among the shard-heap of memories must be a trace of the full and ugly picture. A cryptic utterance, a flared nostril at the mention of Armey's name, a glance at the wall during the Norene-Jaynelle sham argument. She could recall neither when she first suspected the truth nor how she first came to the suspicion. Countless nights, though, she lay in bed and dug through the heap, scouring the shards for atypical markings, but finding only her own emptiness, encrusted by a little girl's terror at her great-uncle's gropings. She believed that when the truth was finally unearthed, the fragments would draw together into a great vessel with no place for emptiness or terror, filled with pain that would soon crystallize into indifference. Now that it was true, and she knew it was true, she found the pain not as full and intense as she had hoped, the emptiness atrophied and calcified, and indifference impossible.

But the other pain, the years of deceit, narrowed to a wedge, like the bow of a boat leaving fresh waters behind to course a purple sea.

TWENTY-FOUR

"A painted bunting, the harlequin of the winged world, boasts a bright and proud, albeit slight, figure, reducing the muted hues of his background flora to tedium. O, a mighty artist is my Lord!"

Pulpwood trucks hulking along Highway 402 blew their horns to oblige the muddy-kneed boys who stood along the road mimicking, with one hand, a railroad engineer pulling down the lever of a steam whistle, the other hand palming a rock to throw as the trucks whined by. Their vibrations rumbled into the propane truck, which sat on the macadam road at the edge of the Francis Marion National Forest.

"I glance above to espy the perfect symmetry of sleek angles, the points of two swallow-tailed kites soaring in slow and tandem spirals, a glorious study of lines against rounded swells of water and tidal arcs imprinted in the bank mud—the geometry of flight above and currents below, drawn by the celestial Draftsman!"

Purvis flipped the page again as he held the alligator clip out the window, dropping the tiny speck of charred paper to the gravel. The sun, though bright, was obscured by a huge rain tree that had started to blossom. Birds jockeyed among the limbs and decorated the truck's windshield with multicolored droppings. This was a side of birds that Purvis had not run across in the journal. Monks don't seem to understand that nothing is all good and beautiful. You need some bad and ugly to complete things. You don't get day without night. You can't live without dying. You won't be sharp without first being dull.

"I have monitored a wafer-sized hole in this living pine with each of my travels of late, and finally, a creature has darted in, doubtless the red-cockaded. I have waited an hour or more, hoping for a clearer view upon her exit, but she does not comply, and the light rapidly fades. Yet, I had the glimpse, and am thus a pace closer to heaven."

Staring at a hole for an hour to see another bird. How different can they be? thought Purvis. What if the old monk had all the birds in the world lined up along the creek? Maybe he'd walk up and down the bank, stroking their little heads, saying "O God." If he caught a stroke from all the excitement before he got to the end, and keeled over and drowned in Wadboo, would he think it was worth all the fuss? Or maybe he'd see every last one plus The Bird right up close and would just sit on the bank and cry cry cry, like the song about the crawdad hole says, because that old monk's creek would sure be run dry then. You can't have the birds without *not* having the birds, and nothing's sadder than a dried-up creek.

The rain tree was filled with noise and motion, and Purvis thought all the birds in the national forest must have been drawn to it all at once. They chirped and cackled in pitches high and low, and they rose and dived, and came at Purvis like arrows and flew away, like hope, all in the same wild motions, and each was a sign that pieced with the others to speak to Purvis. His focus was sharp, and he could see and hear and feel all the things around him, and he was not afraid. He cranked the truck and lurched into a turn, then backed and turned and backed until he was pointed toward the highway. The windshield washer hummed but did not squirt, and the wipers smeared the bird droppings in rainbow arcs, themselves symbols as well. As he stopped at the highway, a pulpwood truck passed, and Purvis closed his fist and pulled down his arm. The trucker answered, his steam whistle sounding off, but Purvis heard only the singing and flapping that passed through his head.

PURPLE JESUS

a novel

The Louvin Brothers' "Stuck Up Blues" praised the virtues of the humble and castigated the haughty.

"I nearly about forgot I'd found that old tape at the flea market last month," Beulah said. "Country singers these days *wish* they could wail like them old boys, you know it? Sweetie, you hear what I said? Listen to that Ira harmonizing. Like a bird is what I'm saying. Sweetie?"

Martha looped a white ribbon around red (for Jesus' blood) and white (for his cleansing resurrection) carnations to form a huge corsage. "I'm sorry. I'm a little preoccupied."

"I know. You're worried about looking for work next week, what with me closing up the shop. Don't you fret it. We'll find you something a whole lot better than rolling flowers, although I got to tell you, you got a knack for it." She rearranged the boxed corsages in the refrigerator. "I'm not saying all the new singers aren't worth a flip. Some are okay. That Vince Gill's all right."

"I'm not worried about that." She put a cigarette between her lips and left it unlit. "Can I level with you, Beulah?"

"Of course you can, baby." She glanced over at Martha's carnations. "That's enough of those," she said. "Maybe a couple more with the roses ought to about do it."

Holding the cigarette low in the fold between her index and middle fingers, Martha made a loose fist. "Money's not it, Beulah. Truth is, I just took this to get away from the house," she said. "But I don't know what I was thinking when I came back here. Mama's hell to live with, and the rest of them are part of the nightmare package."

"I thought you were getting away from your husband," said Beulah.

"I was, but it seems like I just need to get away from everything."

Beulah sat at the table. "I hear you. I don't know how your mama and them can stand each other. You're a very smart girl, and you know there's more to life than sitting around gnawing on each other's nerves."

"It's worse than that, and I can't abide it anymore. I just haven't quite got my thoughts together about exactly where I'm going. What's for sure is that I'm going."

The bell rang, and Bill Cliett came in and bought corsages for his wife and mother. He waved to Martha when Beulah pointed out she was Gamewell Umphlett's daughter. When he left, Beulah reached under the counter and got her flask.

"Sip?"

"You know it," Martha said, taking a long swallow.

"I always said I might not have much sense," Beulah said, "but I do know how to get by on my own."

"That's a good thing to know."

"I got an idea. Why don't you come with me?" said Beulah. "We'll run pick up Vinette, and then you can live with us. Hell, I could use some help, with my wild young'un plus a baby, you know it?"

Martha tied a bow to a rose. "Maybe not a bad idea." She took another pull from the flask. "Let me think about it."

The Louvins began "You're Running Wild." Beulah closed her eyes as she had a drink. "Listen at them. My first husband could sing like that. Last I heard he was doing revivals with a big circus tent and a kangaroo."

Passing water passing—it was an apt object of meditation, whether current, channel, stream, wave, alluvia, littoral. The water passing Andrew would reach Charleston Bay well after dark, carrying cypress needles, hydrilla, fish remains from yesterday's catch, and refuse from Jon boats—beer cans, snuff cans, tangled line cut from the inexperienced's bait-casting reels, styrofoam coolers, countless cigarette butts, netted caps sporting "Daiwa" and "Halvoline" and "REBEL Lures," and the carcass of an arrow-skewered otter that bumped along the shore, pecked by catfish and gnawed by gars until delivered and dispersed into the salt sea.

Sitting upon the bank, Andrew pictured himself among the flotsam, weightless upon the water, and decided to stay past supper—through the entire night if he needed to, even to Resurrection morning, until he felt himself carried far beyond the mouth of the river and into the all-encompassing ocean, beyond all edges.

A sound came from far into the hardwoods. Andrew thought it might have been the *whack whack* of a bird tapping out a great truth.

Purvis sprang through the door and serpentined around the nearly empty display tables. He placed his hands onto the counter and looked as if he might perform deep knee bends.

"Look who's here again," Beulah said. "How're you today?"

"Sharp," Purvis said. "Like a rooster spur."

"Well, sharp's a good thing to be, I suppose. Now, what can we do for you, Percy?"

"Purvis," said Purvis. "Martha told me to come by and get her here, and I also got to buy something for somebody else."

"She right here," said Beulah. "You okay?"

"Just feeling a little froggy, about like I been drinking coffee all day but without all the peeing. Yonder she is." Purvis watched Martha rise from the table and disperse and float about the room. Her arms were already there when the rest of her body pulled together, like acorns rolling into a ditch, to sway before him like a cobra at a flute, or maybe like the flute itself. "Dog, how you do those things," said Purvis. "I'm here and then you're coming together, and arms all arming and symboled up, and *dog*dammit."

Martha steadied Purvis with a hand on his shoulder. "I need to speak with you," she said. "Beulah, we're going to step outside a minute."

A block away, the Last Days of the Redeemer Youth Choir assembled before the courthouse to warm up for its Easter Eve concert. Down another block, a short line of cars filed into Drive-Thru Spirits and Smokes. In the distance, a train whistle blew.

"Did you sleep in those clothes?" said Martha "Did you sleep at all?"

"Yeah, and in the truck, because I didn't want to be late with sleeping all day and then having the old man snatch me into doing something, and then me forgetting and you'd be gone and I'd be drownding again, like I fell off the trestle and drownded with nobody to scoop me up and fly me like up a rope—"

"Hush!" She held Purvis's shoulders, then traced her fingers along his eyebrows. He exhaled slowly as his head settled heavily into his neck. "Now, why are you here so early? I can't leave Beulah now. Besides, I . . . listen, Purvis, I've got to sort through a few things tonight, think about what I'm going to do. I might have to get out of here."

"Florida?" said Purvis.

"That's right. Maybe run down to Florida and leave it all, leave them all—"

"A jacaranda?"

"Yes, lie in the shade of a wide jacaranda and live off love melons and sailfish and no one will know, Purvis. No one will know. Right?" Martha lit her cigarette.

"No one will know. I can get to it. Focus. Sharp."

"Yes, focus. Good." She placed the cigarette in his mouth, he inhaled, and she returned it to her lips. "But you need to go now and wait to hear from me," said Martha. "Are you listening?" She rubbed her thumb across Purvis's lip. A drop of saliva rolled from the corner. "That swelling has almost completely gone. Your ear's about healed up, too. Now, the last-minute Easter rush is about to start, so Beulah needs me in there. You head on home and get some sleep, hear?" she said. "Don't come looking for me. I'll get hold of you tomorrow. Got it?"

"Okay. One more thing. Them FBIs been around here?"

"I'm taking care of it, but the safest place for you now is at home. They won't look for you there." With that, she returned to the shop, as Purvis walked across the street to stand on the propane truck's bumper. The youth choir began "There Is Power in the Blood." He thought he might have heard the song before.

Then, quickly, he crossed the street again and flung the shop door open. "I liked to forgot," Purvis said. "I'm not back to see you, Martha. I'm getting on home like you said. I just need to buy some flowers for Miss Agnes—something cheap. Y'all know about her getting burnt up?"

"Burnt up?" asked Beulah from beside the refrigerator, where she and Martha stacked the last of the corsages. "How you mean?"

"I mean crisp. Building got bombed where she was marching in Charleston, near about took her face off. I'm getting home like you said, Martha. Anyhow, I need something for her—cheap though."

"That poor woman," said Beulah. "Marching?"

"Abortion house."

"Where's she at?"

"Tri-County."

Beulah took a swig from her flask. "I'll make you up something nice for her, Purvis, on the house. Tell her I'm going to try get down there this evening to see her."

"You might not want to. Burnt up like a paycheck. Did you know she was a Pigott?"

✳

The four patients were in various states of disrepair. Five limbs were suspended in traction, two faces covered by heavy bandages. Purvis wondered how the nurses could keep track of which tubes from which beeping machines went to which veins and orifices. As he thought of those puzzles where you have to help the animals find the right paths to their respective dens or nests, a man in hospital scrubs entered with a cart of pans and towels.

"Is this a Pigott?" Purvis asked.

"Excuse me?"

"A Pigott. I can't see her face, but she might be Miss Agnes Pigott." The woman moaned and rubbed at the bandages on her eyes. "If she'd open her mouth, I could tell. Big old pink gum folded over her teeth and like full of blood, like, you know, when you get a fingernail ripped out."

The nurse checked the chart hanging by the bed. "No, sir, she's a Singleton. Let's check this other one." He lifted the chart. "Here we go. Agnes Pigott. I think she's asleep."

Purvis leaned over Agnes. She smelled mostly as she did earlier, but also with a slight odor that reminded him of turpentine. Her head was wrapped in bandages with a small hole left for her nose and mouth. A tube fed oxygen into her nostrils, IVs were taped to her arms, and wires were strapped to her wrists and fingers.

"Miss Agnes?" said Purvis. "You look about like a puppet, with all them lines hooked to you. I believe if I grabbed a clutch of them, I could raise you up like a magician when they do the floating woman trick. Can you hear me in there?"

Agnes wagged her index finger. "I can hear a little." Her voice was labored and dry, as if her tongue, swollen, was sticking to her palette. She inhaled very slowly. "That you, Mr. Driggers?"

"Yes'm, Miss Agnes. I brung you some flowers. I didn't know you was a Pigott."

Agnes reached out with both hands. "So sweet," she said. She inhaled again, a shallow breath, with a whistle through her teeth. "Pigott's my natural name."

"I be dog. I always figured you for a Gaskins. You got ways like them Gaskins out in Bethera," said Purvis. "I thought the woman in that other bed there was you, but she's a Singleton. You know any of them? She might be black." He touched Agnes's hands and softly pushed them down. "You better keep still or you might come loose and set off one of these machines to alarming."

"Flowers." Agnes raised her head an inch and took another long breath. "What kind?"

"Miss Beulah made them up special herself, pretty as all get out. She said she'll try to come see you."

Agnes hummed.

"The big ones are orchids. There's five of them, all kind of purplish, and down inside, there's little parts that . . . Godamighty! You can't believe this, but they look sort of like a mussel, m-u-s-s-e-l, like you can eat." He rubbed his thumb on the folded structures inside the orchid. "Then there's a bunch of tiny little white flowers all around."

Agnes tried to raise up onto her elbows. "Tiny white?"

"Teeny-weeny. Must be a hundred, and with some grassy-looking leaves on the stems."

Agnes coughed. Her shoulders jerked and her neck arched. "Bay, bay." She gagged. "Breath."

"Nurse-man!" Purvis called. "She can't breathe!"

"Baby's breath!" Agnes screamed. Then she settled into the bed, inhaling slowly.

"She says she's got the baby's breath," Purvis said to the nurse, who adjusted Agnes's oxygen feed. Purvis held his asthma inhaler to Agnes's mouth and squirted. "Suck this down," he said.

Agnes coughed and gagged as the nurse pushed Purvis into the hall and other staff ran into the room.

Purvis stroked the orchids and held them to his face, but could not detect an aroma. He stuck his tongue inside of one.

In a few minutes, a man in scrubs approached him. "Mr. Pigott?" said the man.

"Driggers," said Purvis, "but I'm here to see Miss Pigott."

"I'm Doctor Somers. I fear I have bad news," he said. "We did all we could, but she's gone."

"Gone like dead?"

"Yes. I'm sorry."

"All still? body not doing anything?"

The doctor nodded. "Afraid so."

"Lot of that going on," said Purvis. "Hey, you being a doctor and all, let me ask you something." Purvis pointed to the inside of an orchid. "Don't that look like a little Jesus to you?"

TWENTY-FIVE

Martha awoke to a tapping at her window. She slid the pistol and flashlight from her nightstand and sidled along the wall, kneeling at the edge of the window. She leaned away from the wall, pointed the gun, and turned on the flashlight. The face on the other side of the glass winced, and Martha opened the window.

"That's twice you pointed that pistol point-blank at me," whispered Purvis. "You know what that means?"

"It means I about blew your head off again. What are you doing here?"

"You got to come with me. I can't wait no more," said Purvis. "I got something to show you that will say everything. Just come with me for a few minutes and you'll understand."

"Are you still in those same clothes?" said Martha. "Didn't you go home like I told you?"

"For a minute. Please come."

"Where have you been?"

"Right here, mostly. Please come. I got to show you."

"I can't believe this. I'll meet you out front."

Martha dressed and walked out into the first gray streaks of dawn, where Purvis held open the passenger door of DeWayne's pickup.

"Why are you in your brother's truck?" Martha asked as Purvis inserted the key into the ignition.

"The Beasley truck's out in the swamp with the door open," said Purvis, "and probably finally run out of gas and shut off by now." He turned the key, and the Isuzu gurgled. "I figure the FBIs might be tailing the propane truck, and when they find it, they'll look for me out in the swamp for days, and by then, we'll be eating sailfish under them jacarandas." He turned the key again, and the engine popped. "Oh, Jesus on a root."

"We're not going to Florida."

"That's for damn sure, not in this sorry rice-hauler we ain't. But right now we got to get to Armey's. I was there before I was here." He turned the key again. A click, then silence. "Goddamnit Aris-purple-stotle!"

"Purvis, you need to get your brother back his truck, get the gas truck back to town, and then get home," said Martha. "We'll take the van to where you left the gas truck."

He snapped his face toward her. His eyes stretched wide, then sagged. "We got to get to Armey's first. Then we'll go wherever you want. I'll do whatever you want me to do. I been focused all night."

"Do you really think it's smart for you to be at Armey's when the FBI already suspect you?"

"Nothing big can happen on Easter morning," said Purvis. "The whole sheriff's department is at church, and the FBI is federal. The federal government is closed on Sunday."

"Get in," said Martha, climbing into her mother's van. "I'm driving."

Purvis kept his eyes upon her for the entire ride, all the while talking about woodpeckers and metaphors. She asked about Agnes, and he said she was still and gone. Then he spoke of scorpions and otters and secret symbols a woman shows a man.

"Purvis, hush," said Martha. "Are you telling me Agnes died?"

"Got about blowed up at the abortion house," said Purvis, "not dead *at* the house but burnt up and stunk like all forty, and then the hospital wrapped her up like a to-go burger from Fat Henry's Grill, and she died of the baby's breath, flopping like a mullet."

"The clinic blew up?"

"My task."

Martha turned the van into Armey's yard. "We're here. Let's make this fast."

Purvis went around the house, walking backwards to assure himself that Martha followed. She moved like an ordinary woman, her arms folded together to look like only two. She was saving up all her symboling for the proud moment. Purvis wondered how he looked to her, whether his arms multiplied into meaning-givers and whether she was charmed by his serpent movements.

They pushed through the bushes to the creek bank.

"Here," said Purvis. "Look at them."

Near the edge of the water stood a line of towers about two feet tall, made of condensed milk cans stacked in offset layers like bricks. Atop one was the old monk's cypress knee carving; on another sat Purvis's track trophy; on the next was an orchid corsage; another held the Stim-u-Ring; the fifth, the naked woman key ring; and on the last was the monk's journal.

"Oh my God," said Martha. She rubbed her hand over the cypress stump. She picked up the Stim-u-Ring, read the label, squinted at the package, then dropped it, missing the can tower. Purvis picked it up and wiped it on his shirt before returning it to the display.

"What the hell is all this, Purvis?"

"Symbols," he said. "You know, something that means something else, but not the way words do exactly."

Martha pointed. "What's that?"

"My running trophy. I told you I was fast. A track to get you out of here. That's a metaphor, a good one."

"And that?"

"Naked woman from some kind of real pretty wood, with the key to the bathroom at the Venus Parlor. That one just stuck to me like a real sign when it jammed me through my pocket later."

"And that?"

"That's why I was at the Venus Parlor," said Purvis. "It's for when we, when I worship it, you. For your purple, the Jesus folded down in the orchid, in the mussel, m-u-s-s-e-l, of you, of your woman secret, like when you two times symboled it with the pistol. Down where I can crawl in and curl up like a hatchling in a nest, and you can hold me in all those arms and fly me away up, and I'll be out of here and in you and worshipping the Jesus, and I done the task for you to prove that I was right for your secret showing—"

"Jesus, shut up!" Lighting a cigarette, Martha leaned against a sweetgum tree. "Purvis, you're not making any sense. You haven't slept in a couple of days, and you're sounding deranged," she said. "Just gather up your things and let's get going. And you were supposed to take that journal back to that monk."

"Wait." Purvis made tiny adjustments to the objects on the can towers. He looked up, as if correlating the items with celestial markers. He dragged his heel to retrace the lines he had drawn in the sand to outline the display. "I did it for you. They made you abortion your baby and I did it to show you that I will do anything," he said. "I never found Armey's money, but I can take care of us. I can do any kind of work. I can run real fast."

"Jesus, I don't believe this," said Martha. She took a step toward Purvis and stared into his quivering face. "What are you *talking* about? Abortion? Who told you that shit?"

"Miss Agnes."

Martha's head rolled back, then forward. "Agnes is crazy as hell. My fucking God. You blew up the clinic, and *killed Agnes*, by the way, because you thought I was forced to have an abortion? *Agnes* had an abortion, and in her crazy dream world, she's put me in her place. Oh Christ!"

Purvis took three quick paces downstream, twirled, and paced back. "But I still did it *for* you. It was my *task*." A bird with slow, loping wing beats flew just over Purvis's head, then swooped sharply up to land in the gum tree. "Can we go, to the jacarandas? We can look in Armey's house one more time. Nobody's coming out here this morning."

"Listen to what I am going to tell you. Stand still and look at me." Martha took a last, long drag from the cigarette, then blew a smoke ring that trembled like a spring until disappearing over the creek. "There's no money in that house. I took it when I shot Armey. There's more to this than you'll ever know," she said. "I didn't know what to do until you got mixed up in this, and then we got rid of the body."

"But the FBI—"

"Forget that. I used you, Purvis. I felt trapped, and I needed a sap. You did your task for me when you took Armey to the rendering plant, okay? That was what I needed, and you did a great job," Martha said. "You have served me. But now I have to go, and you can't come with me."

Purvis heard a rustle across the creek. He turned as a great blue heron took flight out of the bushes. "I'm going with you."

"If you go with me, they'll think you kidnapped me," she said. "Then the FBI really will get you, and you'll go to federal prison for the rest of your life. Neither one of us wants that."

"No!"

"Let's go get the propane truck before you get in trouble for that, too."

"No." Purvis grabbed Martha's shoulder with his left hand, pulling her to him as he reached his right hand behind her. She slammed the heel of her hand into his nose. He fell backwards, knocking over two of the condensed milk can towers. The trophy stuck upside-down in the mud; the box with the orchid corsage rolled into the water, floating away from the bank.

Slowly, Purvis stood, blood dripping from his nose. In his right hand, he held the Walther PPK, pointing it at Martha. They faced each other parallel to the water.

Martha caught some movement somewhere across the creek. Shifting her eyes, she saw someone at the edge of the vegetation, pointing toward them.

Purvis moved his mouth to say he was sorry for all he'd done, that if Martha wanted him to do so, he would put a bullet into his brain right then, that he was just dull after all and did not want her to suffer for his failure, that he would go to the FBI and tell them that he had done it all. Just then , he felt something strike his right jaw, as if someone had thrown an ice cube and it had stuck. His tongue felt covered by fire ants, swelling and growing numb. His left jaw felt pinched, as if someone was trying to pull him sideways.

Purvis tried to tell Martha to take the gun, but his mouth could not move.

He saw Martha, and she looked horrified, covering her mouth with all her arms at once, and though she may have been speaking, Purvis heard only a buzzing sound in one ear, and the other felt stuffed up, like it always did just before he got an earache when he had a bad cold.

He held the gun by the barrel, giving it to Martha. She took it, then looked across the river. Purvis tried to look, too, but he could not move his head, and when he tried, jolts of pain shot through him. Placing his hands to his jaws, he felt something like a stick shooting out on either side. He pulled on the stick, which only caused more pain. He followed it with his right hand, finding feathery attachments at the end. Then he followed it with his left, to where it was imbedded in the gum tree.

His hearing returned when something splashed in the creek. Martha turned from the creek to Purvis with a desperate expression. The pistol hung by her side. Purvis again tried to speak. He wanted to say, "Am I becoming a tree? Is that what you're making of me?" but only vowel sounds and hisses emerged. He felt blood pouring over his bottom lip and something like pebbles working around in his mouth. He reached in and found three teeth. He held them up to his eyes: molars, one with a large cavity. Purvis wondered why that one had not given him a toothache. He dropped them into his shirt pocket.

Martha turned again to the creek as the hairy monk appeared, holding a bow. He looked at Purvis, then dropped the bow, removing his wet, hooded smock. He wore a white tee-shirt, dungarees, and a necklace with what looked to Purvis like a silver clover dangling just below the beard.

"I," the monk said. He cleared his throat. "I am Tom."

Martha put the gun back under her shirt. "Martha."

"I know." The monk cleared his throat again and coughed. "Anhinga."

"Anhinga?"

"I am leaving," he said, swallowing hard and closing his eyes, as if downing a shot of whiskey after a dry spell. "The abbey."

"I'm leaving a lot of things," Martha said. "There's a conversion van out front with forty thousand dollars in cash hidden in one of its seats. Pick a direction."

"South?"

"Okay."

"Him?"

Martha took Purvis's hands. "You'll be fine, Purvis," she said. "You just need someone else to take care of you. It can't be me."

Purvis pointed at his stacked offerings and moaned. Martha picked up the Cypress knee. "This?"

Purvis managed, "Unh uh," and Martha dropped it. She held up the trophy. Purvis smiled as best he could and pointed to Martha. His "you" came out as "oo."

"Thank you, Purvis," she said. "I'm the fast runner now?"

He smiled and pointed again. Martha picked up the journal. Purvis smiled and pointed at Tom. "Oo."

Tom took the journal, staring down at it with a small smile. "Thank you," he said. He lifted the necklace over his head, passed it around the feathered end of the arrow, and dropped it over Purvis's head. One side of the chain hung over the other side of the arrow. Then Martha and Tom walked out of Purvis's vision.

Purvis stood with the arrow through his jaw and listened. He heard the flowing of the Wadboo Branch, a distant bird singing *meek meek*, and something, maybe a squirrel, moving in the tree above his head. The van cranked, shifted into reverse, whined, shifted into drive, and pulled away. A train whistle from miles away seeped through the damp morning air, blending, like a song, with the faint rumble of the van.

Tilting his head back, Purvis found that he could rotate around the arrow axis without much pain. *Ockham the Arrow.* Purvis chuckled, but it hurt his jaw. He gripped the arrow on either side of his jaw and wondered if he should lift his feet. The arrow was deep into the tree, but would surely break off at the bark. The broken part would probably splinter, especially if it was fiberglass. Purvis could peel the feathers from the other end and slide the arrow through his jaw that way. Then again, that would probably hurt really bad. Besides, the arrow might hold back the bleeding. Perhaps he should just walk the railroad track home with the arrow sticking through him, which would be some kind of sight.

A *whack whack* came from above. A large woodpecker was high in the gum, its elongated head chopping so hard that bits of bark fell onto Purvis, pinned to the tree. The bird appeared to be black and white, with maybe a trace of red, but in the shadow world that surrounded him, Purvis could not be sure.

ABOUT THE AUTHOR

Ron Cooper was born and raised in the South Carolina Low Country. He received a B.A. in philosophy from the College of Charleston, an M.A. from the University of South Carolina, and a Ph.D. from Rutgers University. He moved to Florida in 1988 and is Professor of Humanities at the College of Central Florida in Ocala, where he lives with his wife Sandra (also a CCF faculty member) and their three children.

Ron is a past president of the Florida Philosophical Association, has published philo-sophical essays, and is the author of *Heidegger and Whitehead: A Phenomenological Examination into the Intelligibility of Experience.* His fiction has appeared in publications such as *Yalobusha Review, Apostrophe, Timber Creek Review,* and *The Blotter.*

His much-praised debut novel, *Hume's Fork,* available from Bancroft Press, drew comparisons to John Kennedy Toole's *A Confederacy of Dunces,* and earned him recognition as a finalist for the Bread Loaf Conference's Bakeless Literary Prize.